BURNT BLACK

Also by Ed Kovacs

Good Junk
Storm Damage

BURNT BLACK

A Cliff St. James Novel

ED KOVACS

Minotaur Books ⚏ New York

BURNT BLACK. Copyright © 2013 by Ed Kovacs. All rights reserved. Printed in the United States of America. For information, address St. Martin's Press, 175 Fifth Avenue, New York, N.Y. 10010.

www.minotaurbooks.com

Library of Congress Cataloging-in-Publication Data

Kovacs, Ed.
    Burnt black : a Cliff St. James novel / Ed Kovacs.—First edition.
      p. cm.
    ISBN 978-1-250-02029-1 (hardcover)
    ISBN 978-1-250-02030-7 (e-book)
    1. Police—Fiction. 2. New Orleans (La.)—Fiction. 3. Drug traffic—Fiction. I. Title.
  PS3611.O74943B87 2013
  813'.6—dc23

2013025297

Minotaur books may be purchased for educational, business, or promotional use. For information on bulk purchases, please contact Macmillan Corporate and Premium Sales Department at 1-800-221-7945, extension 5442, or write special markets@macmillan.com.

First Edition: November 2013

10 9 8 7 6 5 4 3 2 1

For Lisa Mary Chan, a fearless, generous soul
and the best writer I know.

And for AJK, the second blood brother I've lost;
his spirit now soars unfettered.

AUTHOR'S NOTE

Thanks in advance to my readers for understanding that while many of the locations described in this book are real and worth a visit, others are purely fictional.

There are many fine officers in the storied New Orleans Police Department. They have my utmost respect and my sincere appreciation for the thankless service they perform. Stay safe, brothers and sisters.

ACKNOWLEDGMENTS

Much gratitude, once again, to the usual suspects: Ed Stackler, Richard Curtis, Christopher Graham, Tony Ritzman, and David Roy. I am truly grateful to the Phoenix Cadre and to the many other helpers behind the scenes who best remain unnamed.

The world would be a better place if everyone had at least one friend of the caliber of Carl Scholl; profound thanks for going above and beyond, partner.

A tip of the hat to the many booksellers out there who have been kind enough to host me at book signings; e-books are great, but please support your local bookstore.

The SMP "krewe" remains awesome. Heartfelt appreciation to Michael Homler, Hector DeJean, and all the other good folks who have labored on my behalf at the Flatiron Building.

Police Detectives Rob Barrere and Reno Bax would make good cops on a reality-TV show; thanks, guys, for all the help down in Sin City South.

Jefferson Parish Sheriff's Detective Myron Gaudet, a tough guy's tough guy, once again deserves special mention for his generous

ACKNOWLEDGMENTS

assistance. Mushin New Orleans Training Center, Myron's cool facility in Harahan, Louisiana, is a must for those interested in learning Mixed Martial Arts and other techniques of the warrior's way.

When Police Captain Eric Morton enters the room, the party starts, and I mean that in the best way. Eric and his late detective partner wrote an unpublished book about a difficult case they had. I have yet to read that book, but Eric gifted me with the kernel of an idea that grew into *Burnt Black*. Eric is a class act, and I thank you very much, my brother.

Lastly, I thank my family for putting up with the considerable demands my dual professions place upon me. It's not always easy to remain sequestered at my writing desk or deployed overseas instead of spending quality time with those I love. I beg forgiveness for my many absences and humbly thank those close to me for their understanding and support.

CHAPTER ONE

Gravel crunched underfoot as Honey and I stepped out of her battered unmarked unit at the end of the drive and threaded through the dark green leaves of wisteria overhanging the walkway. It was only now that the old wooden house came into focus. I turned around, amazed that we stood mere feet from her vehicle, yet this home was almost completely camouflaged by bottomland greenery.

"Private but right off the road. I like that," I said, turning my gaze to the one-story house that had seen better days. "Seems the West Bank has some secrets."

"Real estate agent says this house is haunted," said Honey as she glanced around the low porch. "I don't see the lockbox with the key."

My good friend and fellow New Orleans Police Homicide Detective Baybee had a day off, and I'd tagged along to help her house-hunt for a new place for her mom, who had given up on the government-funded Road Home Program, a bureaucratic nightmare that was supposed to provide compensation to Louisiana homeowners affected by the killer Storm of sixteen months ago. Like many disasters, the Road Home had begun with good intentions, but then again, the government could screw up a lemonade stand.

"If it's haunted, why would you even look inside?" At sixty-five degrees Fahrenheit with a light breeze, today was a classic mid-December day. I felt comfortable wearing a lightweight 5.11 jacket with my Glock 36 subcompact, semiauto concealed in a hidden pocket, but when Honey said the word "haunted," I swear a chill shot up my spine. "Let's go."

She shot me an *Are you joking?* look. "Tell me you don't believe in ghosts."

"I've never seen a ghost. That doesn't mean they don't exist."

"You've got to be kidding me."

"I'm not saying ghosts are real, but I believe some things can't be explained so easily."

"Everything can be explained."

"Explain to me why a real estate agent, who wants to sell this house and make money, would tell you up front it's haunted."

"It means there are a lot of gullible people in the world. That's all."

Cops have an uncanny knack for picking out pertinent radio traffic from the ambient background noise of life. We were both off duty but out of habit and curiosity Honey kept her handheld police radio clipped to her purse, monitoring the main frequency, not Homicide's private channel. Our heads both turned to the direction of the static-tinged dispatcher's voice.

"Ninety-fours in Fourth District, 9997 River Road. See the UPS driver," said the dispatcher flatly.

"That's practically next door," said Honey, craning her neck to peer through the foliage. "In fact, it *is* next door."

"Shots fired, but I didn't hear a thing."

We had a long list of addresses to visit, but the sheer closeness of the "shots fired" location acted as a magnet to our hardwired instincts as cops. If this were the Ninth or Mid-City or just about anywhere else in New Orleans, maybe we would ignore the call and mind our own business. But 94s out here in a bucolic part of the parish didn't feel right, at least not to me, and the adrenaline started pumping.

"So much for this being a quiet neighborhood."

Without another word we raced back to her unit. Honey threw the vehicle into reverse, spraying gravel as she spun onto River Road under an impossibly blue sky, and floored it.

Within seconds we rounded a bend and saw a UPS van parked up ahead in a driveway, right off the road. The long, cement drive wound a good football-field length to an unremarkable one-story house sitting on a remarkably large plot of land, across the street from the inner bank of the levee lushly blanketed with green tufts of soft grass and the Mississippi River just beyond.

"Maybe someone's upset their delivery is late."

Honey ignored me and radioed dispatch to advise them we had responded to the scene. Watching Honey all amped up in cop mode always produced feelings of disconnect, because blue-eyed blondes with movie-star good looks weren't supposed to be tough broads, not in real life anyway, but here she was, performing flawlessly as a consummate law-enforcement professional as she had so many times before.

Being saddled by her father with the unfortunate name Honey

Baybee had created the chip on her shoulder that wasn't going away anytime soon. There was no removing that chip; there wasn't even any discussing it; there was only blind acceptance and unconditional love, which I continually granted my best friend and cuddle buddy. Everyone assumed we were lovers. If my male friends knew I often slept with Honey but we'd never had sex, they would have disowned me. Or had me certified.

Honey skidded the vehicle right up to the UPS van, and I had my door open before we'd come to a complete stop.

"Jackson's the name," said the black UPS driver, climbing down from his big step van to meet me. In his late forties and burly, Mr. Jackson was a salty-looking guy who seemed kind of silly in the brown Bermuda-shorts uniform.

"Three gunshots and screams. Bloodcurdling screams before the shots. From a man."

Honey joined us. "You sure about the shots?" she asked.

"I'm a retired Marine Corps gunnery sergeant. And I grew up in the Desire projects."

Growing up in the projects meant he'd heard more gunshots than a lot of combat vets. "Where were you when you heard the gunfire?" I asked.

"The front door. I rang the bell to get a signature. Heard the screams, then the shots. I hauled ass to my van, drove back out here to the end of the driveway, and called it in. I been watching the house, but haven't seen a thing."

"Thought you guys were always in a hurry," I said, without accusation, as I scanned the distant house, noting a pickup and silver sedan parked out front.

Jackson caught the intent of my remark. "You want to know why I'm standing guard. I been delivering to Professor Drake here for going on ten years. He always tips me big at Christmas, gives me a cold drink on a hot day. Asks about my family. He helped my daughter get a job in the Tulane bookstore. If that was him in there screaming, figured this was the least I could do."

"You know whose vehicles those are?" asked Honey, gesturing with her head toward the house.

"The pickup belongs to some Mexican guys. They been working here off and on since the Storm. The Prius is Drake's. He lives here alone, far as I know."

"Appreciate it if you could stick around, Mr. Jackson. Until we see how this works out."

I extended my hand and he took it.

"Will do."

Honey and I got back into her unit, and she barreled us up to the house.

"What do you think?" I asked. "A little too much tequila for the homeboys, an argument with this professor guy over money, and things go south?"

Honey shrugged. "We'll know soon enough."

"I like this property. If the professor now sleeps with the fishes, your mom should put in an offer."

The driveway widened to accommodate three vehicles, but Honey parked behind a battered old F-150 Ford pickup whose suspension sagged under the weight of power tools and building materials in its truck bed. The silver Prius sat parked closer to the front door. Relatively new pale yellow siding and a new red tile roof suggested this place got a serious makeover after the killer Storm, apparently from the men now inside. Honey gave dispatch a quick heads-up that we were going into the house, a little reminder to any arriving uniforms that there were friendlies inside.

We un-assed ourselves from her unit, drew our weapons, and listened. A couple of yellow-throated warblers played in the trees, a horn blew from a far-off river tug, live-oak leaves rustled in the cool breeze blowing off the river.

Honey's off-duty piece was a .45 SIG SAUER P220 Elite, and she racked the slide back, chambering a round and cocking the hammer, then gestured she would take the back door. We both understood that at a relatively remote location such as this at the edge of the parish, if a homeowner was in the house bleeding out, he had a better chance of survival if we went in now and didn't wait for backup.

I did a fifteen count, waiting for Honey to get around back as I eyed a couple of carved wooden gargoyles with maniacal expressions on either side of the front door. A vertical line of graffiti-like characters painted in glossy black decorated one side of the door frame.

Kind of odd.

I mounted the front steps and turned the knob. The door was unlocked, and I entered the dark room, pistol in hand.

My eyes adjusted to the dim light as I shut the door behind me. It was like stepping into an arts center that just so happened to also have some household furniture. "Cluttered" doesn't do justice to describe the room, and I flashed on a museum I knew: the Voodoo Museum in the French Quarter.

My eyes danced over Native American fetishes, rattles, and drums; African/Caribbean/Asian and other primitive wooden statuary loomed all around, bedecked with bright, primary-colored strips of cloth. The "coffee table" was a glass-topped casket containing a full-size human skeleton that had symbols and text etched on the cranium. Hundreds and hundreds of books jammed shelving, fighting for space with quartz-crystal human skulls, porcelain figurines of Catholic saints painted to wear black robes, polished stone figures that looked Mayan, feathers, exquisite conch shells, and clusters of large semiprecious stones such as amethyst, tourmaline, and malachite. A white wooden cross had unusual symbols and writing painted on it and stood surrounded by vials, bottles, sachets, and black candles of every shape.

Animal heads hung stuffed and mounted on every wall, including the ugliest javelina I've ever seen, and that's saying something.

And then there were the bones. Human bones. Femurs, fibulae, rib cages, pelvic bones, sternums, clavicles, skulls. From adults . . . and children. I had a strong feeling there'd be no more house-hunting today. The bones overwhelmed me with a recollection of mass murderers past. Very sick ones.

I heard a soft footstep and sighted on an entryway. Honey took a quick peek into the room, we made eye contact, then moved off together down the hall.

The rest of the house held more of the same but to a lesser extent than in the front room. We smelled a scent—copal incense?—as we approached the final room to search. This was clearly a new addition to the house. I went in first, crouching, then moved left. Honey jinked right after she cleared the doorway. The high-ceilinged circular room had to be fifty feet in diameter. The floor and walls were black marble, inlaid with all sorts of arcane icons and unknown script. Some of it looked medieval, other images appeared primitively grotesque.

There were sheeted mattresses and large pillows, a couple of big wooden cabinets, a table and chairs. A large red wooden chair, ornately carved and plushly cushioned, sat off by itself, facing the center of the room. An altar—to what I couldn't fathom—was recessed in the wall, contained a human skeleton wearing a top hat,

Mardi Gras beads, and sunglasses. Bottles of rum, packs of cigarettes, candles, cash, and other items adorned the altar.

As Honey and I circled in opposite directions, I saw that the far side of the room held a Bondage and Discipline setup, with all kinds of racks, restraints, chains, and goodies pertinent to a variety of alternative sexual fetishes.

Honey and I silently checked for any other hidden points of egress, since the elephant in the room had made its presence known the moment we had entered, that being a massive circular stone pedestal about three feet high centered in the room. I confidently calculated it could accommodate at least three people, since there were two naked male bodies on it right now. And they weren't moving.

As I approached I saw a drain built into the floor at the foot of the pedestal. *Was this some kind of sacrificial altar?* The stone top was grooved so fluids would easily channel from the altar and drip down to the drain. For blood?

The nude Hispanic guys were freshly dead, but I checked to make sure. We holstered our weapons and scanned the area.

"No blood, no shell casings, no obvious signs of trauma or foul play, no marks, no entry or exit wounds readily visible," I said.

"And no weapon," added Honey. One of the stiffs, who looked to be around thirty, had a skunklike shock of white hair bifurcating his black locks.

Both of their faces were frozen in grimacing death masks, suggesting some kind of horrific fear. *Fear of what?* I'd never seen anything like this, and it made my skin crawl.

Honey unclipped her police radio from her purse. "Dispatch, this is Detective Baybee. Two, repeat, two signal twenty-nine unclassifieds, possible thirties, at the location of the ninety-fours in the Fourth."

Possible 30s, possible homicides? Yes, she had made the right call. My instinct screamed murder, but there was no clear evidence of that.

"What do you make of all this?" she asked me.

"I think the professor has some explaining to do about all the bones. And why he has some kind of altar in a weird chamber with two dead men on it that look like they died of fright."

CHAPTER TWO

Since being recommissioned as a New Orleans police officer a few months ago and given the thing I'd long wanted—a gold detective's shield—I'd kept a low profile. I healed from gunshot and stab wounds and worked myself into the best physical condition of my life. I could kick the bejesus out of testosterone-fueled, overgrown twenty-year-old cage fighters, not only because of experience and strategic fighting techniques but also because I'd become rock-hard strong and super fit. Not bad for a guy in his mid-thirties.

I felt I could take on just about anything or anyone. Kendall Bullard, a UFC fighter whom I'd coached for years, told me a week ago I should go pro. I was that good, he claimed. I'd considered it briefly, only because of the cachet it would add to my dojo, which I had expanded in size and had now fully staffed. Being a pro or former pro was a big draw for students who wanted to learn how to fight.

I ultimately decided I didn't need or want to become a professional fighter. My reputation as one of the best striking coaches in the business was already intact. UFC, Bellator, and other pro fighters were coming to me for instruction. That created a lot of buzz and brought in students. Plus, Kendall trained at my place when he was in town, and he was already a UFC star. So I stayed put, continued to operate my lucrative PI business out of a French Quarter bar (I did that on the sly, as it was against department regs for an officer to moonlight as a private dick), and worked my forty hours a week for NOPD. My bank accounts were fat and life was good.

But now, as I walked the perimeter of Drake's property, looking for signs that a killer might have escaped by running out the back door and into the woods, all of the high strangeness around this case that was only a few hours old hounded me like a thirsty drunk who'd spotted a mark.

Just how tough am I? Truth is, I've always been gun-shy toward the occult. Voodoo and the like kind of spook me. I have no problem with opponents in a physical confrontation, but what if the confrontation is nonphysical? I'm not one to discount the power of shamans and sorcerers, and because I have no skills or knowledge in those arenas, it makes me feel vulnerable now.

Many people opt to take the simple position that witchcraft or sorcery or whatever general, generic umbrella term one chooses to use for the arts of the occultist is just a sham practiced by charlatans. And New Orleans, historically, has had no shortage of charlatans, including those who operated in the past as voodoo priests and priestesses.

But I'd seen some monks do things when I studied martial arts in China that were . . . unexplainable. So I remained open-minded on the subject and strongly suspected there was something to what some call the "manipulation of energy." Personally, I had chosen to ignore those disciplines, to distance myself from them, because they made me uncomfortable. I was—and am—an outsider to such worlds and have chosen to stay that way.

I hadn't been kidding with Honey; I'd never move into a haunted house. Just being in Drake's house was creepy enough. What kind of coward did that make me out to be?

Then a wave of icy chill enveloped me and I almost jumped. I turned to look and saw that a massive cold front had blown in fast from the north and blocked out the sun. The temperature dropped like a stone, and the beautiful blue sunny day of the morning was swallowed by an amorphous mass of angry gray afternoon weather that looked like it had an agenda.

I moved briskly to finish my circuit of the property, searched the shed Honey asked me to check, then made my way back to the front driveway, now choked with CSI vans, the coroner's car, several Fourth District unmarked units, and various and sundry LE—law enforcement—vehicles. How ironic that a couple of misfits like Honey and me were now running a show like this.

One thing I'd learned was to be thorough at a fresh crime scene, to go slowly, get it right, and not jump to conclusions.

As I stood smoking a Partagas mini cigarillo outside Professor Drake's house, I was joined for a confab by Honey and Senior Homicide Detectives Mackie and Kruger, who informed me that conclusions were already being jumped to.

"Coroner confirmed there were no obvious signs of foul play. And there's no evidence of any solvents or chemicals that they used in their construction work that could have caused this. He's speculating the victims were about to have some kinky sex. But overdosed," said Honey. "Even though we didn't find any dope."

"Remember that guy in the news who took some hybrid type of LSD? He stripped naked in a park and ate some chick's face," said Kruger, who was tall and lean and had a permanent look of wariness about him.

"Bad PCP has also made plenty of people take off their clothes," added Honey.

"Toxicology reports will take forever," I said. "And the department won't pop for any elaborate testing."

"The crime lab would probably screw it up anyway," said Kruger.

"So far there's no sign they had sex with each other, even though each of them apparently had an orgasm shortly before death," said Honey.

"So it was, what? A circle jerk?" asked Kruger.

"That's unclear right now," responded Honey.

Kruger shook his head.

"Some of the district-level homicide guys here to do the MORF think it was a double suicide," said Mackie, a short man in his late fifties with a flat head. Mackie was solid as a wall. You might jump over him but you couldn't go through him.

MORF stood for Major Offense Reporting Form. The DIU, District Investigative Unit, was here for that. Honey had put some of them to work helping CSI techs dig up the many small, shallow graves in the backyard that Kruger had discovered. Preliminary exhumations revealed what appeared to be pet remains, but the sheer number of graves boggled the mind.

I consciously shifted my weight onto the balls of my feet as I watched a couple of the Fourth District guys carefully going over the cab of the Mexican victims' pickup truck.

"If it's a double suicide," I said, "how did they time their deaths to happen right after they shot their wad? And if it was an accidental overdose, same question. There had to be a third person involved. How else to explain Mr. Jackson's account of three gunshots? I peg him as credible," I added.

"The CSI folks found no evidence in the marbled room. Or anywhere else in the house. Of bullets bouncing around," countered Honey.

"Since the UPS driver says he heard gunshots, I'm thinking there were gunshots," said Mackie. "He did twenty in the Marines, offered to be printed, gave us a DNA sample, let us swab him for nitrate residue. And he'll take a lie detector test if we want."

"Maybe there were shots, but they came from outside, from out back," said Kruger.

I suspected that Mackie and Kruger, partners for longer than anyone could remember, smelled a rat, and so did I. Honey, well, I couldn't read her yet. I didn't know which way she was leaning, but maybe toward the overdose scenario.

"The way I see it," I said, "the UPS guy interrupted something. The people inside weren't expecting the doorbell to ring."

Mackie and Kruger nodded slightly.

"There are all kinds of nasty poisons that a voodoo practitioner could get his hands on," I pointed out. "Could be these guys were in a lot of pain. That's why the expressions on their faces." I liked this line of logic. The brainstorming session was grounding me to facts and analysis that had nothing to do with spirits.

"The killer then busts a few caps to scare away whoever is at the front door, so he or she can escape out the back. We all know how hard it can be to find a bullet hole when you don't know where to look."

Mackie and Kruger nodded again. The bizarre nature of Professor Drake's home begged the suggestion that something other than suicide had been at play.

As the four of us stood there, I felt thankful that the Homicide Section had been beefed up with more detectives than ever, so officers had fewer cases to handle. The bad news was that overtime had been cut to eight hours a week maximum. That handcuffed a lead investigator like Honey, who could easily put in forty-eight hours of work in the first three days after a murder, meaning she would then have to sit at home for the next four days. I had a strong feeling this was no suicide but the kind of case that would require a lot more than a forty-eight-hour workweek to solve.

"All right. What else do we have right now?" asked Honey. She wasn't showing her hand either way. Good for her.

"I think I figured out who stuffed all the animal heads in the house," I said. "Drake is an amateur taxidermist. He's got the whole setup in the shed out back. As far as I can tell, all the special knives and tools are all there."

"Unusual hobby," said Kruger, lighting a cigarette. "Basically you're taking an animal that someone has killed and then restoring it to a lifelike trophy. It tells me Drake likes to get his hands on and in a dead carcass."

"What about the grounds?" Honey asked.

"I walked the whole perimeter," I said. "There's an asphalt track running along the property line that has to be Drake's own private jogging path. I didn't spot anything unusual, but how about if we bring that Fish and Game warden in, the lady who's so good at reading sign? She could check the fence line, see if anything looks disturbed or maybe pick up a trail. The woods are pretty dense right up against his property on two sides."

Honey nodded. "And K-9s," she said. "We can use Drake's clothes from the house, see if they pick up his scent."

"So why is our professor's car here but not him?" asked Mackie.

"We got his cell number from the Tulane Anthropology Department. But he's not answering," said Honey.

"Imagine that," I said, exhaling bluish smoke from the petite Cuban stick.

"We got about three-quarters of the graves out back dug up. They all contain what looks like cat skeletons," said Kruger.

"How many graves total?" asked Honey.

"Fifty-eight. Some are fresh, but it appears Drake has been burying them for years. And here's the kicker: They're all missing a front left leg."

Honey's face hardened. She loved animals and loved busting those who abused them. And I doubt she cared much for taxidermists.

"That cat thing, I'm not exactly sure, but that sounds like black magic," I said. "I know the voodoo people here in NOLA used to sacrifice black cats and even ate their bones." I had read a few books on voodoo about ten years ago, when I'd first moved to the city and studied its history.

We all exchanged quick, concerned looks, then the meeting broke up and we went back to our individual tasks. I walked over to the pickup, ignoring the Fourth District guys in the cab, and climbed into the truck bed. As I reached for the latex gloves that I always kept in a cargo pocket, I saw Chief Pointer's car turn into the long driveway. Pointer wouldn't show up at a crime scene unless the media were present, and sure enough, I looked over and saw a couple of TV vans being held back on River Road by uniforms.

NOPD Chief Pointer, my old nemesis, had brought me back to the department as a homicide detective under an unusual stipulation: I wasn't to be in the regular rotation, taking on your garden-variety murder cases. Instead, I only worked the Five Alarm cases—high-profile murders—and for those I exclusively partnered with Honey. Since Five Alarm cases didn't happen every day, in order to put in a forty-hour week I'd taken to assisting the other detectives with paperwork and reports. I worked alone, often late at night. To me, a guy accustomed to working eighteen-hour-days, the forty-hour workweek was like a part-time job.

Thankfully, the arrangement I'd created with my homicide peers mitigated what resentment my special status had created. Reports were still typed on typewriters, if one could believe it (and if one could find green typing paper for the "green reports"; I bought my own, since the department was too cheap to provide us with even basic office supplies), so my volunteering to do a lot of other detectives' drudgery went over well. I didn't really mind, because I'm a fast typist, good at writing reports, and the clerical work taught me the strengths and weaknesses of the other detectives in the Homicide Section. I was up-to-date on all of the cases and could offer suggestions for follow-ups or missed leads. Oh, and I'd learned a thing or two about homicide investigation in the process. And politics. Why did major resources get assigned to one investigation but not another? Politics.

I knew no one better at politics than the man whose car pulled up right next to where I stood in the pickup truck bed.

The chief's two huge bodyguards, nattily dressed black men who could intimidate a sumo wrestler, got out of the car. I smiled and nodded hello. The whole department referred to these guys as Heckle and Jeckle, but I liked them. Their boss, Pointer, mumbled into his BlackBerry as he emerged from the backseat.

The chief and I had once been bitter enemies, but we now tolerated each other. Perhaps the millions he'd absconded with from the evidence warehouse a few months ago—money I'd seized and logged into evidence control—tempered his dislike for me. Still, he scowled after glancing my way, then cut off his call.

"Saint James, can't you take a day off?"

"We were literally right next door, Chief."

"I'm told this doesn't look like a double homicide, so I don't think we'll need you on this. Where's Detective Baybee, inside?"

I nodded and Pointer strutted off, flanked by Heckle and Jeckle. The chief had packed on the pounds in the last year and had to be topping 250 now; who needs to work out when you've got two bruisers opening doors for you?

He hadn't officially ordered me to stand down, so I snapped on the latex gloves and turned back to the truck bed. I rooted through pieces of black marble, cans of grout, tubes of caulking, trowels, an electric polisher/sander. A toolbox contained the usual items. I picked up a fifty-pound bag of cement that had been lying on top of a dusty, scratched-up plastic ice chest. I popped open the ice chest and instinctively jumped back.

The decapitated heads of two Hispanic males and one female, probably in their thirties and nicely preserved thanks to some dry ice, told me that both Honey and myself would probably be surpassing our eight-hour overtime limit this week.

Before I could call anyone over, I noticed a man in his fifties, wearing a tweed jacket with patches on the elbows, walk right through the front door of the house, escorted by a uniform.

Professor Drake had shown up to join the party, as if he had appeared out of thin air.

For a moment I was as speechless as my three new friends in the ice chest.

CHAPTER THREE

Kruger was trying to take a statement from Professor Drake in the front room as I entered the house. The professor appeared greatly perturbed to have so many people trampling all over his personal domain.

I ignored him for now and found Honey and Chief Pointer in quiet counsel in Drake's study.

"Saint James, I was just telling Detective Baybee what a good job you both did in responding so quickly, but that I've decided to . . ."

"Wouldn't it be great if we could just call this an overdose or suicide and leave it at that?" I asked. "Sorry to interrupt, Chief, but I'm sure you'll want to know that I just found three human heads in an ice chest in the victims' pickup truck."

Honey's eyes widened a bit. I extended my cell phone, and the chief grabbed it like he didn't believe a word I'd said. As he looked at the phone snaps I'd taken of the heads, I gave Honey a slight, assuring nod. We weren't getting dumped from this case anytime soon.

"Allow me to suggest not releasing this to the press yet, sir," I said. "Or the fact that the victims were naked. On an altar, an altar built like it was designed for human sacrifice." Time to seize the initiative. "The unusual nature of this crime is not good PR for the city, Chief. If you'll assign resources to us, Detective Baybee and I will go balls to the wall and wrap this up fast, on the QT."

With the rug pulled out from under him, a scowl formed on Pointer's lips. "'Fast' being the operative word," he said, slapping the cell phone into my hand. "All right, you're still on the case, even though I'm not convinced the two victims were murdered. The heads might be completely unrelated to the deaths, but find out ASAP."

As he started to leave, he turned back and said, "By the book, detectives."

A moment after he was gone I said to Honey, "That was directed at me."

"No kidding."

Honey nodded for me to follow her, and we walked off to confront the professor.

"Human bones are perfectly legal to own, especially for someone like me," Drake said to Honey. "Please show me the statute to the contrary. I'm a skeletal biologist, for God's sake. I'm a doctor of biological anthropology and a board member of the Society for American Archaeology!"

Drake had a ten-dollar title and acted like a guy who was being inconvenienced. Life would soon be a lot less convenient once we got him downtown and people who didn't give a damn that he has a Ph.D. asked him the same question about fifty times.

"So you can explain where each of these bones came from?" asked Kruger.

"Most definitely," he said, brushing some unseen lint from his tweed jacket. I could see now it was a herringbone pattern, and he looked pretty sharp in it. Crisp chinos, light brown suede shoes, pressed blue denim shirt under the jacket. Black wire-rim glasses, the stubble of a goatee, salt-and-pepper hair over his ears, a Diesel chronograph on his left wrist. It was a cultivated look, the modern anthropologist: urbane and chic yet still a workingman. He was a fairly trim five feet ten, and his hands actually looked like they'd done a bit of manual labor.

"Skeletal biologist means you're a bone specialist, right?" I asked.

"Amongst other things, yes. I used to be an expert witness for the state police lab."

"So you were a guy people like us would use to make a case?"

"That's correct, but that was only a small part of my life's work. My CV is over fifty pages."

"That's impressive. I think my résumé is about half a page," I said, turning to Honey and winking. Drake wasn't sure if I was mocking him, and before he could figure that out, I asked, "So you stuffed the animal heads?"

"That's correct."

"Now that is a skill. But, doc, why a javelina? They are just butt-ugly."

"A trophy of the hunt."

"Yeah? Gee, I always thought killing javelinas was like shooting fish in a barrel."

Drake bristled but didn't respond. We'd already confirmed that his iPhone battery was indeed dead, which is why he said he didn't get our calls. He'd explained his sudden appearance by claiming that a lady friend had picked him up earlier in the day and just dropped him off, unable to drive up to the house due to the police presence.

"What was the name of your lady friend again?" I asked.

"I've already answered that question," he snapped.

"Kate Townsend," answered Kruger. "She used to be his grad assistant at Tulane."

"I hear that at colleges nowadays, the profs get to bang their students and nobody thinks twice," I said, nonchalantly.

Drake started to say something, but checked himself and silently simmered.

"So Kate's your alibi. She was with you all day?"

"No. As I have already explained, something came up for her, so she dropped me at City Park and picked me up after a few hours."

"Okay, so you don't really have an alibi," I said.

"Needing an alibi would connote that I am suspect."

"Make up your mind, Drake," I snapped. "Are you a smart son-ofabitch or are you a dumb bastard? Because anyone with half a brain knows that when the police find two naked dead guys in your house, on a stone altar built to drain off fluids into a floor drain, they're going to ask a lot of questions and have you prove where the hell you've been."

Drake tried to compose himself. "I have no idea what happened here."

"Horseshit," I said evenly.

"Do I need to call a lawyer?"

"Are you saying you don't know the two dead men in your home?" I asked. "Come on," I said, taking his arm and lifting him to his feet. "Let's see if we can jog your memory."

I escorted Drake to the murder scene, followed by Honey, Mackie, and Kruger. The CSI techies were still doing their thing, and the coroner stood off to the side chatting on his cell phone.

"Well?" I asked Drake.

"I know them. They're contractors. They've worked for me on and off for some time. They had almost completed a room addition."

"You talking about this room? The S-and-M sex chamber?"

"Yes, this room." Drake looked over to Kruger. "Is there someone else who could interrogate me other than this offensive gentleman?" he asked.

"You're going to get interrogated by a lot of people, Drake," said Kruger, lighting a cigarette.

"There's no smoking in my home," Drake said, irritated.

"There is now."

"Did the two victims have keys to your house?" asked Mackie.

"No."

"Did anybody?"

Drake looked uncomfortable. "Only Kate." He paused, then said, "Felix and Roscindo showed up for work as usual this morning, to finish work here in the temple."

"Temple?" asked Mackie.

"Yes, temple. I left with Kate, and when I returned home I found half the New Orleans Police Department in my front yard."

"So you knew the Mexican guys pretty well," I stated.

"Well enough."

"And that's all they are to you, just part-time workers?"

"What else?"

"Professor Drake," said Honey, "please don't answer a question with a question."

"They have always been good workers," he said, not answering the question, as he glanced around the room.

"How did you pay them? Check or cash, daily, weekly, or by the job?"

"Weekly, in cash. I paid them twenty dollars per hour."

"So you were all caught up with the payments. You weren't behind or anything. You didn't owe them money."

"I paid them weekly, but not the full amount."

Honey stole a look at me. I had floated the notion of the Mexican workers being owed money as we'd pulled up to the crime scene.

"How much do you owe them, doc?" I asked.

"I can't say exactly, I'd have to check."

"Approximately," said Mackie. "Give us a ballpark figure."

"Eight or nine thousand. I got more ambitious than I'd originally planned and had to put more money into materials such as the black marble. Felix and Roscindo had no problem with carrying the debt."

"So you don't know them that well, they're just workers, they're illegal aliens driving a beat-up pickup truck, and you're a tenured Tulane professor with a nice house and a new, overpriced hybrid car, but they have no problem with you owing them almost ten grand?"

Drake shifted a bit uncomfortably on his feet and didn't answer.

"Professor Drake, please respond," said Honey.

"They were also students of mine."

"At Tulane?" I asked, surprised.

"No, of course not," he said, irritated. "They attended studies here in my home."

"Private lessons?" asked Mackie, pointedly.

"No. I lead a weekly . . . spiritual studies group."

"Spiritual studies. Here in the *temple,* right? You mean voodoo and sex and stuff like that?" I said.

"No, I don't mean that at all, and I can't see why it would have any bearing on this."

"You're being disingenuous, professor," said Mackie.

"I knew them primarily as employees," he said, exasperated.

"Are you feeling okay, doc?" I asked.

"Of course not! I'm upset, as you might imagine."

I had quickly arranged a little surprise show-and-tell with Honey just before we came in to question Drake. I reached into a plastic bag on the floor behind me, pulled out the female decapitated head, and swung it practically into Drake's face. "I'll bet you're feeling better than this lady."

Drake blanched at the head swinging in his face, but his gaze quickly shifted to one of morbid curiosity.

"Friend of yours, doc?" Mackie asked.

"No."

"Funny, but we found a few of these out in Felix Sanchez's truck," I said. "Were you buying or selling?"

Drake suddenly look resigned to the fact that he had a major problem. The wheels appeared to be spinning in his head, but in moments, he settled down completely and looked nonplussed. "I believe you will learn that it's not illegal for me to own one of these, either, detective," said Drake contemptuously. "Now I want to call my lawyer."

"Okay," I said, casually holding on to the head. "You call your lawyer, then we're taking you downtown in handcuffs past the TV cameras and I'll be walking next to you holding this lady's head. We won't leak a word to the press—we won't have to. Let's go!"

Mackie reached to grab Drake's arm—

"Wait. What . . . what do you want to ask me?"

"Just so we understand each other, you *are* going downtown. The way we take you there depends on how you answer my next few questions."

"All right," he said resentfully.

"We want the names and contact info of everyone who attended your 'spiritual study' group."

"That's fine. That's reasonable."

"So now that you can see how your students died here, care to tell us what you think happened? There are no obvious signs of death."

"Perhaps they didn't do a proper banishing."

"A what?"

"They might have summoned a demon but failed to control it. It could have literally frightened them to death. I can tell you that the white streak in Felix's hair wasn't there when I saw him this morning."

Honey, Kruger, Mackie, and myself all exchanged looks.

"Demons don't fire gunshots," said Mackie.

"They can create any kind of sound they want."

"I guess we need to call in Harry Potter," said Kruger.

"The Demon Defense. 'I didn't kill the two naked dead guys in my house I owed money to, Your Honor. An evil spirit did it,'" I said.

"You asked me what I thought and I told you," snapped Drake.

"And you had better hope I can summon it and send it back where it belongs."

"Why is that?" I asked.

"Because it might not stop with Felix and Roscindo."

"Thanks for your thoughts on the crime," said Honey, bringing this line of discussion to a halt. "We'd like you to open the safe in your study. Show us what's inside."

"No, I won't do that."

"Why not?" I asked.

"Because my private affairs are my business. I'll give you the names and contact information of my students, and then I'm calling my lawyer."

Drake wasn't bluffing and wouldn't open the safe. He escaped the silver-bracelet treatment, but the way we manhandled him past the cameras made him look guilty as hell. Oh, and I didn't walk out holding the head, since the chief hadn't left and I had to be a good boy and go by the book.

Honey took me aside as Mackie put Drake into a squad car.

"The guy is hiding something, Honey."

"He's lawyering up. We won't be able to sweat him."

Honey tore off a piece of paper from her pocket spiral notebook and handed it to me.

"Both of the victims' driver's license addresses are bogus. Fake Social Security cards, the usual illegal alien kit. But I called a couple of numbers on Felix Sanchez's cell . . ."

"The one with the streak of white hair?"

Honey nodded. "Got hold of his wife. They all live together out in Kenner on Airline Drive."

"What did you tell her?"

"I told her NOPD has impounded the truck. Which we have."

"I'll give her the news," I said. You always want to give the news to spouses in person, out of courtesy, but also to judge the reactions, since wives and husbands knock each other off all the time. "I'll have Fred Gaudet meet me. He's fluent in Spanish."

"Her name is Gina and she speaks English. But yeah. Maybe Fred can help. Bring her in for a statement. Then to the morgue to ID the bodies."

I nodded. "You know, for a while today, I wasn't sure you thought we had homicides here."

"I'm trying to be open-minded. Except about the demon business. But I'm not convinced we have murders. Poison accounts for less than two percent of all homicides. And I like to play the percentages. These guys could have overdosed."

She turned her back to me and got into her unit.

Great. My partner and I weren't on the same page.

CHAPTER FOUR

The shabby, two-story pastel stucco building housed apartments on the second floor above a Mexican restaurant called Casa de la Carne, or "House of Meat," so my advice would be to skip the fish.

Fred Gaudet, a burglary detective and old friend of mine, who came off more like a soft-spoken, bespectacled librarian than a cop, had met me in the parking lot. The aromas were such that we fought the urge to grab some *carnitas* before interviewing Gina Sanchez and informing her that her husband wouldn't be returning home from work today. Or ever.

Sanchez collapsed into hysterics after we informed her of Felix's and Roscindo's demise, allowing me to casually search the apartment as she sobbed. I sent Fred to interview the neighbors here on the second floor, who were all Mexican and probably illegals.

We'd already been told by Alberto, the paunchy, middle-aged owner of Casa de la Carne, who was also the landlord, that Felix and Roscindo were *curanderos*—folk healers/bush doctors—and that they'd been living here quietly for about a year. The apartment contained, *sans* bones, the dollar-store version of Drake's museum-quality collection of occult objects: dusty fossils, quartz geodes, cheap ceramic figures of Catholic saints with the paint chipping off, *botanica* candles, broken abalone shells, small pieces of agate, rose quartz, and lapis lazuli. Open tins on a shelf held sage, sweet grass, and small vials and bottles of lotions. There was a shaman's rattle made from animal horn, and a stainless steel water drum. Bottles of inexpensive rum and a five-pack of cheap cigars sat on an altar containing figurines, rocks, flowers, and a glass of clear liquid.

I noticed a Snickers bar on the floor near the front door next to a pan full of what looked like sugar. Something had been dropped onto the sugar: blood?

I also noticed lots of dust and grime and grit, which told me that Gina Sanchez wasn't much for cleaning. The dim rooms were the home of working shamans, and while they wouldn't win any *Good Housekeeping* awards, they weren't as eerie as Drake's place.

I looked over as she suddenly stood from the worn red-and-gold secondhand sofa.

"I must cook for Felix."

I usually have a pretty good poker face, but she got me with that remark. I watched dumbfounded as she moved into the kitchen, wiping her eyes, the crying jag finished for now.

"Umm, Mrs. Sanchez . . . I've been waiting to take you downtown to make a statement. And we need you to—if you feel up to it—make an official identification of your husband and Roscindo Ruiz."

"Okay, but I think you search my house, not waiting, okay? So I let you do, and now I must to cook. This no take long."

She busted me straight up on that one, and there was nothing to gain by forcing the issue, so I watched as she lit a stove burner under a pan and set about collecting ingredients from the fridge. She turned on the oven, wrapped three tortillas in foil, and put them and a canary yellow plate inside.

Gina Sanchez was a pleasant-looking woman who I pegged for late-thirties, about five feet two, shoulder-length brown hair, dark brown eyes. Slightly flabby from bad diet and lack of exercise, but not chubby. She wore little in the way of makeup and struck me as being a very determined lady, so I decided to get the ball rolling right here in the kitchen.

"We don't know why Felix and Roscindo died."

She shot me a sharp look as if *she* knew. She spooned lard into the hot pan, then added tomatoes, garlic, chopped onion, oregano, roasted serrano chilies, and salt.

"Did he have any enemies that you know of? People he owed money to, people not happy with the work he did for them?"

"Enemies, no. But many bad people in this world." She spooned some kind of thick sauce out of a bowl into a second pan over very low heat. "About construction, I no think he have unhappy customer. If they unhappy, Felix and Roscindo go back to fix something free."

"So no business records."

"They work for cash. No check, no credit card, no paper."

"Did anybody owe your husband money?"

"I no think so. Felix, he no say that."

Strange. Drake said he owed the Mexicans almost ten thousand dollars. Would Felix have kept that from his wife?

"And the other business they did? They were shamans, right?"

"Yes, but the same—only take cash. People come to them

because of what they hear, what someone tell them. They work seven days and most nighttime. Work construction or work with spirits."

"How long were they doing that?"

"For many year. They help people. People come for reason of love . . . or hate. For health, for happiness. These days, most come for money or luck with jobs." She quickly shelled three hard-boiled eggs and with amazing speed chopped them finely.

"Any unhappy customers?"

"People know is the spirits who can help them, not Felix or Roscindo. Maybe you think Felix was murder, yes?"

"It's a possibility we haven't ruled out. Did they take recreational drugs, or maybe some kind of herbs or something, mushrooms, ayahuasca, as part of their work?"

"Roscindo, I no can say. Felix, never. He no that kind of *brujo*." She stirred the sauce on low heat and stuck her finger in it to test the temperature. "Now I ask you question. You find money in his truck?"

"Money? No. His truck had some . . . interesting things, but no money."

"Maybe the witch steal it."

"Who are you talking about?"

"Same who probably kill him."

I locked eyes with her.

"You have a name?"

"I can no give you name, but she in class with Felix, Roscindo, and others."

"At Drake's house."

Sanchez nodded. "He keep our money under his truck. The rear . . . 'fender' is the word?"

I nodded.

"Felix make some special box there."

"Then maybe it's still there. How much cash are we talking about?"

"Almost fifty thousand dollars. I show you."

A small green candle sat on the kitchen windowsill with a U.S. five-dollar bill behind it. Sanchez retrieved the bill and pointed out a small black symbol that had been written in the lower right quadrant.

"Felix make a mark, like a prayer, on every dollar he save."

The mark looked strangely similar to the glyph I had seen painted next to Drake's front door. I reached into my wallet and gave her a five spot. "I'll trade you, Mrs. Sanchez, if that's okay." I pocketed the marked bill.

"Yes, is okay. This money in his truck—he save everything since we come here to work after the big Storm. We illegal, so Felix no trust banks. I send little money home to Mexico, but Felix no want do that. The money is . . ." She choked back the tears and tightly held the countertop for support. After a three-count, she regained her composure and said, ". . . is for our future."

She bit her lip to choke back sobs. Tears gushed down her cheeks, but she concentrated on the large pan. The tomatoes had released their juices, so she turned off the heat and stirred the ingredients into what looked like a warm salsa.

I hated like hell to ask this question but it had to be asked. "Why would Felix and Roscindo be naked on an altar in a strange room at Professor Drake's house? And they both had orgasms before they died. You understand what that means?"

Her eyes flashed. "If what you say is true, then she use them."

She turned off both burners and removed the yellow plate and the tortillas from the oven.

"Who?"

"The witch."

She dipped the warm tortillas into the sauce using tongs, positioned them on the yellow plate, then spooned chopped egg down the middle of each one. She rolled them up so they looked like enchiladas before pouring the remaining sauce on top. Then she poured the warm tomato salsa over the middle of the tortilla rolls and sprinkled chopped egg on top. "Is *papadzules*. Felix's favorite."

I'd have been a liar if I said I hadn't become hungry as hell.

She picked up the plate, and I followed her into the living room, where she reverently set the food on an altar. She removed a photo of Felix from a shelf, then placed it on the altar behind the yellow plate. And she lit a white candle.

"This enough for now."

She had just made a hot plate of food for her dead husband, and who was to say she was crazy to do it? Not me; I was actually touched. But I stayed focused.

"Mrs. Sanchez, did Felix practice black magic?"

"When he young, but not for many year. He no do bad thing. He try to help people."

"If your husband was so good, why did he have three human heads in an ice chest in his truck?"

Her knees buckled just a bit. "*Ay dios mio*," she whispered, as an expression of extreme disappointment. She shook her head in disbelief.

"You knew about the heads, didn't you?"

After a long pause she said, "I tell him no do that kind of thing. He think he can make easy money."

"I hate to say this, but I need names. Otherwise, I'm afraid you will be in some trouble."

"You find heads in his truck?"

"Yes."

"Then he no get paid for them. So I already in trouble. Better if you arrest and deport me."

"We're not allowed to do that."

"But I am illegal and you are policeman."

"Yes, well, we live in strange times. Tell me, why would you be in trouble because of the heads? Felix is dead."

"Death no erase this debt. Better I go to La Migra myself. They deport me and I find work in Mexico City, where Las Calaveras no have power. But if I stay here, they will come for money. And I no have cash, so Las Calaveras will kill me."

Las Calaveras, or the Skulls, was a bloodthirsty, brutally ruthless Mexican drug cartel. The gang's logo was a human skull with a rattlesnake intertwined through the eye sockets and its hissing head emerging from the mouth cavity. I couldn't blame Sanchez for being fearful of their wrath. "Sorry, but I can't allow you to leave New Orleans right now."

She looked at me with hard eyes for a long moment. She turned away, retrieved a soft box of Swisher Sweets from a drawer, and lit one of the cheap cigars. She then took a swig right from a bottle of Ronrico rum and, taking me completely by surprise, spit the rum onto me.

I flinched. Before I could say a word, she began puffing madly *into* the cigar, never taking it from her lips as she blew smoke up and down my body.

This was all new to me. After several seconds, she stood back and closely examined the long ash on the cigar tip, then fixed me with a stare.

"You are strong, you have much power, much help. Maybe you can find this killer. Or maybe some killer will find you." She crushed out the cigar in the sink. "But the spirits tell me to help you. So let's go."

CHAPTER FIVE

Felix's truck had been towed to the Broad Street evidence cage, part of the police headquarters complex, so I took Gina Sanchez there first to confirm her story about a secret hidden compartment under the rear fender. The compartment was there; the money wasn't. Gina didn't look surprised.

"I searched this truck myself at Professor Drake's house. But we looked *in* the truck, not under the truck. I don't think any police or the tow-truck driver or any of the yard workers looked there either, Mrs. Sanchez."

"I know who take it."

"I need a name."

"She just want money and power."

"You're talking about one of Drake's students. Which one?"

"If I help you, they kill me!"

"The Skulls? Las Calaveras?"

"No, this different." My built-in bullshit detector started to beep inside my head. Sanchez was now claiming that if she talked, she'd have *two* groups out to kill her.

"We can protect you, put you in protective custody," I said, thinking it would be a good way to keep an eye on her and keep her from skipping town or sliding into the netherworld of illegals. The truth was, there was very little a police department could do to stop a foreign national from leaving.

"You can protect me from demons?"

I gave her the blankest look I could muster.

"What kind of police can do that?" she asked as a follow-up.

I'm not a religious guy, even though I go to church sometimes. I like to think I'm spiritual, but what exactly is a spiritual person, anyway? My smart-ass response to Gina Sanchez, which I kept to myself was, *Due to budget cuts, we shut down the unit that used to protect people from witches.*

I had my superstitions, true. Compared to Honey, I was a true believer. But in a million years I wouldn't believe what Drake had said about a demon or that somebody could send demons to kill Gina Sanchez. But I had to honor the notion that *she* believed it. In fact, I respect the superstitions and beliefs of all cultures, because not to do so is to stake out a platform of arrogant scientific materialism, an intellectual superiority implying that "we know better." Well, the physics and history and archaeology textbooks keep getting rewritten, don't they, by smug academics who never pony up any mea culpas? So I don't know who holds any ultimate truths. I simply try to avoid exercising cultural imperialism.

Sanchez feared the Skulls cartel would kill her for the money owed. There was nothing arcane about that organization: They were psychopathic killers. A simple Internet search would turn up numerous videos made by the Skulls of them torturing and beheading their opponents. They often displayed the decapitated heads of their enemies on poles or hung from trees or public monuments, and were rumored to be involved in sorcery.

Demons sent from a witch, however, was an issue I would use only to the extent that I wanted the name of Drake's student, whom Gina believed killed her husband, Felix, and their friend Roscindo.

Gina Sanchez didn't have an alibi. She claimed to have been at home all day, but Fred Gaudet told me the neighbors couldn't confirm that. She and Felix were a one-vehicle family, and she said she usually got around by bus. I placed her in an interrogation room at Homicide, and Mackie took over to get her statement. I'd given her chewing gum and a soft drink so we could get her prints and DNA if she refused to submit a sample.

Drake sat parked in an adjacent room with his lawyer. They were trying to come off as cooperative without really cooperating. Kruger, maybe the best interrogator we had, was handling the questioning when Honey returned from the autopsies. After she checked in with Kruger, I caught her in the hallway and filled her in on what I'd learned from Sanchez.

"The Skulls are some bad mothers," said Honey. "My SWAT commander had some ICE agents come in and give us a presentation. There's a small group of them that come in and out of NOLA. Since the Storm. Bringing in dope."

"And heads, apparently."

"Apparently. Will she accept protective custody?" asked Honey. "Or is she a top-tier suspect?"

"I wouldn't make her a prime suspect, but we can't rule her out yet. And no, she won't accept protective custody. But I do believe she's scared: She wanted me to arrest and deport her. Does the VCAT have a line on the local Skulls gang? Maybe we need to go proactive."

The Violent Crime Abatement Team follows and apprehends the most vicious local thugs. Since the chief had, de facto, made this a Five Alarm case, Honey and I would have a free hand in using other NOPD resources for the investigation.

"I'll find out," Honey said, walking into the big office toward her desk. "Is Fred Gaudet here?"

"I cut him loose after we finished up at Sanchez's place."

"Tell him he's on assignment with Homicide for now. I need a Spanish speaker to run down all the numbers in Felix and Roscindo's phones."

She handed me two cell phones in evidence bags.

"Any duty that gets him close to Mexican food, he likes. Hey, did anything new turn up with the coroner?" I asked.

She shook her head. "He's still thinking overdose but will run broad tests for poisons."

"Since these guys were bush doctors, and considering Drake's background and all this talk about witches, there may have been some very esoteric herbs or plants used on our victims, assuming they were poisoned. Not sure how much help a broad test will be."

"Agreed. But we got what we got."

"So you want to start with Drake's students?"

Honey nodded and handed me the list of names that Drake had provided.

As I scanned it, Sgt. Penny, a black lady in her fifties whose uniform had the sharpest creases in town, walked up, holding a parcel. I liked Penny; she'd been a good street cop back in the day and always looked ready for a uniform inspection.

"You two newbies probably never met Tony Fournier, retired homicide detective," said Penny, without preamble. "He was the department's unofficial occult specialist once upon a time. Been out for at least six years or so. He dropped this off for ya'll. His old case files on Professor Robert Drake."

"Case files? But Sarge, Drake doesn't have a record," I said, a little confused.

"No thanks to Tony. He tried to put Drake away for over a decade. Mostly on his own time." She hoisted into my hands a huge manila envelope that weighed about the same as an old Los Angeles phone book.

"The department needs a new expert on hoodoo and all that spooky stuff. Which one a' you will it be?"

"Not me," said Honey quickly. "Who wants to be an 'expert' on something that's a load of bunk?"

Sgt. Penny noted Honey's reaction with a raise of her eyebrows. "My great-grandma knew Marie Laveau, so I will just have to bite my tongue, detective."

Marie Laveau (there may have been more than one Marie Laveau) was the most famous, and infamous, voodoo priestess in New Orleans's long line of occult personages. A larger-than-life legend, for many decades in the 1800s she wielded enormous influence over the police, city officials, and the movers and shakers of high society. And to the true believers, her power was unequaled.

"Is Fournier still in the building?" I asked, ripping open the envelope and eyeing the files.

"Wouldn't know. His number's inside. He said to call if you wanted to talk." Sgt. Penny winked at me, then started to slowly saunter off as I thumbed through the folder.

"Thanks, Sarge. You still using hairspray and a hot iron to make those pants creases so sharp they could cut a poor boy like me?"

"Mop & Glo, not hairspray, newbie," she said, and shuffled off.

I was still absorbing the sheer magnitude of the files in my hands when I heard Honey ask, "You coming or not?" with an impatient bite to her tone.

"You don't want to look at the files first?"

"I want to interrogate suspects. Living and breathing ones. Looks like you could spend a week reading all that."

I arbitrarily opened a folder and saw something that caught my eye. I pulled a newspaper clipping.

"Okay. Let's go." I checked my curiosity, put the fat envelope of files under my arm, and followed her out. "Where to?"

"Crafty Voodoo in the Quarter."

"You want to go to a voodoo store?"

"Kate Townsend, the first name on Drake's list, is the owner and lives upstairs," said Honey.

"Allow me to suggest making a stop first. Drake owns a curio shop over in Riverbend. A curious curio shop. Selling occult items." I handed her the clipping from Fournier's files. "This old *Times-Picayune* article mentions that Drake had a lamp for sale with a special lampshade. A lampshade made from human skin."

CHAPTER SIX

Late autumn darkness swallowed up the residential Riverbend street, and the brisk wind nipped like a cold, hungry dog. Honey and I got out of her unit, and I zipped my jacket all the way up. Damp cold could chill you to the bone, and the strange weather front that had snuck in earlier today loomed over the city with the welcome of an icy blanket. The street lay black and quiet, and as I glanced around I saw lights shining in some homes but no one outside on porches, in yards, or on the street.

We approached Drake's curio shop, a faded-gray, two-story wooden corner structure that bore no signage. Honey shined her xenon flashlight on the windows. The glass looked like it hadn't been cleaned since the Korean War, making it hard to see beyond the dusty window displays of Black Cat Oil, Lucky Jazz, Get-Together Drops, Hell's Devil Oil, and Drawing Powder. These old voodoo potions stood like a presentation frozen in time. Maybe the place used to be a drugstore.

The windows and doors were securely barred, and the crud

collected around the front suggested the doors hadn't been open for business in a long time.

"Sure would like to see what's inside," I mused.

"Don't get any ideas just yet," said Honey, looking at the second-story windows, which were heavily curtained. "I'll talk to Second District. Get the four-one-one on this place."

"You're not suggesting I would commit an illegal act to gain entry, to get the unvarnished truth of what's inside before Drake walks out of police headquarters and has a chance to sanitize the interior, are you, detective?" I asked with mock indignation, as I pulled a lock-picking tool from a cargo pocket.

"I might feel different if Felix and Roscindo had their heads cut off. But what if the coroner is right? What if they OD'd? Gives us zero excuse to 'accidentally' break in here."

I put the tool away. We rounded the corner to check the other street side. There were two heavy doors locked tight. "One of these doors is probably a separate entrance for the upstairs, but I doubt anyone lives here."

The other, unseen sides of the building directly abutted neighboring homes, so entering or exiting via a door could only be done street-side. I quickly calculated the best way to break in, since I held no hope Honey could get us a search warrant and didn't even bother asking about it.

"What did the article say about the human-skin lampshade?"

"It said that Saddam Hussein had owned it. That some guy approached Drake needing money, and so Drake bought it. If you read the article you get the idea that Drake thought he was talking to a customer in his shop and didn't know he was talking to a reporter. He didn't want any publicity."

"Even though the heads were in Felix's truck? They were on Drake's property. I'll try to get us a warrant. So keep your lock picks in your pocket."

Not likely.

Honey and I parked across the street from Crafty Voodoo on Chartres just after 9 P.M. We could see from the car that the joint was still busy with tourists looking for a unique souvenir from Sin City South.

Voodoo shops were the new spin on the corner drugstores of old that used to sell physical gris-gris items, such as oils, bags, dolls, powders, ad infinitum, which were used to achieve some specific purpose, like success in gambling or luck in matters of the heart. With the acceptance of voodoo and every other kind of religious or spiritual practice, Louisiana voodoo, or hoodoo, became a local cottage industry. So aside from all the usual gear, such as ritual candles, charms, talismans, jujus, mojo bags, statues, and books, one could buy key chains, bracelets, T-shirts, bumper stickers, and every other conceivable piece of merchandise that could be tied to voodoo, however tangentially.

Maybe Drake's curio shop had once been one of those corner drugstores selling gris-gris to wives hoping to keep their husbands from straying, and to men trying to win the affections of young ladies. If so, the owner might be turning over in his grave at how mainstream voodoo paraphernalia had become. The commercialization of the religion seemed to almost take the mystery out of it. Almost.

As I got out of Honey's unit parked in front of Townsend's shop, I caught sight of a solitary figure in a second-floor window above the store. Even from this distance I could tell she was a pale beauty, with long, wavy black hair cascading down her back, a diaphanous gown backlit by a soft light, a long, lithe figure that somehow seemed very alone. *Kate Townsend?* I couldn't take my eyes off the woman, and she finally stepped aside and disappeared somewhere into the room.

Honey hadn't noticed the figure, so I didn't say anything as we crossed Chartres and entered the store.

Like other voodoo emporiums I'd visited in the Quarter, Crafty Voodoo also had an on-site psychic to give readings, had a separate room where various herbs and concoctions could be conjured up to order, and had several very large and unique voodoo altars, one of which looked surprisingly like the one in Drake's "temple" chamber.

I couldn't help but notice that all of the clerks were extremely attractive females wearing short shorts and matching Crafty Voodoo polo shirts that showcased their ample bosoms. Perhaps that could help explain the crowd. A sign prohibited any kind of photography, which seemed petty, especially since the feel of the place was extremely commercial, kind of like walking into a Hooters franchise.

Once Honey saw I was no longer checking out the store's merchandise but the employee's merchandise, she flashed her badge at the cashier. "We need to speak with Kate Townsend."

Before the cashier could respond, a tall, long-haired redhead confidently strode through a doorway covered by a colorful bead curtain. "I've been expecting you. Shall we go upstairs?"

Townsend was a striking woman of about thirty, but I felt a pang of disappointment that she wasn't the female I'd seen in the window. No, the woman in front of me looked more like a banker than a voodoo shop owner. She wore a sharp charcoal-colored business suit, black heels, and her trendy eyeglasses looked like real tortoiseshell, a PC no-no. Pale blue eyes, ghost white skin, and facial freckles told me her red hair color was natural.

Honey and I followed her through a doorway and up a narrow flight of stairs. As a man mounting steep stairs below a woman in a skirt, I couldn't help but notice that her shoes were Kenneth Cole and had to cost at least five hundred dollars for the pair.

You never know what you're going to get in a French Quarter apartment, and Kate Townsend's place was a surprise: The front room featured mid-twentieth-century modern furnishings flanked by stark white walls. Even with the crown moldings, the baseboards, the pocket doors, and the ceiling medallions in place, the room felt ultramodern. Honey and I sat on a sofa upholstered in white suede, as Townsend settled into a chair.

We had already introduced ourselves as we walked up the staircase, and Townsend began talking before we could ask a question.

"I met Robert, Professor Drake, five years ago when I was twenty-five and came to Tulane to get my Ph.D. I became one of his graduate assistants and fell in love with him. He's been a mentor, close friend, financial backer, confidant, and lover ever since. But not a husband. We both like our independence too much for that," she said, smiling. "So we're nonexclusive, sexually."

Honey and I both looked on stoically, but she took out her pocket spiral notebook even though she knew my pocket video camera and voice recorder were committing everything to digitized memory.

"I picked him up this morning around eight," Townsend continued. "We were going to spend several hours in City Park gathering herbs and other items we use in our magical practice. Certain grasses and flowers, bark, things like that. Well, I got a call from my Webmaster that the business site had crashed, so I dropped Robert off at the park and then came back here to work on my computer. I picked him up at the park around noon or so, drove him back to the West Bank, and that's when we both saw that something was very wrong at his house."

"Are you aware of what happened?" I asked. Honey and I had already agreed that I would take the lead in the interrogation.

"I saw it on the news, yes."

"You haven't spoken to Mr. Drake?"

"He called me from the police station after his lawyer arrived."

"What did he say, exactly?"

"That Roscindo and Felix were found dead in his home and he feared that the police thought he killed them."

"What else?" I asked quickly.

"I don't think I'm required to give you that kind of private information. But I'll tell you that you're wasting your time if it's a murderer you're looking for. Roscindo and Felix were *brujos* who experimented with all kinds of plant medicines, psychotropic drugs, and sexual stimulants, both natural and synthetic."

"You've witnessed that?" asked Honey.

Townsend hesitated for a moment. "They told me so. Many Latin American healers and shamans use drugs during the course of their work. That's nothing new."

"And you got to know them how?"

"There's been an ongoing study group at Robert's house since before I knew him. Meditation and other spiritual work. Sending healing energy to sick people. I got to know them a bit chatting during the breaks."

"So you don't know them well?" I said.

"Not really."

"You never saw them outside of Drake's classes?"

She paused for a moment. "That's correct."

"So you didn't know them well, but they told you they used Viagra?"

"I didn't say the word 'Viagra,' but, yes, we would talk about our mutual spiritual work, our techniques, tricks of the trade. If you've been to their home, then you will find all of their tools and medicines."

"How would you know that? You said you've never seen them outside of Drake's house."

"It's logical to assume . . ."

"Miss Townsend, we're not asking you to assume anything. So please don't. Please just give us facts as you understand them."

Townsend visibly flushed but said nothing.

"So you saw Felix Sanchez and Roscindo Ruiz this morning when you went to pick up Drake?"

She answered but with a decidedly less friendly edge to her voice. "Their truck was there, but I didn't see them, no."

"You said Drake was your financial backer."

"He loaned me seed money to help get the shop off the ground."

"Do you know if he owed Sanchez or Ruiz any money?"

"I don't."

"Are you or Drake voodoo practitioners?"

"Not exactly. The gris-gris I sell downstairs is only part of the equation. The other part is the nonphysical part, the invocations one has to say to call upon the magical properties of voodoo. I've used voodoo but I don't consider it my religion because that's too limiting. Robert and I are fusionists, interdisciplinary sorcerers, if you will. We use many techniques and modalities from many different belief structures and cultural systems. It's all about the manipulation of energy, and there are many ways to achieve that."

"So could someone have killed Sanchez and Ruiz with voodoo or black magic or one of these 'techniques' you mentioned?"

"Theoretically, it's possible, if you believe what's in the literature."

"But not to your firsthand knowledge?" asked Honey.

"That would be some very dark work. It doesn't interest me."

"Know anyone who's talked about doing that kind of work, someone who knew our victims?" I asked.

She hesitated, thinking. "Hans Vermack. He owns the Voodoo Cave on Saint Peter. But I'm not saying he had anything to do with . . . what happened today."

Hans Vermack was on the short list of students Drake had given us. "So both you and Hans own voodoo shops?"

"There are a half dozen in the French Quarter alone. It's a good business."

"Tell us about the stone altar in the middle of the temple chamber," I said.

"That would seem odd to you, wouldn't it?"

"The grooves and floor drain suggest . . ."

"Something sinister?" She laughed heartily, tilting her head back, revealing a soft, lily white neck. "We sometimes do ceremonies of a Hindu nature. We'll pour honey, milk, flower essence, scented oils, and so on over a large, smooth stone representing a lingam."

"Lingam?"

"A phallus. The stone altar has a concave area where the stone sits, and it represents the yoni—the female. We used to make quite a mess, so Robert had the grooves etched in and the drain installed. Easy cleanup."

Honey was nodding like she wanted to believe it. I wasn't so sure.

"That sounds harmless," I said, "but what do you know about decapitated human heads? You or the professor wouldn't buy those, now, would you? To fill a special order perhaps? Or to use in some ceremony?"

Her face froze, but her eyes darted from myself to Honey and back as she seemed to gauge a response. "I don't know what you're talking about."

Kate Townsend had just lied, I felt sure of it. "I'm talking about human heads brought into the country from Mexico."

She said nothing.

"Would you mind if we took a look around your place?" I asked.

"I'd have to insist on a search warrant, first. You're on a fishing expedition. No, a witch hunt. People of my belief have suffered and been discriminated against and have been tortured and killed for centuries by those looking for scapegoats. So no, I won't play that game."

"That's fine, but Robert Drake suggested that Sanchez and Ruiz summoned a demon that they lost control of. That the demon killed them. Does that sound sinister to you?"

"I think it's time for you to leave."

Kate Townsend stood up, as if dismissing us.

"Sit down, Miss Townsend, or we'll finish this conversation downtown in a dreary room next to your boyfriend," I said.

Honey looked at me and then looked over to Townsend, who

sat back down. "Is there someone who can confirm that you were here in your apartment this morning?" asked Honey.

Kate pretended to think for a second. "Yes, Sheri was here. She saw me several times this morning. Sheri Myers. She has a room here and works for me downstairs."

"So Sheri is . . ."

"I provide rooms for battered women. Free of charge. I help get them off the street, give them a job if I can. Get them away from drugs, the strip clubs. Sheri shares a bedroom with another girl and pays me a modest room-and-board fee out of her earnings."

"Really? How do you find these girls?" I asked.

"They find me. It's on the street, what I do. And I don't take any money from the government for it."

"Bringing strangers, transients into your home like that can be dangerous."

She gave me a look like she wasn't worried about it. "I can handle them."

"We'll talk to Sheri on the way out," said Honey, who looked like she was ready to go.

"If it should turn out that the two men were murdered, Miss Townsend, then how would you explain it?" I asked.

"I couldn't say. I liked them. I don't know anyone who didn't."

Honey's cell rang and she checked the caller ID. "Excuse me, I have to take this." She stood up, crossed the room, turned her back, and spoke softly into her cell.

"You know, for such a fearless man, you're terribly afraid," Townsend said to me softly so Honey couldn't hear.

"Is that right?"

"You don't believe in witchcraft or sorcery, do you?"

"A lot of people don't."

"Because they've never experienced it."

"I used to believe in the tooth fairy, until I lost all my baby teeth."

"You're being flip to hide your fear. I can see into your psyche, detective. I see that you're afraid of your own true power. Of your sexuality. Of the spirit world and what it has to offer you. At the root of all that is a fear of losing control. Surrendering to the unknown is not something you will countenance."

I felt defensive, but I couldn't disagree that I liked to be in control of most situations; seems like a good way to stay alive in my kind of work.

"I see your spirit guide standing behind you. Some kind of Taoist magician. You have very strong protection you can call upon, but you could be doing so much more. The spirits are waiting to work with you."

"I prefer dealing with the living, Miss Townsend. But I'll take what you said under advisement."

"You prefer the living? Is that why you're a homicide detective, dealing with the dead on a daily basis?"

For once, I didn't know what to say.

"I can also see people's sex lives."

"In my case, there's not much to see."

"You're repressing yourself. You're carrying a torch for someone. It's unrequited lust. For your partner, isn't it? I can see that this is not healthy for you. She'll never be yours."

"Sorry, but you couldn't be more wrong."

Honey rescued me by turning back to Townsend and saying, "Thanks for your time, Miss Townsend."

We made our way downstairs. Sheri Myers, one of the Crafty Voodoo clerks, backed up Townsend's assertion that she was home for most of the morning. Myers would have every reason to provide a phony cover story to the lady that rescued her from the streets.

Honey and I walked outside and waited for passing traffic to clear on Chartres, then crossed toward her police unit. A frozen blast of air caused me to hunch my shoulders in protest.

"That was the chief who called my cell. Did you get anything out of Townsend while I was on the horn?"

"Nothing you wouldn't laugh at. She told me . . ."

My peripheral vision picked up a blur as I heard the throaty rumble of a growl. I pivoted to my left, standing in the middle of Chartres Street, and looked straight into the eyes of a huge German Shepherd that had just taken a running leap toward me, its front paws extended, ivory-colored claws knifing toward me, saliva dripping from discolored fangs, demonic eyes fixated with conquest.

I heard Honey call my name in the second it took me to compute what was happening. Time slowed to a crawl. The flying mongrel was now feet from me, barreling for my chest with a blow that would surely knock me down.

I turned to face it at a 45-degree angle. Was that instinct or training? No time to run, no time to pull a weapon, no time to get Honey out of harm's way—I did the only thing I could think of. Except I didn't think of it, I just did it.

I raised my hands and grabbed both of the huge paws rocketing toward me. The enraged canine's momentum carried its frothing mouth to inches from my neck, when I snapped the legs with all my might, jerking the shepherd to my left, away from Honey. The snap of bones breaking split the silence that had descended on me. Saliva sprayed onto my body but not into my face as I threw the dog down onto the street with brute force.

The dog's screaming howl felt like it was ripping into my soul. I stepped back in semishock. The animal shrieked as it tried but failed to stand, to attack me, to somehow get to me in spite of having two broken front legs. The whole surreal moment struck me as inexplicably bizarre. Why was this crazed animal intent on attacking me? How did I even react in time? I've never had any training to defend against something like this.

A gunshot blasted next to me, and the animal went silent. Screams from some bystanders on the sidewalks. Honey had put one round from her duty weapon into the dog's heart, killing it.

She quickly holstered her gun. I saw tears running down her cheeks as she steeled herself, then said, "It was the humane thing to do. And the safe thing. There are kids on the street here."

I looked over to Crafty Voodoo Shop and then to the windows above, where I had seen the haunting figure of the pale, black-haired beauty. Kate Townsend stood in the same spot now, and when our eyes met, she pulled the curtains closed.

CHAPTER SEVEN

It took a couple of hours before we were clear of the animal shooting on Chartres Street. Honey had discharged her weapon in the line of duty, necessitating all kinds of reports and paperwork to be filed, not to mention the response of various agencies and mucky mucks in the NOPD. The dead dog was carted away to be checked for rabies. No one seemed to care that it hurt Honey like hell to kill an animal.

We stood at her unit, ready to drive off after having called Mackie and Kruger to confirm that both Professor Drake and Gina Sanchez had given their statements and left Broad Street headquarters. Curiously, Gina Sanchez had refused to voluntarily be printed or have her DNA swabbed, so Mackie had retrieved her Coke can and chewing gum for those purposes.

When Mackie took her to ID the corpses, she had made positive identifications and confirmed what Drake had told us: When Felix had left the house this morning, there had been no white streak of hair on his head. Honey had just relayed that info to the coroner, but the doc had no explanation for it.

Lastly, Drake and Kate Townsend were both put under twenty-four-hour surveillance, at my suggestion and Honey's request, by undercover members of NOPD's Intelligence Division.

I checked my TechnoMarine chronograph; it was now too late in the evening to call on any other names on Drake's list, and the dog shooting had made an already long day seem like an eternity.

"I could use a stiff drink," I said.

Honey nodded. "Remember all the dogs that got shot after the Storm? Their frigging owners had left them. They evacuated their own asses before the Storm hit, but left their animals to fend for themselves."

I remembered only too well. Some irresponsible owners had abandoned domesticated animals. Hundreds, if not thousands of them. A lot of those pets drowned. And many animals who had survived the floodwaters ended up dying from conditions such as heartworms because they drank bad water. In the post-Storm rescue, Honey and I had encountered dozens and dozens of hungry, sick, disoriented pets, many in shock.

"I remember when packs of dogs approached National Guard units, the 'weekend warriors' shot them," said Honey.

"The soldiers were afraid, just like the dogs. And some of the dogs attacked them. It was a lose-lose situation for all of us." Honey had been a uniformed patrol officer then, and we had worked closely together in those horrible days after the Storm. We kept a fifty-pound bag of dry dog food in the trunk of her squad car. It felt so much better to feed the animals than to shoot them.

"What do you make of that dog coming out of nowhere like that?" I asked her. "I mean, right here in the middle of the Quarter. I don't remember hearing about anything like this ever happening."

Honey said nothing, keeping her thoughts to herself.

"And it happened right here in front of the voodoo shop, as soon as we walked out. Did you happen to see Kate Townsend standing in the window watching, after you fired?"

"She heard the shot and looked out her window. And the fact is, there are rabid dogs in New Orleans. Okay? Easy explanations." She opened her car door. "Let's go get that drink."

No doubt Honey was right. But as I got in the car, I doubted there would be any easy explanations in solving this case.

Honey and I sat at my rented, permanently reserved table in the rear corner of Pravda on Decatur Street. I ran my sideline private-investigation business from here and had a locked Russian antique cabinet containing some office equipment and supplies right next to us. I liked the arrangement. The quirky, Russian-themed French Quarter bar was well known for its selection of vodka and absinthe, but considering the weather and other events, tonight felt like a single-malt-scotch kind of night. Three fingers of fifteen-year-old Dalwhinnie for both of us should help take the edge off.

I slipped the thick stack of Fournier's old case files from the manila envelope as Honey sat quietly.

"You did exactly the right thing. Thank you," I said, anticipating that she was second-guessing her actions. "That dog was about to rip me apart even with two broken legs. Animal Control would have put it down if you hadn't. Period."

She nodded. I wanted to get her reengaged on the case. I was all too familiar with how one can be consumed by guilt after killing a sentient being.

Tony Fournier's files on Drake were neatly organized and

thorough. I sat looking at fifteen individual file folders—one for each year Fournier had been tracking Drake.

"He's got the skinny on Drake broken down chronologically, going back fifteen years." I slid a few of the folders to Honey. After a moment, she seemed to snap out of the funk that had hit her and started to plow through the files.

"The name of his little group is the Crimson Throne. Sounds devilish," I said, quickly reading. "Alleged antiquities smuggling, alleged drug dealing . . ."

"Drug dealing?" asked Honey.

"Psychotropic plants, mushrooms, peyote . . ."

"That's stuff shamans use."

I rifled through several folders quickly, barely scratching the surface. "You were right. It'll take a week to go through all of the material here."

"Let's meet with Fournier and have him give us the bullet points," said Honey, closing a file. "Seems like if Drake had been guilty of even half of this? He would have got busted."

"Get this. Fournier has tied the disappearance of dozens of transients to Drake. People who had attended at least one of Drake's classes, then disappeared."

"Interesting, given what we saw today. But New Orleans is full of transients. They disappear all the time—usually to go back home."

"That's true." I closed a file. It was late, and I suddenly didn't feel like tackling the mountain of material any more than Honey did. I grabbed her keys from the table. "I left my smokes in your vehicle. Be right back."

I bounced out to the street and caught sight of the usual long line of people waiting on the sidewalk to get into Coops, a joint with great bar food, then noticed something that stopped me in my tracks.

A strange symbol was freshly painted on the exterior wall, probably by using a stencil and spray paint, right next to Pravda's front door.

It hadn't been there just a few minutes ago when Honey and I walked in. I took a quick cell phone snap, and then scanned the street. The Quarter was jumping tonight; there were easily a hundred people on this block of Decatur in various states of sobriety. Trying to spot any possible surveillance wouldn't be easy.

I stepped back into Pravda's doorway and waved for Honey and Michelle, the twentysomething Goth chick owner, to come join me.

"What do you ladies make of this?" I said, showing them the vandalism.

"It's a sigil," said Michelle, unhappily. She frowned and tugged on an earlobe that had been pierced about twelve times. Her brown eyes stared out intently from circles of heavy, dark eye makeup on her pale white skin as she studied the symbol.

"A sigil?" asked Honey.

"A sigil is any glyph or symbol with a magical or mystical root or intent. They are used in all different types of magic to represent a specific resolve, such as, 'My will is to be rich,' or they can be used to summon demons and so on."

"This is voodoo?" asked Honey.

"To my knowledge, this is not a voodoo sigil. It looks vaguely familiar, but I can't place it. I'm sure as hell not thrilled somebody put it on my bar."

Honey instinctively did the same thing I had done and scanned the street.

"It wasn't here ten minutes ago when we came in. Sorry to tell you, Michelle, but it might be directed at us. Due to a case we're working."

"I'll have one of the guys use rubbing compound to remove this, then I'll join you for a drink."

"I see sigils around the French Quarter all the time, but not this type. It looks like some medieval symbol or even a partial ancient symbol, like maybe a piece from one of the seals of the Lesser Keys of Solomon."

I knew Michelle lived an alternative lifestyle and I wasn't too surprised she knew a little something about the occult. Maybe more than a little something.

"You mean King Solomon of the Bible?" asked Honey.

"Exactly. He was quite a black magician with a powerful *grimoire*."

Before we could ask, Michelle continued, "A *grimoire* is like a how-to book—how to make talismans, how to cast a spell, how to summon a spirit. Solomon used magical symbols quite effectively, if you believe the Old Testament. Moses used magic, too, and had his own book of spells and probably his own *grimoire*."

"I saw something today next to the door of a suspect's house."

I quickly sketched out the unusual glyph I'd seen when I first paused at Drake's front door.

"That looks like a typical self-generated sigil, maybe something that came from chaos magic."

"Chaos magic sounds modern. Is that a more recent type of magic?" I asked.

"Exactly. It evolved out of England in the 1970s. To use a bad example of chaos magic, let's say your intent is 'My will is to marry a millionaire.'" As she spoke, Michelle picked up a pen and wrote on a cocktail napkin MY WILL IS TO MARRY A MILLION-AIRE. "After you write your intent, remove the vowels." She wrote M WLL S T MRR MLLNR. "Then remove any repeating conso-nants." This time she wrote MWLSTRN."

"So this kind of a sigil is really just compressed writing?"

"Exactly. From this last group of letters, it's up to you to ar-range them into a single cohesive symbol. After you do that, there is an elaborate process one has to go through to energize or charge the sigil."

"So the sigil on Drake's house could mean anything," I said.

"I wouldn't be surprised if it's a statement of protection of some sort."

"That sounds harmless," said Honey.

"Like any tool," said Michelle, nodding, "sigils can be used posi-tively or negatively."

"We need to figure out what this means," I said, referring to the sigil left at Pravda's front door.

"What it means is somebody is trying to spook us. No pun intended," said Honey.

After getting Michelle's promise of discretion, I filled her in on what had transpired in the last twelve hours, leaving out only the part about the human heads, since those details were not going public yet.

"It might be helpful to find Drake's journal of his workings. Most serious practitioners of magic keep a very detailed account of what they did and of the results," said Michelle, finishing off the last of her Ketel One martini.

"That might be what was in his safe," said Honey.

"Or in his laptop or maybe stashed at his curio shop," I speculated, again tempting myself with the notion of a black-bag job.

Honey must have read my mind and looked me in the eyes. "Please avoid stopping at the curio shop. Okay? Just get a good night's sleep."

I lifted my glass toward Honey. "Yes ma'am."

The last sip of scotch went down easy. I damn sure felt exhausted but had a feeling I wouldn't be sleeping well at all.

Honey declined my invite to spend the night. It hadn't escaped my attention that she'd been somewhat of a contrarian all day, since we first spoke of haunted houses this morning. I guess the whole business just rubbed her the wrong way, but it felt odd to be slightly out of tune with my partner. So she wasn't with me when I discovered the sigil painted on the wall next to my front door, the same as the one we found at Pravda.

I lived in a former warehouse just up from Ernst Café in the Warehouse/Arts District, so there were still pedestrians noodling around on my street and no one appeared out of place. What really bothered me was how the vandal got my address. And he or she got it fast. My name wasn't released to the media as being connected to the investigation.

Who did I deal with today who might have a reason to intimidate me? Robert Drake, Kate Townsend, Gina Sanchez? It would be difficult for someone to get this address, since one of my corporations had purchased the old building and my utilities were also in the name of a corporation. The IRS and the Feds, the DMV, my bank, the credit-card companies—almost no entity or person knew my actual home address. I have made plenty of bad-guy enemies so I take my privacy very seriously.

An elaborate alarm system confirmed my loft was secure, but still, based on some past bad experiences, I logged on to the Internet using my smartphone and accessed my security system remotely. I wouldn't enter until I checked the CCTV security video of my front door. Footage clearly showed a person wearing a long, dark cape and the "Anonymous" Guy Fawkes mask made famous by a graphic novel. The disguised figure approached my door and then used a stencil to spray-paint the symbol on the brick wall; it took 3.5 seconds. I checked my roof-mounted cameras and watched the suspect walk up South Peters Street and go left and disappear on Girod Street. The time stamp told me the deed had been done about ten minutes before Honey and I had gone to Pravda.

I entered and climbed the stairs to the living area. Even though two Russian assassins had been shot dead in my loft a few months ago, I really liked the place. All of my stuff was now unpacked and neatly arranged to best showcase the masculine features of supple brown leather furniture, exposed red brick, and polished oak flooring.

Ignoring Honey's admonition to get some sleep, I brewed up a pot of Pakxong Bolovens Gold Lao coffee, grown in the mountains outside of Vientiane. I dialed up Miles Davis's 1970 *Bitches Brew* double LP on my music player and set about downloading onto my e-reader half a dozen e-books on the occult. I spent the next several hours closely reading select files Fournier had assembled on Drake or skimming chapters of the e-books.

I dragged myself to bed around 3 A.M. and, as per usual, within fifteen seconds of hitting the sheets had a hypnagogic jerk—an involuntary myoclonic twitch—as I fell into a light sleep.

The next thing I knew, I was fighting for my life.

CHAPTER EIGHT

The hypnopompic state, which I was now trapped in, is a fancy name for a person's state of consciousness when he or she is emerging from sleep. I had no clue what time it was or how long I had slept, but I desperately tried to wake up and prevent something terrible from happening to me. For I was about to be sexually violated by some unknown female form who didn't have my best interests in mind.

So it was a dream but it wasn't. It felt strange to be able to control my mental faculties but not my physical self. It occurred to me that depressed frontal lobe activity in the hypnopompic condition causes slowed reaction time—sleep inertia—whereby one can feel frozen, perhaps from fear. This kind of waking can be an emotional, confused experience, especially if you are coming directly out of REM sleep. I knew all of this intellectually, but it didn't help me in the here and now.

I couldn't say what my condition truly was; I simply flashed on the term "succubus" and felt without question that if I allowed sexual union to transpire in this bizarre, delusional experience, I was a dead man. That made no sense, but I knew it to be true.

An erection strained at my boxers, which were drenched in sweat. *How can that be?* It was a cold night, but I kept the thermostat set at seventy-two degrees. And yet an unmistakable wave of stifling heat enveloped me as if trying to melt my will.

What a messed-up dream. It occurred to me I could just surrender and have the orgasm, and so what? But then a different thought muscled that aside and reaffirmed I was doing battle here and there was no surrender, no prisoners taken, no quarter given or asked.

I strained with every muscle to pivot my hips away from the descending beauty who seemed to be in a slow-motion downward float to mate. I tried to form a scream but couldn't, wanted to slap her but couldn't. She smiled, although her features were unclear, and cooed a lulling melody, softly urging me to come, come into her sweet caress.

I flashed angry on how hunters sometimes use a similar technique to lure prey.

Somehow that anger exploded, instead of my lust, and it propelled me up and out of bed. I now stood wide awake, panting, sweat literally dripping from my brow. The room felt unbearably hot, and I scrambled over to the thermostat and saw that it was still set at seventy-two but that the actual temperature was over ninety degrees. Out of habit or fear, I retrieved my Glock, which I always put on my nightstand before going to sleep, and pounced into the front room, keeping the lights off. The large room felt twenty degrees cooler. Street lighting shone through the tall front windows, giving me more than enough illumination to confirm the place was empty.

I padded over to the windows and looked out. A lone figure stood on the street corner staring up at me, a figure wearing a long, dark cape and the Anonymous mask. I bolted for the staircase barefoot and in my underwear, bounded down the stairs, and hurtled through my first-floor door, past the sigil, and into the middle of a deserted South Peters Street. The sprint had taken no more than twenty-five seconds, but the dark figure was nowhere to be seen.

I called the Eighth District station at 5:13 A.M. and reported the vandalism and stalking. Patrol units would now pay extra attention to my immediate neighborhood, and anyone seen wearing an Anonymous mask was going to get some unfriendly attention.

Pent-up adrenaline continued coursing through my system, so I biked up Magazine Street in the dark to Audubon Park on my Cervélo R3 racing bike, locked the expensive bike to a lamppost, and then started one of my thrice-weekly five-mile runs on the asphalt track.

While I ran, Honey texted me that she had to meet with the chief this morning, and could I go out to Tulane alone and meet with Drake's boss, the chair of the Anthropology Department? The fact that Honey sent a text and didn't call me was itself strange. And why wasn't she sending me to interview any of Drake's students? That would have been my call for our next move, not background stuff at Tulane. Was she giving the plums to Mackie and Kruger and relegating me to second string?

The Zen of my running regime always helped me to get organized mentally and prepare for productive analysis. My first mental item was Drake's curio shop. If Honey hadn't ordered me to stay away from the curio shop, I would have absolutely done a bit of B&E—breaking and entering—just to satisfy my curiosity. Regardless, it was a moot point now: Honey was always lead investigator when we worked murder cases, and since she wasn't even convinced this was a murder case, I'd just have to keep my trap shut, do what she asked, and hope I could bring her around, with hard proof, of my suspicions.

The vandalism, stalking, and mad-dog attack I put aside to focus on Kate Townsend. She lied about the human heads. Did she have some on her premises? Was she selling them to special clients? She wielded the same kind of smugness as Drake did, and when the interrogation took a turn against her, she retreated to the business about being a victim. I couldn't begin to count the number of times I'd seen the guilty do the exact same thing. Somehow I knew that the "witch" Gina Sanchez had referred to was Townsend.

Feeling great in spite of lack of sleep and the terrifying dream, I finished the run strong and raced the bike back to the loft, where I took my usual hot/cold shower as a placating salve for my many injuries collected over the years. After dressing quickly, the remnants of last night's coffee tasted just fine as I threw them back.

First thing on the agenda was to beat feet to the Eighth District cop shop and pull all the recent FICs and MICs—Field Interrogation Cards and Miscellaneous Incident Cards—for my neighborhood, checking to see if there might be a connection between the stalker and any suspicious persons who got jacked up by a patrol unit. I desperately wanted to know who was shadowing me, but the FICs/MICs didn't help.

Following Honey's orders, by 10 A.M. I stood in front of Dinwiddie Hall, a handsome pale-stone four-story building right off St. Charles Avenue on the Tulane campus. Donna, the smiling secretary and only person present in the anthropology office, perked up when I introduced myself. I pegged her for forty-five, lonely, and bored to tears.

"Dr. Sharte, the department chair, is running a little late. Would you like some coffee, detective?"

"No, but can I ask you a question?"

"Sure."

"How long have you worked here?"

"Forever and a day. I'm retiring next year."

"So you probably know how this place runs better than anybody. In fact, you probably run the place. Just like in the military, it's the sergeants—the noncommissioned officers—who really get things done, not the ego-heavy generals. Or ego-heavy professors."

She smiled even bigger. "Flattery like that can get you all kinds of things," she said coyly. She leaned in closer, her voice lower. "I saw it on TV. Professor Drake is in a lot of trouble, isn't he? And you want some inside poop."

"I'm not asking you to rat anyone out, but some serious crimes have been committed. If Drake is clean he won't have any problems. I'd prefer to get some real background information and not the brochure version that the department chair will try to give me. I understand about protecting the integrity of Tulane, providing cover for a colleague and all that, but I don't have time for it. So what kind of dirt can you dish me on Drake?"

"You get right to the point, don't you?"

"Life is short and then we die."

"Maybe I could tell you over a drink?"

"We can have that drink after I close the case. Then it won't be rushed," I said, winking unintentionally. I could be a shameless flirt and sometimes used it as a tool.

She smiled like the cat who swallowed the canary, then looked around to make sure we were alone. "Drake puts on a good front, but after I got to know him, he started to creep me out."

"Why?"

"His weird hobbies like taxidermy, collecting human bones. Jokes he would make about dead bodies. But believe it or not, he's a very successful ladies' man. Tries to sleep with just about every straight female student he has. About five years ago he had a pretty young girlfriend who was one of his graduate assistants. She got pregnant, but he cheated on her like crazy. She went ballistic up in one of the second-floor research labs. But I heard they stayed together."

"Remember her name?"

"Kate Townsend."

I nodded. *Kate, my new best friend.*

"Did she have the child?"

"She dropped out of the program, but Drake never spoke of a baby, and it would be rude to bring it up. Anyway, rumors are that any girl who accepts an invitation to go to his house understands she is going for some sort of sex party."

"Sounds like the professor is a bad boy. You haven't been to his place, have you?"

She smiled but didn't answer the question. "We can joke about it, but one student complained about an 'event' at Drake's place. It was investigated by campus police and then dropped."

"How long ago?"

"About this time last year."

"What was the event?"

"Wouldn't it be better if you got that from campus police?"

"Rape?"

"That's part of it. She claimed she was drugged and then raped by more than one person, including Drake. Anyway, the people at the party all said it was consensual. And the girl had signed a release."

"What do you mean she signed a release? An agreement to be raped?"

"I got a good look at the document because I see everything that crosses my boss's desk. Drake had provided a copy of it to campus police during their investigation. It was a consent form to have group sex, basically, that she was partaking of her own free will, and that no one had coerced her to participate."

"I need the girl's name and the names of the other people who were present when she was raped."

"Can't help you with that, but if you're a man of your word, I'll see you sometime soon for that drink you promised."

She handed me a campus map and drew a circle on it. "Campus police office is right here."

CHAPTER NINE

Campus police were going to be problematic. I would be viewed as an interloper trying to encroach on their little fiefdom, and, hey, they controlled the fiefdom. Many public and private universities have their own police forces—sworn, commissioned law-enforcement officers possessing all the same arrest powers as big-city cops. Smart campus cops, however, understand they serve at the pleasure of the big shots holding the reins of power: chancellors, regents, presidents, trustees. It's a scenario ripe for abuses of authority, although I had no such information that this was the case at Tulane.

To their credit, Tulane coppers were better equipped and trained than NOPD. I mean, hell, my department won't even pay for our business cards. And NOPD has to be unique in being a big-city department that doesn't even have its own shooting range; we have to drive to Slidell or Plaquemines to use their ranges. Even more frustrating is when homicide detectives need to respond to a murder but there are no units in the car pool available for them to use. When cars are available they're old, outdated pieces of junk. The unmarked cars don't have police radios installed, so detectives have to rely on the handheld radios they are issued.

I signed several waivers of liability and got permission to drive my own Bronco as my duty vehicle. Honey was fortunate to have a car assigned to her, but its beat-up condition exemplified a lack of concern the department had for its own officers. The Tulane police vehicles were newer and better maintained than ours. I could only imagine how else their small department trumped our large one, equipment-wise.

But I wasn't sure they trumped us street-smarts-wise.

After making a very detailed and pointed call to the executive secretary to the university president and saving her number to speed dial, I decided on a simple tactic to use with campus police that I could defend if called on the carpet for it, which I probably would be.

Within ten minutes I had bullied my way through their headquarters building and into Police Superintendent Rob LaChappelle's office. I've seen pickup trucks smaller than LaChappelle. I sat down and very respectfully and courteously told him what I was doing and what I needed, and of course he tried to blow me off. So I went right at him verbally, like a self-righteous attack dog. Homicide detectives like me are known as being arrogant prima donnas, and I didn't want to disappoint.

"The files you want to see on Professor Drake are sealed," said LaChappelle, with a look so sour I grew concerned for his pH levels.

"Oh, bullshit. No charges were ever brought, so nothing can legally be sealed. You are stonewalling me and impeding a homicide investigation with some chickenshit, two-bit, university cover-up." I stood and silently congratulated myself, thinking I was putting on a nice show, as I whipped out my smartphone and speed-dialed.

I engaged the speakerphone, and the executive secretary to the president answered: "President Miles's office."

"This is Detective Saint James, NOPD Homicide, calling back regarding the matter with Professor Drake. I'm just now leaving the office of Campus Police Superintendent LaChappelle to come see President Miles."

"President Miles!" LaChappelle shot out of his chair like he'd just sat on a tack.

"Detective, as I already explained to you, that won't be possible . . . ," came the secretary's voice over the speakerphone.

"President Miles will see me right now, or my message to her is two words: 'exit strategy.' Maybe she's heard about some college sex-scandal cover-ups that have come to light over the last few years, costing the universities millions and the university presidents their jobs and reputations? Ring a bell? Come to think of it, I'm not going to waste my time to walk over to your offices. Put the damn president on this phone right now, miss, or my next call is to *USA Today,* just in case you people have *The Times-Picayune* and the local TV stations in your pocket."

LaChappelle looked like he wanted to jump me, so I gave him my best *Don't even think about it* stare, and this time, I wasn't acting. He literally took a step back.

"This is President Miles," came an angry but steely female voice on the speakerphone.

"President Miles, you know who I am and what I want. Quite frankly, I will destroy you and Superintendent LaChappelle if I don't get it. Your position is untenable, and I'm not bluffing. But to help you say yes, I have just e-mailed you a photo of three freshly decapitated human heads that were found on Professor Drake's property yesterday. That's Drake, spelled D-R-A-K-E. Get the picture? Does Tulane want to be dragged into this kind of mud, or do you want to cooperate with NOPD and see if we can minimize a university connection to some pretty sordid shit? Like the rape of a Tulane coed that got swept under the rug by your police department here. I want everything this department ever generated on Drake: raw notes, interview transcripts, draft reports, final reports, memos, evidence—everything. And I want it now, understood? Mr. LaChappelle is standing right here, waiting for your orders."

There was a pause, then, "I'm going to put you on hold, detective. Please don't hang up."

I turned to LaChappelle, who had somehow summoned a couple of officers into the room when I was jawboning the president. He looked like he was getting ready to have them throw me out.

"She's checking with a lawyer, is my guess. It's all about CYA, as you know. Nothing personal, LaChappelle. I understand you're just a flunky for the mucky mucks. Nice office, though. You must pull down six figures, or—"

"Superintendent LaChappelle, are you there?" said President Miles over the speakerphone.

"Yes I am. I'd like your permission to have Saint James removed from—"

"Shut up and listen. Give him what he wants concerning Professor Drake. Everything. Full cooperation. Starting right now. Is that understood?"

LaChappelle hesitated. "Yes, ma'am. Understood."

"Detective Saint James, I wonder if you could please stop by my office as soon as possible."

"Madam President, I'll have to give you a rain check, but you have my word that however this plays out, my issue is with Drake, not Tulane."

I terminated the call and then turned to a scowling LaChappelle. "While you get me the files, I'll just set up here in your office."

As expected, that hurried things up considerably.

I tossed a plastic tub filled with campus police files and evidence into the back of my 1986 midnight-blue-and-white Ford Bronco just as Honey called.

"Hey, I was about to—"

"Could you please shut up?" Honey yelled into the phone.

I blanched.

"I asked you to interview the chair of the Anthropology Department. Not threaten the university president and police superintendent." Honey could barely get the words out coherently, she was so angry.

"That's why I'm such a good value; I always give so much more than asked," I cracked. Honey didn't respond. Her silence just hung there as a reminder that she wasn't in my corner on this case. "Look, I came on strong to get some information we needed. You know that's how I operate." More silence from Honey. "The chief crawl up your ass?"

"Unless you got a smoking gun, as of midnight, Felix Sanchez's and Roscindo Ruiz's deaths will be classified as accidental drug overdoses. That's from the chief, and I agree." She said it perfunctorily. A done deal.

Damn. The whole case was being driven by public relations. I'd seen no smoking gun in the Tulane files as I'd skimmed them in LaChappelle's office, so I quickly sketched in for Honey what I did have, knowing that the rape of a young female was not something she would easily gloss over.

"What did you find out that was worth causing me all this grief?" she finally asked.

"Kate Townsend was one of the people involved in the alleged rape of"—I checked the file for the name—"Georgia Paris, age nineteen at the time. Paris subsequently dropped out of Tulane and disappeared. She's an orphan, but a guardian in Hattiesburg filed a missing-persons report on her."

"Yet another missing transient tied to Drake," said Honey.

"No kidding. Drake was the guy mixing drinks all night. I bet he slipped her some 'roofies.'" Rohypnol, the "date rape" drug was as insidious as it was ubiquitous.

"Maybe," said Honey. "I heard back from Second District. Drake's curio shop used to be a corner drugstore. They sold voodoo stuff. But that was fifty years ago. They have no current info on the place."

"Great," I said, not bothering to hide my disappointment.

"Stop by your loft and get your tactical gear. VCAT located the Skulls' hideout. We'll hit them later today."

"Well, that's good news."

"But for now, just get your gear and meet me at the Voodoo Cave on Saint Peter."

"The one owned by Hans Vermack," I said.

"We'll talk to Hans first. Then go see Becky Valencia, the last name on the list of students Drake gave us. Try and use what you uncovered as leverage."

So Honey hadn't given the job to Mackie and Kruger after all.

"Honey, I'm sorry my Tulane stunt caused you trouble. It gave us one more piece of a very large puzzle."

"True. But we don't have enough time to put the puzzle to-gether."

CHAPTER TEN

The Voodoo Cave had a handful of customers browsing the gris-gris, and its clerks were severely pierced and tattooed. They weren't the kind of people you'd want walking behind you on a dark street. The merchandise on the whole felt a lot scarier and a lot less cutesy than at Kate Townsend's place. If I were looking for a way to put a curse on someone, I'd do my shopping here.

Hans Vermack was a tall, rail-thin forty-year old with salt-and-pepper hair tied into a ponytail using a cheap scrunchie. He wore gold and silver rings of esoteric design on all eight fingers and was heavily tattooed with bizarre symbols I'd never seen before and a few, like death heads, that I had seen but would never want permanently displayed on my skin. He wore a tattered black Rob Zombie T-shirt, and blue-tinted wire-rim glasses made him look like, at best, an aging hipster, and there's not much worse than an aging hipster.

Vermack was a chatty guy who still maintained his Dutch accent and seemed genuinely troubled by Felix Sanchez's and Roscindo Ruiz's deaths. He readily agreed to speak to us about the murders but insisted we convene in a back workshop where he could fulfill orders while answering our questions because, "Time is money."

"Speaking of time, where were you yesterday morning?" I asked.

Vermack poured out a gallon of low-grade olive oil from a large tin into a bowl. "I was . . . sleeping in. I live with my girlfriend upstairs."

"So your girlfriend is your alibi," I stated, unimpressed.

"Not really. She's quite insane. Certifiable, actually. Too much mescaline. But she can still function within the narrow parameters I impose on her. And she's a good worker, a good cook—although I had to remove all of the kitchen knives from the house. No reason to tempt fate a second time."

"She knifed you?"

"No, but in a way it was worse. I woke up one night and she was straddling me in bed holding a butcher knife over my head. Anyway, I taught her how to satisfy me sexually and she does what she's told. But try to interrogate her and she'll go catatonic."

I glanced at Honey, not quite believing what I'd just heard.

"What's her name and where is she?" asked Honey.

"Patrice!" yelled Vermack, at the top of his lungs. "One diet Dr Pepper! Tall glass! Two cubes!" He looked up at us. "Patrice Jones. She'll be along in a few minutes."

After draining out the last drops of the cheap oil, Vermack unscrewed the cap from what looked like a dollar-store bottle of bootleg perfume and dumped the contents into the oil, then stirred with a single wooden chopstick from a moldy bag of Chinese takeout. "Any kind of love oil has to smell good," he said, mostly to himself.

"Tell us about the group you belonged to at Drake's," I said.

"Not much to tell. A small weekly study group. We talked about spiritual ideas, practiced different kinds of meditation. Felix and Roscindo were members."

"Who were the other members?"

"I'm sure you know the names already, but regardless, I can't reveal that. I took an oath of secrecy about our group."

"Why would that be necessary?" asked Honey.

"To keep powerful techniques out of the hands of amateurs and fools. Robert Drake facilitated the sharing of a lot of special knowledge. Only adepts who had reached a high level of awareness were allowed to become actual members, which is why the group was small."

"So, based on your explanation, how could the *number* of members be something you couldn't discuss?" I asked.

"I didn't write the oath, I took it. I vowed not to discuss specifics of the group, and I won't. Many groups such as ours over the millennia have had similar vows of secrecy. It's nothing new, officers."

"Murder has been around for millennia, too. And for thousands of years, the guilty have been held accountable by people like me," I said, pointedly.

"I doubt they were murdered. They were fearless *curanderos,* and my guess is someone from south of the border brought them some kind of herb or plant and they tried it, with unfortunate results."

A very pretty and petite woman of twenty-five appeared in the doorway holding a cold drink. A heavily dreadlocked Creole girl, she avoided making eye contact with anyone. On closer inspection, her green eyes looked like sunken pools, dead and vacant, and I couldn't detect the slightest flicker of life behind them.

"Bring it here," demanded Hans.

Honey and I couldn't help but stare as she carefully placed the drink in front of him.

"I'm counting five ice cubes in the glass," he said, practically snarling. "Do you think ice is free, Patrice? You're costing me money again!" he snapped at her, and she flinched. "Just get back to work, quickly."

She slowly, almost robotically retracted her arm and left as quietly as she had entered.

"Forgive the lack on introductions, it would just confuse and frighten her."

I gave Honey a look that would roughly translate as *Just when you think you've seen it all . . .* , then I turned to Vermack. "We checked out your Web site, but I'm curious about what you're making right now."

"Lesbos Love Oil. Follow the instructions for usage and a female can bed another female. Four ounces for twenty dollars."

I looked back to the low-quality olive oil and cheap perfume, silently calculating the high profit return for Vermack. "What gives it its power?"

"The intent I'm charging it with right now using my mind. And the hour of the day and the day itself that I have chosen to perform this work, ruled by certain planets and angels and spirits, as it were."

I saw that Honey wasn't interested in this line of questioning. "How long have you known Professor Drake?" she asked, a little impatiently.

"I met him in Mexico almost seventeen years ago. After that I visited him here in New Orleans and never left, not even for one day. I quickly realized voodoo was my destiny, although I practice many forms of magic now. Maybe one day I'll become legal, but probably not, and I'll likely remain in New Orleans forever."

"You're an illegal alien?"

"Sure. I get free medical, food stamps, all kinds of assistance. I used to live in Section 8 housing till I bought this shop and the building. Now I *own* some Section 8 housing units, thanks to the Storm, and I make a killing. America is a great country," said Vermack, as he expertly used a specially designed ladle to fill small bottles with the love oil. "The state pays me to take care of Patrice. Why would I want to become legal, and why would I want to leave?"

"Glad to hear that, because we want you to remain in town until we clear up these deaths," I said.

"I'm not going anywhere, except maybe over to Chartres Street to burn down Crafty Voodoo. Kate Townsend copies everything I do. She's selling this oil now, too. In fact, her whole business model is a copy of mine, except I don't use cheap whores in tight shirts to sell key chains."

"Sex sells," I said.

"She should know," retorted Vermack.

"Care to elaborate on that?"

"I'm just calling her a bitch, that's all. She posts YouTube videos with her priestesses in costume as they prepare and 'charge' the gris-gris. What's next, a concession at Disneyland? My business is down thirty-six point two percent since she opened last year."

"And you spend one night a week in a small group with her," I stated.

"I'm dedicated to the work. I remain in the group due to my loyalty to Robert and our long-term friendship. I can tolerate a lot. Just look at Patrice."

Who is tolerating whom?

"So when Drake hooked up with Townsend, did that strain your friendship? He got her pregnant, right?" I asked.

"So I understand."

"They didn't have the baby?"

"About this I cannot speak with direct knowledge. That's a very private affair and not my business. Do I like her? No. Do I understand why he keeps her as his high priestess? No. Perhaps she has bewitched him. But Robert has counseled patience. He says change is coming."

"What does that mean?"

Hans suddenly looked like a guy who knew he'd said too much. "We'll just have to wait and see."

"For a guy who says voodoo is your destiny, you must know that it's always been the voodoo queens who held the real power. The men, well, they were kind of window dressing," I said in a deliberately offhand way.

"There are no absolutes," said Hans gruffly.

"Do you fill unusual special orders?" asked Honey.

"Such as?"

"You tell me."

"I don't personally find very much in this world to be unusual. It's said that in the 1800s, a voodoo priestess's home here in New Orleans was searched and many dead babies were found, charred black and hanging like hams inside the chimney. I once got a request from a client for a human fetus with a high price to be paid for its delivery."

Vermack didn't say whether he filled the order or not. Either way, I was liking him less and less.

"I'm talking about human heads," Honey said. "Freshly decapitated."

"I hear it's lucrative, but no, I don't deal in those." Vermack didn't appear surprised by the question. Drake probably forewarned him of what was coming.

"Who does traffic in that kind of thing?" I asked.

"Greedy people. Maybe Kate, but I really can't say."

"Not Drake?"

"I wouldn't know."

"Any idea what this is?" I handed him a photocopy of the sigil painted on my door and on Pravda's.

"Sure. It's a sign of Lucifer, also known as the Seal of Satan. This is maybe five hundred years old. It was used to help invoke Lucifer—a visual form of him."

"So it's a tool to use against someone?"

"Of course. Who would want Lucifer sicced on them?"

"You're set up pretty good in New Orleans, Hans. May I call you Hans?" I asked.

"I don't mind."

I leaned forward, getting in his face. "So why risk all this by raping that young girl at Drake's?"

Vermack bristled, backing away. "I don't know what you're—"

"Georgia Paris," I said loudly. "The statute of limitations hasn't expired yet, Hans. A conviction means hard time in a state penitentiary like Angola, where I could make sure it's known that you raped a teenager. That'll go down real well with all the fellas inside with you. And you'll have to register as a sex offender for the rest of your life if you ever got out of that hellhole alive. Think you'll still like America then?"

"I didn't rape— She participated voluntarily! And without her testimony, you have no case." He looked at me with contempt. "And believe me, she won't testify. She dropped the matter, to say the least. Now get out."

The massive, low-hanging, roiling black front of a storm cell charged in from the direction of Lake Pontchartrain and filled the sky with a premature darkness, leaving only fringes of lighter gray on the horizon. Night falling during the day always felt like a cheat to me, as if I were getting shortchanged by the weather gods for reasons not of my doing.

I watched all this transpire as I stood at a corner of Jackson Square waiting for Honey to wrap up a cell call. I was on my second cigarillo when she finally finished.

"And?"

"The surveillance of Drake and Townsend has been pulled. Mackie and Kruger are off the case. Fred Gaudet has been sent back to burglary. You and I have until midnight."

"The witching hour," I said, looking into the sky. I felt frustrated by the chief's decision to close the investigation. "The Tulane president probably came down on the mayor, and the mayor came down on the chief. Politics holds the high hand right now."

"We could trump politics with damning evidence," said Honey. "But I don't see any."

"What about the gunshots? No one has yet explained away the gunshots."

"You know that eyewitnesses provide the least credible evidence in most murder investigations."

"The UPS driver, Jackson, is not the kind of guy to mistake

gunshots for something like a truck backfiring. And I'm sure you heard that Mackie and Kruger paid a surprise visit to his house. He's clean as a whistle, and I can't believe that he imagined the gunshots or made them up or is somehow involved in all of this."

"Whatever Jackson did or didn't hear is not enough to hang a case on. You and I were next door, and *we* didn't hear gunshots."

"'Next door' is a relative term. We were hundreds of yards away, and the shots could have been fired before we got out of your unit."

Honey shrugged. I glanced around Jackson Square. Bundled-up tourists ambled by smiling, not a care in the world except where to stop for the next cocktail. In a way I envied them.

"Are we still on for the raid on the Skulls gang?"

Honey nodded. "SWAT, the VCAT animals, Homicide—the gang will all be there."

"Maybe we'll get lucky with something."

"This doesn't feel like the kind of case where we get lucky."

I smiled in spite of myself. "I had a sigil on my door when I got home last night. How about you?"

"Yeah. I painted over it before I went to bed. But this morning? It had bled through the paint."

"Easy explanation," I said with a grin. "The spray paint our vandal used is metallic based. It's not so easy to cover with regular paint. Michelle had the right idea last night—use rubbing compound."

"I don't like that they found my house."

I nodded. "Yeah, I know." Since there was no ashtray around, I snubbed out my butt in a small Japanese-made pocket tin I carried for such occasions. "Somebody really doesn't want us nosing around, which is why I want to keep nosing."

"Hans Vermack is a grade-A prick," observed Honey.

"You think? And telling us he's an illegal scamming the system. Suggesting he's trafficked in fetuses. He acts like he can't be touched."

"It's a contempt some people have toward NOPD. Like we're too incompetent to do anything." Honey paused, shivering against a stiff, cold breeze. "He said Georgia Paris wouldn't testify. Should we try to locate her anyway?"

"How? Nothing came up when I put her in the system. I called the number of her guardian in Hattiesburg, but it's been disconnected. I've gone through all the Drake material from Tulane PD and didn't see anything to follow up on."

"We're still at Ninth and Nowhere," said Honey.

"I know. All we can do is go balls-out until midnight."

CHAPTER ELEVEN

Honey and I took separate vehicles to South Carrollton. Becky Valencia's address was a beautifully refurbished double shotgun nestled between commercial enterprises, including a bank and an auto-parts store. The interior looked as good as the outside: Hardwood floors glowed with polish, bold paint schemes matched perfectly with trim colors, all of the original architectural details were present, and large paintings of Native American art—impressive, powerful images of everyday reservation life—resonated with the interior design. Native basketwork, silversmithed items, fetishes, rattles, and drums of exquisite caliber sat well placed like museum pieces throughout.

"Half the house is my acupuncture office, the other half is where I live," said Valencia as we all sat in her front waiting room. "I used to have an office over in the Triangle, but the rent was high and business not that good."

"I don't see any gris-gris," I joked as I scanned the room. A bank of shelves was weighted down with various types of Chinese medicines and other products.

Valencia was an exotic Native American/French/Irish mix. We had quickly learned that her father was a Yaqui Indian medicine man, silversmith, and artist (he had painted all of the artwork in her home), and she had lived on the reservation just outside of Tucson for years as a child. A big-boned female, she had high cheekbones, long black hair, sparkly eyes, and an easy laugh. She came off oddly feminine for someone as tall and solidly built as she was, and I liked her immediately.

"I suppose I'm the only member of the group who doesn't sell voodoo gear or power objects of some sort, now that you mention it," she said, smiling. "Just the stuff you'll find any acupuncturist hawking anywhere in the world."

"Why did you join the Crimson Throne? And how long have you been a member?" asked Honey.

"It's been four or five years now. I come from a long line of Yaqui medicine people. My husband and I moved to New Orleans because we felt the city had a dearth of healers and that there was a need. I've known Robert Drake most of my life, so naturally I was drawn to the group. I'm not much of a party person, and that's what New Orleans is all about, so I suppose I had a need to find like-minded people. I don't care for the black arts, I just want to help people. At first I thought Crimson Throne was a good fit. All of the members had advanced skills, so the level of the work appealed to me. The group was small but powerful. Egos aside, when it was time to do the work, everyone got along."

"How did you meet Drake?"

"My father met him over thirty years ago in Mexico. Drake was in college then and researching ethnobotany. Over the years, Drake bought artwork my father made, so he was something of a family friend. You see those sterling silver baskets on the mantel?"

"They're beautiful," I said. "Exquisite craftsmanship."

"And worth a small fortune now. Robert has been trying to buy them from me for years, but I won't sell."

"You've heard me explain the details of Felix and Roscindo's deaths. What do you think happened?"

"Sounds like they were doing sex magic," she said simply. "As to what killed them, wouldn't it have to be an overdose?"

"What do you mean, 'sex magic'?" asked Honey.

"Sex generates some fabulous energy. If you train yourself to focus that energy, you can use it to achieve goals or desires."

I could tell Honey thought that was bogus, but she took notes anyway.

"Why do you suspect our victims were doing that?" I asked.

"Because it's what the Crimson Throne was all about—sex magic. Once a week. All of the members are bisexual. Robert usually led the work, so he didn't always engage in sex himself."

"So Felix and Roscindo were naked on the big altar in the room, had orgasms as part of some magical ceremony, but something went wrong?"

"Well, I'm not a policeman, but since you told me there were no signs of foul play, that would be my guess."

I was starting to think Honey was right, that there was no murder here, and that I needed to have a talk with my instincts.

"Why would they do that when they were supposed to be working on Drake's house?"

"Not sure, but it seems odd to me. I also don't understand the gunshots and screams. But it wouldn't have been unusual for someone else to have been there during the ceremony."

"How do you mean?"

"Well, in almost all of our rituals we use a guide. The guide isn't always involved in a sex act. Felix and Roscindo may have sent their orgasmic energy to a third person, who would then direct it to whatever the agreed-upon goal of the group was."

"If you had to take a wild guess as to who this third person might have been, who would you guess?"

"Kate. She really liked working with Felix. But that doesn't make her a murderer."

I flashed on Gina Sanchez's assertion that "the witch" from Drake's group killed Felix and stole his money.

"You're telling us a lot about the group," said Honey. "Didn't you take a vow—not to speak?"

"When I heard about Roscindo and Felix's deaths, I decided those vows were null and void. It was time to leave forever. There has been too much dissension, and . . ."

Valencia just shook her head sadly.

"Could you please expand on that, on why you chose to leave?"

Her conflicted look told me she wasn't sure if she should tell us more.

"Ms. Valencia, we need your help. Understanding the truth of what happened can lay all this to rest," I said.

"Kate is always jockeying for power over Robert. She resents his leadership role, I think. Robert himself is fed up with her, and he's extremely manipulative. As for Hans, he's only out for himself. Why can't the members, coming together to supposedly do good deeds, just do the right thing?"

"You said 'supposedly.'"

"Every week, the group would agree on where the energy would go. So one week, maybe the guide—the leader of the sex-magic session—would send it to a sick person for healing. The next week, maybe someone had a nephew who needed a job, for instance, so the guide would send our collective energy to help the man find work. But I began to suspect that . . . well, the guides can send the energy wherever they want, can't they? And there's no way for the other members of the group to know."

"Okay, I think I follow you. Let me use the example of money. If the group members do some work to raise money and then hand it over to the leader, the leader is supposed to spend it in an agreed-upon way. But the members don't really know how the leader is spending it. The leader might be using it for partying or whatever. Is that what you mean?"

"Yes. And Felix and Roscindo were starting to wonder about this, too. I think it's one of the reasons the group has always had such a high turnover of members."

"Who were the guides suspected of this wrongdoing?"

"Kate . . . Hans . . . and Robert. If Robert hadn't been a family friend, I would have left long ago."

Honey shrugged. I knew what she was thinking. "Stealing energy" is not a bookable offense, and none of this meant much to a homicide investigation. At least not yet.

"Did anyone ever confront Kate or Robert or Hans about this?"

"Many times. People who did always left the group."

Something about all of this bothered me, but I couldn't put my finger on it.

"Why the BDSM set-up in the temple room?" asked Honey.

"It produces very intense sex energy for the magic. Kate and Hans liked to play with that. They can both be very cruel."

"You've had sex with every member of the group?"

"Yes, and every week we usually have a guest join us. Robert is constantly grooming new potential members."

"Your husband doesn't mind," asked Honey, "that you have sex with all these people?"

"Maybe he did. He left me six months ago. He's disappeared, actually. And when it's my turn to request where the group energy be sent, I always ask for it to go to heal my relationship with Shane. At the very least I ask for him to make contact and let me know he's okay. But I don't think the guides have been sending the energy to achieve my goals."

"Because your husband hasn't called?"

Again, she simply shook her head sadly. "Excuse me, but I've said enough. And I'm not feeling very well now."

Honey joined me at my Bronco as a light, cold rain began to fall, sprinkling absolution on a city that needed all of the cleansing it could get. My thoughts drifted back to the Storm that almost wiped us out, and I remembered talking to some coppers from out of town who had been sent in to help us through the horrible aftermath. They were religious guys and absolutely believed that the hurricane was some kind of Storm karma, divine retribution upon a city with a bad reputation and a violent and corrupt history, including plenty related to voodoo.

I didn't embrace their position, but I saw their point, because I'm a guy who believes that—generally and eventually—what goes around comes around, in ways unimaginable. We all know about the corruption of our political and religious leaders, but how spiritually bankrupt are we if the persons who are supposed to be our local "adepts" are just shysters preying upon the all-too-human weaknesses of followers like Becky Valencia?

Gee, a person could almost become a cynic.

"How many people did we have to interview before we confirmed it was a sex group?" I said, shaking my head.

"We're going nowhere fast. But it explains the Georgia Paris business. They bring fresh meat in every week. Georgia went to Drake's willingly. Maybe Drake drugged her, or maybe she just had too much to drink."

"And woke up bound and gagged with Hans standing over her holding a cat-o'-nine-tails. At least that's what she told Tulane PD. She hadn't bargained for that, but as Carole King once sang, 'It's too late, baby.' So afterward, Paris was righteously angry and wanted to get even with Drake."

"Vermack's comment that she'll never testify?" asked Honey. "Maybe she was paid off. And signed a covenant not to sue or press charges."

I nodded, now in full retreat from my surety that Georgia Paris had been raped. "Even Donna, the secretary at Tulane, told me anyone going over to Drake's house knew what was going to happen. And if somebody in Drake's group was doping unsuspecting females, I think we'd have more than one complaint on record by now." I had already checked NOPD databases for just such complaints. And there were none mentioned in Fournier's files, either. "I'm surprised Tony Fournier's files missed the Georgia Paris affair. And Valencia clammed up before I could ask her about the rape allegations."

Honey just shrugged as she checked an incoming text. "Good news. We have a confirmed appointment with some badass Mexicans. Let's hit them." She looked up at me. "But unless we uncover crucial evidence, screw midnight. I say we call it a wrap on Felix Sanchez and Roscindo Ruiz."

CHAPTER TWELVE

The eight NOLA-based Las Calaveras—the Skulls—had taken over a dilapidated two-story apartment complex in New Orleans East called Tequila Flats, so I guess there was some irony at work. The twenty-eight units were all studio apartments with a bathroom, most of them still uninhabitable following the Storm of nearly a year and a half ago. All of the units of the U-shaped wooden structure were accessible from open first- and second-floor walkways, either street side or courtyard side—there were no interior apartment halls. VCAT believed the Skulls occupied seven or eight units but were only certain about five.

Those five rooms would each be hit by a SWAT strike team. More SWAT members acted as a ready reserve. Other officers would provide cover, maintain the large perimeter, and act as a backup reserve force. They would be joined by commanding officers from different divisions and units: SWAT, VCAT, the Intelligence Division, and Seventh District. In addition, undercover officers were already in position providing surveillance.

That left twenty other officers to clear the remaining twenty-three rooms plus common rooms and areas. We were coming in with a large force, but I figured we could have used a dozen more bodies, even though we were hitting them during their siesta time. Between six and eight Skulls gangbangers were known to live at the complex, though it wasn't believed they were all present.

Most relevant to Honey and me was the fact that Fred Gaudet had found the cell-phone numbers of two of the Skulls in Felix Sanchez's cell. Relevant to everyone was the fact that these perps were known to be armed and extremely dangerous.

At the staging area I saw that Honey wore her SWAT BDUs and was geared up in full tactical-assault mode. Since she was a member of the SWAT team, Tactical Platoon Two, she'd been assigned for this assault to Strike Team Charlie, second position.

I, being a lowly homicide detective and not a member of any special fancy team, was assigned to the ad hoc group called Sweep Team Two along with three uniformed cops from Seventh District. One of them was a Vietnamese American officer I knew and liked named Kevin Lee. Lee had helped me on a case that launched my career as a PI. We were to clear the rooms in an upstairs corner of the complex that was damaged and where no activity had been seen.

I felt like a kid in gym class, whom the cool jocks didn't want on their team. The SWAT team commander had a crush on Honey, and I hadn't exactly impressed him as being a man of action in a confrontation a couple of months ago, so I had to bite my tongue and accept my fate. And try not to worry about Honey.

We timed our silent arrival at Tequila Flats perfectly under battleship-gray skies, and coppers bailed out of cars, vans, and wagons in unison around the complex. With my reconditioned Colt M1911A1 .45 in hand, I led my team up a concrete slab staircase with wrought-iron banister, and we hustled toward our little corner of the assault above the inner courtyard. We all wore heavy exterior Kevlar vests with our badges prominently displayed. Like the other officers, I wore my police radio on my belt with an external microphone clipped to the top of my vest.

Kevin Lee was behind me on the stairs and carried a Remington 870 combat shotgun, and the last two men of our little stack held M4 ARs with thirty-round magazines. Before we got to our first target room, flash bangs broke the silence: SWAT was softening things up on the other end of the building. That was normal, but then gunfire broke out. Lots of it. And our radios squawked with frantic traffic. It sounded like more than one strike team was engaged in a gun battle.

We had all paused for a moment to look toward the shots, so I snapped, "Faces forward, hit your targets!"

Lee and I would clear one room at a time; same with the other two members of our sweep team. There was no need for Thor's Hammer, a WallBanger DoorKey, or any kind of breaching tool because all of the apartment doors in the complex were flimsy old French doors. I kicked open the door to apartment 20, and Lee entered yelling "Police" and covered the left side of the room. I followed him in, covering the right side. The other two members of the team ran toward a nearby apartment assigned to them.

The room was a shambles and stunk to high heaven of garbage. A grimy mattress leaned against one wall. As I stepped forward to carefully pull the mattress back and make sure no one stood behind it, Lee ran to the closed bathroom door, instead of remaining in position, covering me. Before I could yell for him to hold up, he threw open the door—

—and was promptly shot.

Lee staggered backward and slid down the wall to the floor. As I bolted toward Lee I put five rounds into the wall between me and the bathroom, knowing the .45 slugs would blast through the drywall and plaster and, at the very least, give me a moment of cover.

I pointed my .45 into the bathroom as I reached down to grab Lee and pull him out of the line of fire. A quick look showed me the small room was empty, but I also saw a gaping hole in the wall leading into the bathroom of the unit on the other side of this unit.

Damn, they've turned the place into a labyrinth.

I keyed my mike: "Officer down, officer down! Sweep Team Two, Unit—"

Before I could finish the transmission, in my peripheral vision I saw the mattress I had wanted to check drop down from the wall and a man run forward, shooting at me.

I put three rounds into his center mass. My ears rang from the gunfire as the slide locked back on my cannon. One mag expended. Instead of inserting another magazine, I pulled my backup Glock and holstered the .45.

Scratch *uno* dirtbag. Then I saw the hole in the wall that had been covered by the mattress.

I rekeyed the microphone. "Officer needs help, Sweep Team Two, unit two-zero, unit two-zero, officer down."

Lee was out cold but was one lucky SOB; his vest had stopped a slug right over his heart. I felt responsible for Lee, but there was nothing I could do for him now except take out the guy who drilled him, so I bolted for the hole in the bathroom wall.

I stuck my gun through the hole, chanced a look, and a round exploded into the plaster inches from my face. I squeezed off two unaimed shots in the direction the round came from, and then looked again. Clear. I scrambled through the hole.

Two caps busted, four left in the stick, one up the pipe.

I stood up and stopped at the open bathroom door. After a beat, I chanced a look into the main room, with my Glock leading the way. This unit looked almost identical to unit 20, except a pissed-off three-hundred-pound Mexican with rheumy eyes and three-day stubble had a 9mm pointed in my direction, and damn if the guy wasn't shy about shooting it.

Time slowed down, sound deadened and elongated. Rounds whizzed past as I pulled the trigger, but I knew it was a miss because I jerked the pull.

I squeezed the trigger to fire again, but nothing happened. I looked and saw that my spent round hadn't cleared the ejection port. I had a stovepipe! I couldn't believe the bad luck. Glocks don't have stovepipes. I'd put thousands of rounds downrange in Glocks over the years without a jam or malfunction of any kind. My guns were always squeaky clean, my ammo top of the line.

No way this guy can keep missing me, even if he is a hung-over druggie, was replaced in my mind with *tap and rack, tap and rack.* I tapped the butt of the Glock hard with my free hand. Sometimes this alone will clear the jam, but it didn't. So I tilted the gun slightly then racked the slide hard. The cartridge flew free just as the Mexican slammed into me, causing me to fire wide.

At least it was him that slammed me and not a bullet. His breath smelled of tequila and cigarettes and bad cheese as we grappled standing and stumbling in a death dance, his weak-side hand wrestling for my gun as my weak-side hand did the same with his pistol. He was trying to work his gun barrel into the armhole of my vest. If he could do that and squeeze off a round, he'd punch my ticket.

I wormed my Glock toward his chest and pulled the trigger.

But the gun didn't fire. Damn if I didn't have another stovepipe! Which put us in Guinness book of World Records territory, because Glocks don't do this. Why had I even pulled it? Why hadn't I just reloaded my Colt?

I head-butted him to not much effect and kneed him in the groin to even less. We started to spin, and I put my shoulder into his chest to drive him into the wall.

But my aim was off and we exploded through the French door and out onto the second-floor open-air walkway. Our momentum smashed us into the wrought-iron railing, knocking a section free and dropping us and the railing toward the parking lot below. I remember sliding my forearm up toward his throat as we fell and hoping I'd just have broken bones and not be paralyzed.

Fatty hit the pavement flat on his back. I landed on top of him, his considerable blubber providing a nice cushion as I bounced off, but not before his rib cage made the Rice Krispies sound and my forearm bones crushed his windpipe.

I sprawled on the pavement, going through a little checklist I'd developed over the years. It included remembering who I was and where I was and gently moving parts of my body. I felt dazed but strangely okay. EMS arrived in seconds along with other officers.

Although I insisted I was okay, a paramedic told me to "Shut up and go along with the program." I just smiled, and within four minutes they loaded me onto a gurney as I heard other paramedics pronounce the Mexican guy dead.

"How is Officer Lee? Kevin Lee, upstairs in unit twenty?" I asked insistently.

"His vest saved his life," said some copper I couldn't see.

"You can ask him yourself at the ER," said a female EMS paramedic. "That's the next stop for both of you."

"What about Detective Baybee? Any other officers hurt?" I asked as they started to roll me toward a meat wagon.

"Just you two," said a black man who was head of the Special Operations Division. His name didn't come to me, but it should have. "All four of the gangbangers here died fighting. So there are four more out there somewhere, but we'll find them."

Four dead cartel killers. That sounded real good. But no one knew just how close we had come to a very different outcome. I'd had two stovepipes, and I just couldn't wrap my mind around that. And I could easily have died in the fall or been hit by numerous bullets. I had a hard time understanding why I wasn't dead, since bad luck and bizarre occurrences seem to have become my constant companions since this case began.

CHAPTER THIRTEEN

The docs were surprised, but except for a badly bruised left forearm, I was fine. Officer Lee would remain hospitalized for a few days as they monitored his internal workings. Honey hadn't turned up at the hospital, at least as far as I could tell. I called her cell but got dumped to voice mail. Before I could call Homicide to bum a ride back to the Tequila Flats complex, Kruger walked in.

The good news was the press was going apeshit for the story; bad news was the chief wasn't sparing me the Officer-Involved Shooting process. Kruger took possession of my Colt and my Glock for forensic checks. We drove back to Tequila Flats, where TV talking heads did stand-ups with cameras rolling on the perimeter of the grounds. A cute blond reporter from a local network affiliate recognized me from previous run-ins; the press office must have released my name as being one of the injured, because she yelled at me, waved her arms, and shouted questions as she tried to get my attention. I ignored her and spent over an hour with Lt. Carondolet, a beefy guy who ran every investigation in which an officer had used deadly force.

I answered all of his questions without mouthing off and walked him through the whole scenario several times. He claimed to be satisfied that we had a "clean shooting." He wasn't too impressed with the fact the fat guy and I did a half gainer off the second floor, but better that than a slug in my forehead.

Carondolet informed me I was confined to desk duty until the investigation was complete—standard operating procedure for everyone in the department . . . except Honey and me.

Until now, anyway.

Previously, when working a Five Alarm case, I had always escaped this scenario. I understood that since the chief was shutting down the Sanchez/Ruiz investigation, this would be a good excuse to put me on ice.

"Look over there," said Kruger as we walked toward his unit in the Tequila Flats parking lot.

"Chief Pointer?" I asked. A mob of TV and print reporters had surrounded someone for an impromptu press conference.

"Who else? The chief is better at working the media than anyone I've ever seen."

I turned away from the spectacle. "Call me crazy, but why can't I escape the feeling Sanchez and Ruiz were murdered?"

"It's the roll of the dice, ace. You know how many cases I've worked where there was no question we had a homicide, but we couldn't find the shooter, or couldn't make charges stick, or witnesses recanted, et cetera, et cetera? Those are the cases that keep you up at night. This one . . ." Kruger lit a cigarette as he stood next to his unit. He absentmindedly ran a hand through his slightly wavy salt-and-pepper hair. "Believe it or not, I think another shoe is going to drop."

"What do you mean?"

"I mean enjoy your time off while you can. Because my gut tells me the defecation is about to hit the oscillation. Every occult murder I ever worked, shit just gets strange. Separate and completely removed from that line of thinking, let me ask you: You got another piece?"

I nodded. "Handgun-wise, I have a Ruger nine mil at home and a Browning three-eighty stashed in my truck."

"Good." The lean, perpetually hungry-looking detective took a long drag on his cigarette and tossed the butt. "Start carrying them both. With plenty of extra mags. The Skulls aren't stupid. They'll connect the names of our two injured officers to the deaths of their four guys. I'd be expecting trouble if I were you."

I texted Honey that I'd be at my dojo. After years of leaving it unnamed, I now officially called it Sōhei, which literally means "warrior monk." I'd just completed a quick expansion by buying the building next door on Magazine Street in the Lower Garden District, which tripled the size of the training area. Big Bob, an ex-felon pal, lost the lease on his gym out in Fat City, so I made him a junior partner, maybe the smartest thing I'd ever done. He hired a cute, smart, buffed-out receptionist who was great at multitasking, and we made deals with a cadre of outstanding instructors to come in and teach classes for us.

Sōhei still offered kickboxing and MMA training, but now we offered classes in jiujitsu, sambo, octagon training, women's self-defense, boxing, a kid's program, yoga, and specialized tactical instruction from edged weapons to weapon retention. I popped for expensive new equipment, put in a juice bar, big-screen TVs, Wi-Fi, and a cushy locker room. The buzz spread like wildfire, and in two weeks my membership roll had quadrupled.

This new arrangement took a lot of pressure off me, since I was no longer a one-man band; I now taught less than 10 percent of the classes, and when I got wrapped up on a case, it was easy for other instructors to step in and cover for me.

And while I still privately called it my dojo, my thinking had changed; Big Bob and I wanted to create the atmosphere of an old-fashioned boxing gym, but in a state-of-the-art training facility. We wanted Sōhei to be a place where you could find a dedicated community of fighters or lovers of the warrior's arts who were supportive of each other, a place where people with raw talent could be refined and molded and even develop as human beings, not just wrecking machines.

We also started doing some community outreach, offering free classes for underprivileged kids; if we could help even one kid avoid joining a gang, then we would have succeeded.

But tonight, as I stepped onto the Zebra mats and strapped on fourteen-ounce Hayabusa Tokushu gloves, the only thing on my mind was the high strangeness of my life since Honey and I answered the shots-fired call. We'd been off duty, so if we'd ignored the call, other homicide detectives would have handled it.

I'd come tonight to work off some stress on the Thai bags, siphon off some adrenaline, and maybe clear my mind as I delivered various kicks and punches. I'd shot a man dead today, and while that didn't make me feel good, it didn't bother me as much as it used to. The sad truth was, I had grown accustomed to killing. Today, I'd had no choice in the matter, with either of the cartel killers. And as to the caliber of the deceased, well, basically, I'd squashed a couple of bugs.

As I began with simple jab/punch combinations, my mind wandered away from today's violence to more peculiar considerations that I'd avoided thinking about. *How to account for the attack dog that had come out of nowhere? The overheated dream I was about to be killed? The stovepipes? Or the new wedge that seems to exist between Honey and me? Coincidences? An overactive imagination? Did I have that dream because I'd been reading Fournier's files and books on the occult before drifting to sleep?*

The sigil and the mysterious figure on the street corner were obvious attempts at intimidation by someone related to the case. Kate Townsend? I had to admit she'd gotten under my skin with her conclusion that I needed to be in control, that I feared losing control. And she'd been spot-on regarding my feelings for Honey and how I wasn't very sexually active as a result.

As I tagged the Thai bag with a left-leg front kick leading into a combo jab/right cross/jab, I knew I wasn't afraid of physical threats, but having a black magician curse me with Satan, well, it bothered me, because I couldn't simply ignore it, as Honey could, and I didn't know what to do about it. I felt as if . . . as if I had no control of that situation, thank you very much, Kate. So I decided on the spot to go see Tony Fournier first thing in the morning, as a private citizen, and see what I could find out.

To emphasize my decision, I executed a quick front-snap kick, then followed with a solid front-thrust kick, driving my foot hard into the heavy bag.

"Hey, Brutus. That kick combo? Didn't look like it came from a guy who just fell off a two-story building."

"Yeah, but I landed on a tub of lard."

Honey wore black Revgear training shorts and a sports bra, which answered in the negative the question of whether she had much in the way of body fat. "Grab a pad, I want to get in some upper body," she said.

I found an MMA Elite Muay Thai training pad, slipped it over my right forearm—the arm that wasn't bruised—and we moved into an open area. "Sorry I couldn't come to the hospital," she said, "but I heard you were okay."

"No worries. I figured you had a SWAT debriefing, after action reports." I held up the pad and we faced off.

"Our guys only killed two of the Skulls, so we matched your score." Honey assumed a guarding stance, her legs a natural walking step apart.

"One-one-two," I said, calling out a punch combination. I held the pad firmly, in front of my face, and Honey thumped it with two jabs and a right cross.

"Chief got himself into trouble with the press. He said a homicide detective had been injured. A sharp reporter from the AP wanted to know why Homicide was involved in the raid. Pointer tried to BS her but it didn't work. Now that reporter's like a dog with a bone. News of the raid went out on the national wire. So we're back on the Sanchez/Ruiz case. Just you and me. But no more grandstanding, like out at Tulane."

"One-two-one-two," I said, nodding, as Honey's left-jab/right-cross punches tagged the pad with a healthier bite. Kruger's words echoed in my brain: "Enjoy your time off while you can."

"Drake's home-phone number?" said Honey. "We found it in two of the cell phones the Skulls carried."

I nodded, not surprised the Mexicans had Drake's number. "Interesting. One-two-three-two." Jab, right cross, left hook, right cross. Honey quickly warmed to the task. I'd seen her kick more ass than most men I knew had.

"And we found a certain business card."

"One-six-three-two. Business card?" She stung the pad with a blistering jab/right uppercut/left hook/right cross.

"For Crafty Voodoo. With a cell number on it written in a woman's hand."

"One-one-two. Whose number?"

"Kate Townsend's," said Honey, drilling the pad. "The chief wants us to make lemonade out of this lemon. Pronto."

"Then I know where we're going right now."

Tony Fournier lived in LaPlace, in sleepy St. John the Baptist Parish. Honey had asked me to drive her unit, but first we stopped at my loft to retrieve my Ruger; I now carried it and the .380 with extra mags.

I turned onto Fournier's quiet street of single-family, middle-class homes with large yards just before 10 P.M. I held fond memories of attending countless Andouille Festivals in LaPlace, where the thing to do was guzzle beer as you munched on the spicy sausages. They even crowned a Teen Andouille Queen, although why a girl would want to be named the "spicy sausage queen" is beyond me. My less-fond memories of LaPlace were of making banzai shopping runs to the Walmart in the aftermath of the killer Storm, since it was the closest business to New Orleans that was open and had toilets that worked, electricity, and goods for sale.

"Tell me again why we're showing up late without calling first?"

"You mean aside from the fact I don't trust anyone but you?" I joked. "The guy has been obsessed with Drake for how many years?"

"Fifteen."

"So he's got an agenda with us. I guarantee he wants to insert himself into the case, make himself invaluable. So I want an un-edited look at Mr. Fournier before we consider taking him into our circle." I'd gotten his home address from NOPD personnel and wasn't surprised he lived out of town, since many New Orleans cops who retire tend to settle elsewhere.

Honey nodded. "We going to share what we got?"

"Let's play that by ear. Kruger didn't exactly sing his praises yes-terday when I asked if he knew him. Said he was an okay homicide dick but kind of an odd-duck loner."

"There's the address," she said. "The big lot on the corner with all the fencing."

"And security lights. Maybe Tony's expecting trouble, too."

"What do you mean 'too'?"

I didn't answer, as I slowed the vehicle. Fournier's front door suddenly opened and a woman bolted out. But not just any woman.

"Honey . . ." I said, not quite believing what I saw.

We both watched as a man who had to be Fournier hustled out of the house yelling after the woman as they argued. They stood engrossed in a back–and-forth and hadn't spotted us yet, and we were far enough from them that I couldn't make out what they were saying.

"This is beyond strange."

"What?"

"That's the same female I saw the night we went to Crafty Voo-doo. She was standing in the window of the apartment on the second floor when you parked your unit on Chartres." Without a doubt, the same haunting, pale beauty with long, black hair now stood on the front lawn arguing with the former occult specialist of the New Orleans Police Department.

"You sure?"

"I'll never forget that face. At the time, I thought it was Kate Townsend."

"But you didn't get a close look."

"I'm telling you, it's her."

The young woman, whose high heels and short skirt suggested she was heading for a night on the town, stormed over to a new Lexus parked in the driveway, and Fournier doggedly followed.

"Then what the hell is going on?"

I watched as she opened the door to the Japanese sedan. "Good question. Let's make her acquaintance."

I turned on the wig-wag headlight flashers and parked in front of the gate, blocking the driveway. We got out holding our gold shields in the air.

"NOPD Homicide," I announced. "Sorry to interrupt, but we drove a long way out here and don't have much time."

I figured I'd put the ball in Fournier's court. After all, it was he who had approached us. As Honey and I stood there watching through the automatic gate, the two of them very consciously altered their body language and hid the tension between them.

"You must be Baybee and Saint James. Tony Fournier."

Fournier couldn't be more than five feet five and one hundred and fifty pounds, and his pale face had more deep wrinkles than a balled-up wad of cellophane. I knew him to be in his late forties, but his thick, sandy hair hadn't even hinted at turning gray. The incongruity of a middle-aged guy having young man's hair and an elderly man's face struck me as weird. He wore neatly pressed jeans, sneakers, and a cardigan sweater.

"Guess we missed you at Broad Street," I said.

"Can you move the unit? My niece has a party to go to. That's why we were arguing. I told her she had to be back before dawn and she didn't like that." Tony's remark had sounded like a joke, but he didn't smile.

The pristinely beautiful woman, who I pegged for early twenties, possessed a haunting sadness. I instinctively felt she didn't smile naturally but "remembered" to do it now and then. As if reading my mind, she showed her perfect white teeth and flashed me a smile that could melt diamonds.

"My uncle worries too much."

I riveted her with my eyes. Her outfit left little to the imagination; the short, tight skirt showcased firm, nicely rounded buttocks; a sheer celadon-colored silk blouse revealed substantial breasts and a thin waist. Her shapely legs sealed it: She was an absolute stunner.

"I'm Detective Saint James, Miss . . . ?"

She never took her eyes off of me, but I didn't see a spark of recognition. Maybe she hadn't noticed me on Chartres Street. "Anastasia Fournier."

"This is my partner, Detective Baybee." As the ladies exchanged brief nods, I memorized her license plate number. "Please drive carefully. There are a lot of crazies out there."

"So my uncle tells me."

I forced myself to break eye contact with a woman who I could simply look at for days. Charisma? Sensuality? I wasn't sure what the word was, but Anastasia Fournier had exotic good looks combined with a raw animal magnetism—a dangerously addictive combination.

CHAPTER FOURTEEN

Fournier's home was a completely unspectacular middle-class abode furnished with the kind of cheap pressboard furniture that looks good from a distance. Considering how elaborate his security system was, you'd think he was sitting on Fort Knox, which told me his concern was personal safety and not the safekeeping of material goods.

Anyway, bargain-basement furniture or not, it was comfortable enough, and his living room had no obvious occult artifact collection or display. Emphasis on *obvious*. I spotted small talismans here and there—basically miniaturized versions of what Honey and I had seen elsewhere in the last two days. I even noticed a tiny sigil wood-burned into a window frame.

After spending five minutes with the guy, it became clear Fournier was the bookish, serious type. He hadn't smiled, but then I'm not sure I would have seen it since his door knocker of a nose dwarfed his face. The guy seemed to be carrying some awful unseen weight on his shoulders, and I had little doubt but that the weight was Professor Robert Drake.

"Your security lights and fencing remind me of an FOB. Expecting trouble?"

"I wish I was as secure as a Forward Operating Base. And yes, I'm expecting trouble. Always. I've made enemies. They probe me from time to time."

"You mean like attempted burglary, or mugging—"

"I wasn't talking about a physical probe," he barked.

Okay. Seemed like Tony was a little out of sorts tonight. "Sorry if our timing was bad here. We didn't know we might be interrupting something."

"Anastasia's father Tom is . . . *was* my older brother. He married a gal up in Alexandria, and they both died in a boating accident about three years ago. Tom was an old hippie—no life insurance, retirement, investments, didn't even own his own home. Their daughter had just turned eighteen but had no place to go. She's been with me ever since."

Honey and I just nodded. We would have to learn for ourselves why Fournier's niece had been in Kate Townsend's apartment, because we sure as hell weren't going to telegraph to Fournier that we knew that. The fact that I couldn't make sense of it completely derailed the line of questioning I had worked out.

"Mr. Fournier—"

"Call me Tony," he said without an ounce of warmth.

"Your files on Drake were . . . exhaustive. Why put so much time into the guy?"

"You probably heard that I had been the department's de facto occult expert."

"Why was that?" asked Honey.

"My father was a minister, my mother a folk healer from Lafayette. So at a very young age, I was already mixing 'alternative' beliefs with Christian, kind of like the way the voodoo folks mix things with Catholicism."

Fournier tended to speak slowly, as if parsing his words carefully.

"My mother had more influence on me. As a teenager I read esoteric books—Rosicrucian writings, treatises by Manly P. Hall, works by British occultists, Egyptian mythology and magic, and so on. People in the department knew I had these interests, and so when presented with strange cases—I worked narcotics at the time—they began to consult with me. I moved into Homicide about five years before I retired."

"But your obsession with Drake goes back fifteen years," I said.

"I wouldn't call it an obsession."

Honey and I didn't respond and just stared at him.

"Anyway, your question was why did I put in so much time and effort on Professor Drake? Fifteen years ago I worked patrol in the Second. My partner and I came across a homeless kid one morning. Right outside Drake's curio shop in Riverbend. He was half naked, pretty scraggly. I say 'kid,' but he was nineteen. Honest to God, the kid was terrified. Not completely coherent. He talked about his friend Jimmy, and said parts of him were for sale inside the curio shop."

"'Parts of him'?"

"Exactly. Now maybe the kid was high on drugs. But he talked about Drake, said he'd been to his house. For sex parties. Said that he and his pal Jimmy had argued with Drake. He told me there was a lampshade in the shop made from Jimmy's skin."

Fournier placed his hands over his water glass for a moment and closed his eyes as if performing a blessing, then took a sip.

"The shop was closed, so not much me and my partner could do. I called my sergeant, and he told me to write up an MIC and forget about it. I wrote the MIC, and we gave the kid a ride to his apartment. But I couldn't forget about it, so I passed on a detailed report to a homicide detective I knew. A week later, the kid's body was found in the Seventh Ward with a wooden stake through his heart. Cold-case detectives still have it."

"And you think there have been dozens more like this kid."

"Yes, I do."

"Does Drake fit the profile of a serial killer?"

"I suppose he does, if that would include ritual human sacrifice as part of his religion."

"You believe that?" asked Honey.

"Yes. He's not a pure voodoo priest, he's an amalgam. He's definitely into Palo Mayombe."

"Palo Mayombe?" asked Honey.

"Some refer to it as the dark side of Santeria, but that's being unfair. Slaves from the Congo imported the religion to places like Brazil and Cuba. It's an animistic, a shamanistic religion where you communicate directly with the spirits. Human bones are one of the tools of Palo, so more than a few practitioners have gotten into trouble by digging up graves to get at some bones."

"Seems like a natural fit, since Drake is a bone specialist."

"Yes, but he also studied certain Aztec and Maya sects that performed human sacrifice by drugging an unwilling young person, putting him or her on an altar and then cutting out the heart in front of the gathered masses. The priests would place a human skull carved from stone, usually quartz, into the victim's body cavity, then would use the skull as some kind of religious icon. Drake has a collection of human-size quartz skulls, and he has privately stated that some of them were used in such rituals. He's a powerful sorcerer and he's not squeamish about shedding blood. Both of you are in grave danger."

Honey didn't hide her derision. "I think I'm in grave danger of being talked to death. No offense."

"None taken. Drake is going after both of you. With red magic. Trust me. Just as he's been after me for many years."

"You look pretty healthy," said Honey.

"I take countermeasures."

"What is red magic?" I asked.

"Let's just say he's coming after you to kill you, but he's letting you know up front what's coming."

"How would you know he's doing that?" asked Honey.

"I'll answer that by asking you to tell me about the strange oc-currences you've had in the last couple of days. Bad luck, acci-dents . . . ?" said Fournier. "I still have friends in the department. I heard about the mad-dog attack."

Fournier saw that I had raised my eyebrows just a bit.

"I'm sure there's more, but keep it to yourself if you want," he said.

"Okay, look," I said, "I've read your files. If something comes up—"

"How do you figure Sanchez and Ruiz were killed?" he asked.

"It's an open question as to whether they were murdered," said Honey.

Fournier looked at the two of us and shook his head. "You're keeping me out of the loop."

"You're retired. We came here because you approached us. It's a courtesy call. Not a recruitment gesture."

Fournier sat silently for several long moments, just looking at us. "I'll be happy to check your houses, apartments, wherever you live. Look for items they placed there to attack you."

"Thanks for your time, Mr. Fournier," said Honey, standing up from the sofa.

"You two have a pretty good rep and track record," said Fournier. "But it's important to know what you don't know. And right now, you're both clueless. No offense."

"None taken," I said, parroting his earlier remark. "If you weren't able to nail Drake, and you think we're clueless, why contact us?"

"I try to remain hopeful. In spite of everything."

Honey and I crossed to the door. Fournier moved quickly to join us and took my hand. I could feel something in his palm as we shook hands.

"For good luck," he said.

I looked down and saw a black stone pendant on a silver chain. Some kind of mystical symbol was etched into the stone.

"What could it hurt?" he asked.

Honey looked on disapprovingly, but I kept the charm.

"Guess we'll find out."

Honey took surface streets up to the I-10, then kept it at seventy as we headed south across swampland and skirted Lake Pontchartrain en route to New Orleans. I ran Anastasia's plates, and dispatch informed me the Lexus was registered to Tony Fournier at the LaPlace address.

Honey looked at me askance when I hung the talisman pendant from Fournier on her rearview mirror.

"That's against regulations."

"Please humor me."

She shook her head. "Except for seeing the girl? This trip was a waste of time."

"Wish I could have put a GPS tracker on her Lexus."

"You're working as a homicide detective. Not as a PI. We can't do that."

"We just can't get caught. I mean, it's only you and me, but we need to be running surveillance on about five people."

"Ruling out coincidence, what could Anastasia have been doing at Kate Townsend's?"

I didn't have an answer and exhaled audibly. "It's been a long day and I didn't sleep much last night."

"Me either. Bad dreams."

I didn't ask. I knew I'd be up late again, reading FBI reports on ritualistic murder and other accounts of the occult. A couple of theories had started to form in the dark corners of my brain. Theories that put the lie to the innocent notion that Honey was right and we had overdoses on our hands, and not some sadistic killer.

I just had to make sure I didn't become the new Tony Fournier.

CHAPTER FIFTEEN

Dead bodies in New Orleans were no big deal, unless maybe you're the stiff lying facedown in your own blood. Becky Valencia lay faceup on her acupuncture table, but there was no blood. She had dozens and dozens of needles in her naked body. Needles in her ears, above and below her eyes, on her torso, arms, legs, hands, and feet. I'd had plenty of acupuncture and didn't see anything that looked wrong, needle-wise, although she had a hell of a lot of needles in her.

But she was dead, so something had definitely gone wrong.

Honey had called me at 9:05 A.M. I'd had vivid dreams the night before but generally slept okay. I'd hit the dojo at seven for an early workout and then back home for a shower. The coffee was brewing when Honey had called. It was now 9:30, and, damn it, we could see no sign of foul play.

Except there were these black candles. Thirteen of them, all lit. In a circle around the acupuncture table. I put on latex gloves and carefully examined the underside of one of the candles.

"Uniforms are out canvassing the neighborhood. In case some-one saw something."

"It's possible to die from acupuncture," I said. "Usually from infection due to poorly sterilized needles, so death is not quick. But misplaced needles can puncture your heart or collapse your lungs and kill you."

The coroner and crime-scene techs hadn't arrived yet, or they might have chimed in with more information.

"So these needles could be used to murder someone?" said Honey. "Or to commit suicide?"

I nodded. Honey had explained to me on the phone that a patient had showed up promptly at nine for her appointment. The door was unlocked, she let herself in, and found the corpse. She was already downtown in an interrogation room with Mackie but wasn't a suspect.

"Except I'm not buying suicide, and I'm not buying that Becky Valencia allowed a killer to put needles in her. It's got to be poi-son," I said.

"So how was it administered?"

"Look at the needles. These are not the packaged, disposable needles used on patients ever since HIV came along. You couldn't poison those, because you'd have to rip open the package to get at them. Valencia used old-fashioned, reusable needles on herself." I pointed to the antique wooden box on a small table next to the body. "That's probably her personal set. The killer could have predipped the needles in poison."

"Okay, let's say we run with the poison scenario. The killer ei-ther broke in and planted the poison, or Valencia knew the killer and let him in. Someone she would be comfortable enough with to get naked in front of. But why focus just on the needles? The killer could have doped her coffee, a glass of water. Then cleaned the glass or took it with him."

"You're talking like someone who doesn't think this was an overdose or suicide."

"I play percentages. Three students of Drake's dead in a couple of days? That spells murder to me. And the candles are . . ."

"Spooky?" I asked. "Why surround yourself with black candles if you're administering a healing, right?"

Honey nodded.

"And another thing," I said. "Remember those silver baskets she showed us the other day in her waiting room?"

"The ones her father made. Expensive pieces that Drake wanted to buy."

"Take a look at the mantel. They're missing. I doubt she would have gotten rid of them."

"She said Drake always wanted them. . . ."

"Plus the professor may have been pissed Valencia broke her vows and quit the group. Did you find an appointment book?" I asked.

"No. And no cell phone either. She might have kept track of her appointments in her phone."

"The bank, maybe the auto-parts shop next door will have security video," I said. "Might show us something."

"Go for it."

I started to walk out, but Honey touched my arm. "I'm sorry. I could tell you liked her."

"She seemed like a good person. She's a doctor of Oriental medicine. She wanted to be of service. I was going to book an appointment when this was over."

"So let's find her killer. Chief said to forget about going by the book."

Just don't get caught, right?

"He also promised search warrants for Drake," said Honey quickly. "So hold off on him for now."

I nodded. I'd already worked out some special surprises for Townsend and Vermack.

"There's something else," I said. "The nature of Valencia's death here." I'd been boning up on all this and knew Honey didn't want to hear what was coming; I also knew she needed to hear it. "These are ritualistic killings. They have all the hallmarks. So the question is Do we have a secular killer, you know, a serial killer or sexual sadist using ritual, but not because it's part of his religion? Or is the killer coming from a religious place? Are these killings fulfilling responsibilities to the killer's beliefs, like certain Satanists or sects of Santeria and Palo Mayombe?"

Honey shrugged. "A killer's a killer. Let's nail him."

"Or her."

One of the security cameras from the bank and one from the auto-parts store showed angles of Becky Valencia's front door. I made copies of both, but the auto-parts-store camera had the clearest footage, so I concentrated on that video. The person I assumed to be the murderer arrived at 7:05 wearing a long raincoat with an open umbrella. The killer walked with a slow, exaggerated shuffle, with head bowed, making it impossible to determine the individual's true posture and gait. And the umbrella stayed strategically placed to block the auto-parts-store camera view, so the perp knew the placement of the closest camera, making this a very premeditated affair.

But just before mounting the front steps, for only a moment, the umbrella lowered, revealing the killer wore an Anonymous mask. Same as the stalker who put the sigil on my building.

From my desk at the Homicide Section, I sent a copy of the surveillance video of Anonymous to Honey's smartphone. I made a spate of other calls and arranged to have twenty-four-hour surveillance put on Drake, Townsend, and Vermack. I gave our guys the info on the Lexus that Anastasia was driving; if sighted, they would follow her and notify me immediately. I had a special GPS tracker ready with her name on it. If I could have gotten away with putting a spotter at Fournier's house in St. John's Parish to watch for her, I would have done that too. I still had no logical explanation—none—as to why Fournier's niece would be in Kate Townsend's apartment. And that bothered me. A lot.

Fred Gaudet was happy to come back onto the team, and I asked him to check in on Gina Sanchez out on Airline Drive. I knew Fred would return with several orders of *carne asada* and plenty of chips and fresh salsa for the Homicide Section.

VCAT and the narcotics folks hadn't been able to locate the remaining Skulls members believed to be in the NOLA area. As for the suspect in the black cape and Anonymous mask, I'd sent out a description in an e-mail addressed to "NOPDALL," which included every officer in the department, asking them to "apprehend the murder suspect, if sighted, who is considered to be armed and dangerous." I also had dispatch put out a BOLO, a "Be on the Lookout" alert that broadcast a description of the suspect on all district patrol channels.

I made a number of other urgent calls, and my last one was to Kendall Bullard, the UFC fighter I had coached for years and who had more girlfriends than a rap mogul and about a gazillion followers on Twitter.

"Coach, what up?" came Kendall's thick NOLA accent over my smartphone.

"Three dead bodies. Some spooky hoodoo cult is buying the farm, one at a time."

"Man, don't be messin' wit hoodoo."

"Never. The UFC still got you in Cleveland?"

"Yeah. Got me doin' more promotin' than trainin'."

"You're a valuable commodity now, so they're squeezing you. Speaking of your popularity, I need a flash mob in Crafty Voodoo in the Quarter in thirty minutes. Can you make it happen? Be great if they were all asking to speak to Kate Townsend and wouldn't take no for an answer."

"For you? Easy as pie, boss."

We rung off. I knew Kendall would deliver a boisterous crowd to Kate Townsend's place of business, probably by using only one tweet on Twitter, the social networking Web site. Since the chief had now unofficially loosened my reins, and the rules now served more as suggestions, I'd decided to go on the offensive, and Townsend was the first target in my crosshairs.

I muscled my way past at least a hundred people milling outside Crafty Voodoo and found another hundred crammed inside, all insisting on seeing Kate Townsend. I smiled, silently thanking Kendall and the clout he had with his fans. The buxom clerks were overwhelmed, and I caught a glimpse of a flummoxed Townsend trying to convince a group to leave.

Thanks to the mayhem, I easily retraced the path Honey and I had taken just the other night, and walked through the bead curtain unseen, through the wooden door, and silently mounted the stairs. Before entering the store, I had checked out the private parking for the building; no Lexus, but I ran the plates on a jet-black BMW 750i sedan, which was registered to Kate Townsend.

She had money and wasn't afraid to spend it, and I was reminded of that as I entered the upstairs rooms. A quick walk-through suggested she either had a lot of roommates—three bedrooms had three beds each with connecting bathrooms and all looked lived in—or she'd told the truth about providing rooms to transient females.

The freezer and huge fridge in the kitchen didn't contain any human heads or body parts, but both needed to be cleaned.

A soft beep from my chronograph told me I needed to hurry the hell up. I moved through Townsend's private quarters looking for a computer or any other tempting sources of information or evidence. When I'd visited Crafty Voodoo the other day with Honey, I'd established there was no office downstairs. I had to believe there was some space with office equipment and a computer/printer, unless she ran everything from behind her front counter.

I entered the last room, the master bedroom. A massive four-poster bed with canopy, all done in red satin, looked terribly inviting. There was no office setup. Damn, she must be a techie running a virtual office from wherever she was with a laptop. Then

I noticed two different makeup vanities on either side of the room. A quick check revealed different choices in beauty products.

Kate Townsend shared this room with another woman.

Anastasia Fournier?

I swept the room again and spotted a red notebook computer, almost the same color as the sheets, sitting right on the bed. I needed to act fast and started for the bed.

"Stop right there or I'll shoot you dead."

I stopped and slowly turned around to see Townsend with a 9mm pointed at me. Her hand was shaking just a bit, but was it because she felt nervous or angry?

"I've been looking for you, Miss Townsend. Please point the gun down."

"Shut up," she practically spat. Okay, it was anger. Guess she didn't appreciate the flash mob. "Those are all your friends down there, aren't they?"

"My father said that if you have more friends than you have fingers then they're not really your friends. I swear to you, I don't know a single person downstairs."

"You're a liar. I think I'm going to have to shoot you."

"That would be a mistake. I'm here on official police business."

"You broke into my apartment!"

"Not at all. I entered your shop downstairs and found a wild party in progress. I couldn't get anyone to help me, so, having visited your home before, I noticed the door to the stairway was ajar. I merely came up to find you."

"That's your story? Well, here's mine. I took you for a burglar and, fearing for my life, I shot you. No, I thought you were a rapist. It'll fly."

With her free hand she ripped at her blouse, popping off all the buttons and tearing the sheer material. She wore the kind of bra you could open from the front, and she did so, revealing pert, pale breasts with pink nipples. She then slapped herself in the face so hard her nose started to bleed, but she kept the semiautomatic leveled at me the entire time. I was impressed.

"Wow," I said. "Cool, but I'm afraid I have to take you into custody."

"You don't get it." She raised the gun.

"Look at the small lens just above my jacket pocket. Looks like a button to the casual observer. I've been streaming video ever since I walked in. To two officers sitting in a van around the corner."

She wavered as she looked at the lens. "I'm digitally recording this conversation," I said. "Audio and video. And even if I weren't, do you really think you could kill an on-duty NOPD detective who's been dispatched to question you in the murder of Becky Valencia?"

Townsend's jaw literally dropped, and her eyes went wide. "Becky? That's not . . . possible."

I took a side step, then lashed out with both hands, grabbing the gun and bending her wrist. She yelped as I removed the handgun. I pocketed the piece, wrenched her right arm behind her back, and snapped on the cuffs.

"What's this?"

"You don't use handcuffs in bondage and discipline?"

"You're arresting me?"

I pulled her left arm behind her and finished the process. "Um, well, if you insist. I don't like people pointing guns at me. Like your two pals from Las Calaveras—the Skulls—who I had to kill yesterday."

"The Skulls?" She looked like someone desperately positing an alibi in her mind, running the pros and cons.

"Never heard of them, right? Then why did they have a Crafty Voodoo business card with your name and cell-phone number written on it? You're just like Drake. Make up your mind: Are you stupid or are you smart?"

She just stared at me.

"Where were you this morning at seven o'clock?" I demanded.

"In bed," she said coldly.

"With who? Somebody shares this bed with you. What's her name?"

Townsend dropped her head. "How was Becky killed?"

"You tell me. But why would you use thirteen black candles that came from your own store?"

She looked up at me unpleasantly surprised. I pulled her toward the bed, retrieved her laptop, then guided her toward the stairs.

"Put a jacket on me or something. My blouse is all ripped."

"Yeah, and your boobs are hanging out and your nose is bleeding, too. You look like a cheap floozy. But don't worry, we're two blocks from Bourbon Street. No one will notice."

CHAPTER SIXTEEN

No way the New Orleans district attorney would press charges against Townsend for pulling the gun and threatening to kill me, but I arrested her for resisting a police officer with force or violence just to get her behind bars for a while—and to use as leverage. We let her reexamine her life's priorities in a holding cell with a group of female felons who looked like they could bench-press Buicks.

Townsend had lawyered up quickly and refused to answer any questions. Her attorney had a reputation of being a fifteen-hundred-dollar-an-hour high-rent wonder, good at getting felonious politicians, investment bankers, and CEOs released scot-free. *How could she afford the sleazebag?*

Honey was still at Valencia's crime scene with the coroner and CSI techs, so with Townsend incarcerated and refusing to talk, I left Broad Street and invaded Hans Vermack's Voodoo Cave with a small army I'd quickly cobbled together: ICE agents, reps from the Section 8 Housing Choice Voucher Program, a city building inspector, a member of the Vieux Carré Commission, a fraud inspector from the Louisiana Food Stamp Program, two inspectors from NOFD, half a dozen uniforms, and myself.

A squad car with lights flashing now sat parked at Vermack's shop entrance, and two nasty-looking NOPD coppers stood like gargoyles of a different sort on either side of the front door. Not likely too many customers would run the gauntlet, and those who were inside when we arrived quickly left.

All of Vermack's employees, including his girlfriend, Patrice Jones (a state psychologist was standing by to evaluate her, and a nurse would examine her for signs of physical abuse), were being escorted downtown to be interviewed by homicide detectives. I knew Honey would appreciate my little display of authority, all perfectly legal. And considering Vermack's track record, appropriate.

"Verdomme het allemaal naar de hel! Dit is onzin!" he yelled, storming around his shop. "Somebody is going to pay. This is discrimination because I'm a minority. This is harassment! I'm losing money here!"

"What minority are you from, again," I asked, with my hands crossed.

"I'm a Wiccan. We have always been discriminated against. I'll be filing complaints and"—he pointed his finger at each of us, then—"you will all regret this day. I'm going to teach you a lesson," he said, stepping toward the black female rep from Section 8 Housing. Her name was Janean Bayham, she had a little meat on her bones and didn't look intimidated; in fact, she put her hands on her hips and stared at Vermack.

A few of the LE folks in the room looked like they were ready to grab him, but I gestured for them to wait.

"I'm going to put a curse on all of you that will make your lives a living—" When he tapped Janean's chest with his fingertip, I pounced, wrenched his wrist into a very painful compliance hold, and dropped him to his knees, screaming.

"That was misdemeanor assault." I quickly cuffed him. "As soon as all of these nice people are through with you, you're going to jail. Why we don't deport scamming douche bags like you is beyond me."

Two uniforms stepped forward and lifted him to his feet.

"Where were you at seven this morning? Poisoning Becky Valencia, right?" I asked.

"What?"

"No alibi again, Hans?"

"Patrice can—"

"Patrice doesn't know what decade it is. Becky told us how you and Kate and Drake were shafting the other members of the Crimson Throne. Did you kill her for breaking her vows?"

Hans stood speechless, like a confused man.

"You are in a world of trouble," I continued. "A little later on, you are going to talk to me truthfully, or it's going to get much worse for you. And trust me, your magic won't save you. *Begrijpen?* Understand?"

I'd visited Holland a few times and loved it. And I like Dutch people too, especially Dutch ladies. I just didn't like Hans.

I gestured, and the coppers led him back toward his office, where the assembled investigators would be asking him questions while he sat handcuffed waiting for the ride downtown. I hadn't planned on arresting him, but it suited me just fine.

By the time I made it back to headquarters, Townsend had been released, and Honey was now at the morgue with the coroner for

Becky Valencia's autopsy. Hans Vermack, however, had lost most of his piss and vinegar once he understood just how much trouble he was in. I barged into his interrogation room alone, like I owned the place.

"You," he said, glancing at me, and then shaking his head.

I slammed my fist down so hard on the table in front of him, his coffee spilled in his lap. "Hans, shut the fuck up." I went nose to nose to him with my best criminally violent insane look, a look that has frightened more than a few people when they saw it, including myself, because I knew I was capable of performing the kind of violence the look advertised.

Vermack was no fighter, not a physical one. He might be a ferocious sorcerer—if that kind of thing was real—but he was no fighter. My killer persona intimidated him, and he cast his eyes downward.

"What you have experienced today is just a taste, a sample, of how I plan to ruin your life. Tomorrow is a new day, and I'm going to bring a whole new world of trouble down on your head." I waited a couple of beats, then sat down across from him. "Unless . . ."

I left it hanging and started ferociously jotting notes on a pad, making sure he couldn't see what I wrote. I opened the bottle of water I'd brought in and sipped, then lit a cigarillo, ignoring him. And that drove him crazy.

"Unless, what?"

"The Crimson Throne is finished. Drake's going down, I promise you that. And Townsend just made bail." I slid him a copy of her mug shots, but didn't tell him what she'd been arrested for. "Tomorrow, your bank accounts will be frozen and deportation proceedings will begin . . . if I give the word. Or I could have you arrested for *murder.* An arrest doesn't mean a conviction, Hans, but your picture would be on the front page of the paper, your business would have to close, you'd have to give a fortune to a bail bondsman because as a noncitizen you're a flight risk. Plus, I'll talk to your bank about those real estate loans for the Section 8 houses. Oh, and the IRS—I'll dime you out to the Feds."

He started to say something, but I held up my hand. I talked about sex magic and made out like I knew a lot more about the Crimson Throne than I actually did. I used Tony Fournier's file as show-and-tell, flipping open one folder to reveal the photo of a missing transient, a person who had once upon a time been a guest at a Crimson Throne sex session. "There are dozens more like this girl, but then you know that. You had sex with her, right?"

"I vaguely remember her, yes." Hans rubbed his eyes. He looked like he could go to sleep sitting in his chair.

"Tell me about what happened to Felix Sanchez and Roscindo Ruiz at Professor Drake's house the other morning. I remember what you already told me, but that was bullshit. There was no overdose. Who was the guide that day?"

"I would have to guess Kate," he said quickly. Hans had broken. He was mine now, and it hadn't taken much; all it had taken was going after his pocketbook in a major way. "Felix and Roscindo liked her, and the feeling was mutual. If you have some kind of toxicology report proving there was no overdose, then the explanation is easy. She summoned a killer demon but lost control of it."

He noticed my skeptical look. "That's the same thing Drake told us. But let me humor you. Why didn't the demon kill Kate?"

"She was probably wearing something to protect her. For example, the Third Pentacle of Jupiter—one of the seals of Solomon—something the Mexicans didn't have."

"So according to your beliefs, could Kate have ordered the demon to kill?"

"Yes. She is an advanced-enough practitioner to do that. But . . . I don't like Kate, okay? Even so, I can't believe she would kill them or anyone else."

Hans hadn't seen her pull the pistol and work out a scenario to justify whacking me.

"So she must have made some error," he said. "The demon could explain Becky's death, also. How was she found? In what position?"

"I can't give out those details yet," I said, exhaling a long plume of smoke.

"Okay, it doesn't matter. The point is, if the demon got into Becky's body, it could make her do whatever. Even kill herself. You have heard of the expression 'The devil made me do it'? There is more truth to that than you might care to consider. Demons attach themselves to people at bars, nightclubs, concerts. People who use drugs or drink too much are more susceptible, as are the weak-minded, weak-willed, and the overly emotional personalities. I can't count how many times I've heard on the TV news, when they interview a family member or friend, the person says, 'I can't believe he's guilty. He's not like that, he's never hurt a fly.' Well, some entity jumped into the guy's body, caused him to do the deed, then jumped out."

"How could that theory apply to Valencia? You Crimson Throne people are advanced practitioners."

"Yes, but if she were attacked and her guard was down, she

would be vulnerable. I now have to worry that maybe I will be next."

"This is all interesting, but I can't arrest anyone for losing control of a demon. Three people have been murdered. Our courts don't recognize 'evil spirit' as a murder weapon. Let's talk about the heads. You lied to me earlier."

Hans sighed. He was about to start ratting out his friends. "Over the years, Robert has sold hundreds and hundreds of body parts and human bones. You know about Palo Mayombe?"

"It's called the dark side of Santeria. Some sects supposedly perform human sacrifice, but most if not all members use human bones in their ceremonies."

"Most members of that religion are perfectly fine people and not doing evil deeds and so forth. Only some. But yes, there is a demand for human bones. You can buy older human skulls on the Internet for around a thousand dollars. Fresh heads are something else. I'm not sure Robert sold human heads, but Kate, absolutely. She sells them for five to ten thousand dollars each."

"Where does she get them?"

He shook his head. "This I cannot tell you. It could cost me my life."

"Las Calaveras. The Skulls."

Hans remained silent.

"How did she connect with them?"

"Please, I can't answer that question, but let me tell you this. I called her a whore, before. It wasn't an exaggeration."

"You're saying she's a prostitute?"

"It's not like she's selling a human head for ten thousand every day or even every month. Yes, she does well with her business, but how do you think she can afford the clothes, furniture, jewelry, the luxury car? She's a madam, with a stable of girls."

It struck me like thunder. *Anastasia Fournier.*

"Escort service?" I suddenly understood the high-priced criminal lawyer representing her.

"Yes, but also she rents out a nice four-bedroom apartment. Sets up the girls to see clients there. After a few months, they move to a new location."

"What's the current location?"

"Ask your vice officers. I heard from Robert that several of them get freebies on a regular basis."

That could explain how my home address came into play. Townsend's vice buddies could have gotten it from the NOPD personnel office, or from any number of coppers who know where I live.

"Kate's call girls come and go quickly, the same as her shop clerks. That's why she's always recruiting new girls from the streets. I think she got the idea from Marie Laveau."

"The famous voodoo priestess from long ago."

"Yes. Laveau was said to have had a house in the New Orleans area, where she provided the sexual services of young ladies to gentlemen of means. It was a moneymaker. Then for Laveau, now for Townsend."

A plan for Kate Townsend already started to form in my mind, but I needed to focus on questions for Hans Vermack.

"I asked you before about Townsend's pregnancy."

"She had an abortion," he said, shrugging. "Because Robert insisted. She was much younger then and foolishly thought she could ensnare him with the child. But he is too much of a philanderer.

She had to adjust her thinking, and their relationship changed. Now, to be honest, they're not close. Not even a little."

"She said Drake has been her boyfriend for years."

"In name only. Long ago he got fed up with her ambition and greed. It's been a long process to extricate himself from her clutches."

"Drake told you to be patient, that change was coming. What did that refer to?"

"The big dump. He's leaving her. No more financial support, advice, no more spiritual work together, no nothing. Anyway, she's got money now, she doesn't need him. Robert will disband the Crimson Throne for a time, then begin anew with a new high priestess he can trust. It won't matter to Kate. She'll start her own group."

"Seems like a long and drawn-out way to end a relationship."

"He's afraid of her."

"Afraid of her because of what she knows? Crimes he has committed?"

"Possibly. So sure, she could ruin him. Tulane would disown him and he'd go to jail. But certainly he fears her power as a dark magician. She is formidable, in spite of her sloppiness."

"Think Drake will skip town?"

"I doubt it. He loves New Orleans too much. And he is too proud. He won't run away. Yes, Kate is powerful, but so is Robert. He'll probably work some incredible magic to make her think it was her idea to leave him."

"Hans, put aside the demon explanation. Murder usually happens for a very specific reason. But I can't determine a motive as to why anyone would want to kill our victims. Unless it was because they were leaving the group."

"Leaving the Crimson Throne is not a killing offense. That's preposterous. No member is given some kind of knowledge that, were it revealed, could ruin Robert or anyone else. People left the group all the time, usually because of ego clashes."

"All right, then, what if it was religious, ritualistic homicide and they were killed for their death energy?" This was one of the theories that I was still working out.

Hans paused thoughtfully and chewed on a fingernail. "Yes, that's possible. Ritual human sacrifice is largely about absorbing the energy of the deceased. Some radical vampire cults, Satanists, and certain sects of Palo Mayombe make no secret about this kind of killing. Satanic groups like the Order of Nine Angles and the Friends of Hecate advocate human sacrifice under certain conditions.

"Ritual killing generates powerful medicine, but it is very dark work," said Hans, continuing. "That wasn't what the Crimson Throne was all about, although I can't speak for Robert or Kate or anyone else in this regard. Remember, our individual members all practiced other types of magic. Voodoo, hoodoo, Santeria, Palo Mayombe, ritual magic, folk magic, qigong, Asian shamanism, and all kinds of neo-paganism. So, yes, I suppose your theory about ritual killing is legitimate."

Vermack furrowed his brow. "And now that I think about it, maybe that's exactly what it was."

CHAPTER SEVENTEEN

I checked with Janean Bayham, and she agreed to drop the assault charges against Hans Vermack. While he got processed out, I ran a check on Anastasia Fournier and came up with nothing but a DUI on her DMV record. When Kruger popped into the office, I buttonholed him.

"I'm trying to run down Tony Fournier's niece, Anastasia. You know anything about his family?"

"I didn't know Tony had a niece."

"He told me his brother and sister-in-law were killed in a boating accident a few years ago. Anastasia is the daughter."

"I vaguely remember him mentioning a brother. I know he had a sister, career army officer, stationed in Germany. But that was years ago."

"I'll check with personnel."

The personnel office was closed, but my gut told me that Tony Fournier was up to something, and I needed to find out what. So I walked out of Homicide and popped in to the Vice offices. I approached a detective I didn't know at his desk.

"Saint James, Homicide. Listen . . ." I handed him a copy of Townsend's mug shots. "A reliable source tells me she's running girls out of an apartment in town. My guy is on tape accusing detectives from this unit of stopping in for freebies. My partner and I report directly to the chief, so Pointer is going to either listen to the tape or read a transcript. I'm going to make sure that any false accusation against your unit gets edited out. Okay? You have my word."

The vice detective looked at the mug shots but didn't say anything.

"One way or the other, I'm bringing this chick down, maybe for Murder One. If someone were protecting her, and I'm sure no one here is, they would get tarnished. And who wants to see that? What I need is the current location of her brothel. Off the record, of course."

I scribbled my cell number on the copy of Townsend's mug shots.

"I'll ask around," said the vice dick, coolly. "Give it a day or so."

Honey came back from the morgue, and I waved her over just as I took a call from Fred Gaudet, who had gone out to check on Gina Sanchez. I put the call on speaker.

"Fred, I thought you'd be back here with some *taquitos* by now."

"Gina Sanchez has disappeared."

My smile faded quickly as I looked to Honey. I remembered Sanchez's fears of being targeted for death, concerns that seemed exaggerated at the time.

"Fred, this is Honey. What happened?"

"She wasn't grabbed, she cleared out. Didn't even ask for her rent deposit refund. Landlord says a couple of Mexican guys in a beat-up van helped her move. Her place is empty except for the furniture that came with it."

"No forwarding address, phone number? The owner get a van description, plate number?"

"Zip, zero, *nada*. Sanchez had a state ID card, so I pulled her photo. Been showing it to my Mexican contacts, at the *mercados,* the markets, and the *panaderías*, the bakeries. Someone will spot her."

"Don't forget the check-cashing service she used."

"I'll go there right now."

I rung off and looked at Honey.

"She might have left the state or the country. She even talked about surrendering to Immigration."

"Maybe Fred will turn something up," said Honey, who looked a little sad. I knew she didn't like attending autopsies, especially when the victim was someone she knew.

I briefed her on arresting Townsend and the interrogation of Vermack. "I'm waiting to hear back from Vice, but it should be easy to bust Townsend for promoting prostitution."

"And maybe set up a sting. Buy one of those heads."

I nodded. "Wish we could sting Drake somehow, but I think that would be a long-term operation. Wonder why Tony Fournier never did that?"

"Any why is his niece hooking for Townsend?"

"We're not certain of that yet. Maybe that's why Fournier was arguing with her when we showed up. It would have to hurt him like hell if Anastasia has linked up with the girlfriend of the guy he's been trying to put away for fifteen years."

"No doubt," said Honey, crossing to her desk. "As far as Valencia? The findings are preliminary. Coroner says he found exudate indicating she had an orgasm before she died. But no positive sign of intercourse."

"Strong similarity to Sanchez and Ruiz."

"The needles went in before she expired. The coroner is sure about that. Cause of death was pneumothorax."

"That's a new one on me," I said.

"No it's not. You just didn't know the name. Air gets between the membranes that separate the chest wall from the lungs. Then the lungs collapse."

"So it was an acupuncture needle that allowed the air to enter?"

She nodded.

"One reason I was gone so long is I had an acupuncturist from Metairie take a look before we moved Valencia to the morgue. Korean guy. He confirmed the needle placement was wrong."

"So maybe the killer mildly sedated Valencia, then there was some kind of masturbation or something, then he puts the needles in once she was incapacitated."

"The killer knew where to place the fatal needle," said Honey.

I grimaced and shook my head. "You realize how painful collapsed lungs are? Even if she'd been lightly sedated, that was a torturous death. We have to stop this person."

Hans Vermack was under surveillance as soon as he left Broad Street headquarters, but Professor Robert Drake could not be located. Kate Townsend had ridden with her attorney to his penthouse offices in the Central Business District, but she must have left via a private elevator; our team lost her.

I seriously wanted to break into Drake's curio shop, but since the chief had promised warrants, I decided to hold off.

Even though she'd been going nonstop all day and hadn't eaten, Honey declined my dinner invitation. So I headed to one of my neighborhood haunts for a quick bite. After dinner I intended to make an unannounced visit to Tony Fournier. Tomorrow we'd be hitting Drake, so I wanted to work a few things out and see if the puzzle pieces fit together.

The guy on the Hammond B3 organ at Tommy's Wine Bar made some fast runs on the keyboard that almost made me forget all the bad luck this case had brought. If the music couldn't make me forget my troubles, maybe the Pali Keefer Ranch Vineyard Pinot Noir would lend a hand. I noshed on a plate of Oysters Tommy— oysters baked in the shell with Romano cheese, pancetta, and roasted red pepper—and asked myself a series of questions.

What exactly connected Valencia's strange death with Sanchez's and Ruiz's? Was someone killing all of the members of the Crimson Throne? If so, maybe our surveillance teams should be acting as protection details. Was it mere coincidence that three of Drake's students had been killed in ritualistic fashion, albeit using different rituals?

Anastasia Fournier's presence on the scene still made no sense, and I'd forgotten to ask Hans about her. I'd try to do so tomorrow. And what about the mad dog, the bad dreams, and the sigils? Who was the disguised person who'd stalked me and killed Valencia? Were they even the same person?

What was the lyric from the old Albert King blues song? "If it wasn't for bad luck, I wouldn't have no luck at all." I knew things could always get worse, but I didn't think they would here in my sanctuary for good music, food, and wine.

Until Twee Siu sat down next to me.

Twee Siu, the New Orleans CIA station chief.

A former client and lover, Twee had once saved my life. But another time, in a suite at the Hotel Monteleone, she'd come close to gunning me down in cold blood after she murdered her husband, who had preceded her as NOLA's CIA station chief.

A beautifully put-together thirty-year-old Vietnamese American with fashion-model cheekbones, she always elicited conflicted feelings of lust and repulsion from me. We hadn't seen each other recently, but she regularly sent me classified intelligence reports in hopes of recruiting me to spy for the Central Intelligence Agency.

For her to show up like this at one of my neighborhood haunts told me something was up. Something connected to this damn case. I casually looked around to see if she had backup. Nobody stood out, and thanks to the cozy nook we sat in and to the music, we could speak openly.

"You don't look too worse for the wear," she said. "Although I heard you fell off a two-story building."

"They didn't teach you tactical jumps like that at spy school?" I asked with a straight face. I motioned for a cute waitress to bring another wineglass. "This pinot is very nice. Please have one with me." I looked at her as I fired up a cigarillo. "Is this about Drake, Townsend, or Vermack?"

She smiled. "I have a sitter for Brendan until eleven. It's been too long. Even single moms deserve to have a social life."

I didn't believe for a second this was just a social visit.

"Come to my dojo and meet the gang. We'll do some upper

body on the Infinity Rig. And I'll only charge you twenty percent more than everyone else," I said, smiling. Twee was worth over thirty million, but that was another story.

"Drake is a company asset and has been for something like thirty years. Since he was a grad student on digs in the Yucatan. His hobby back then was ethnobotany, and the Agency was very interested in synthesizing unknown native plants into drugs that could be used as truth serums or for mind control. He helped the scientific directorate in those days."

I shook my head. Bad luck squared. "Okay."

"But that was just a hobby. His field of study was bones. In Mexico he befriended a young American-born thug named Tico Rodriguez, who years later became a top leader of the San Leon Drug Cartel."

"And the San Leon Cartel begat Las Calaveras, who are now the largest cartel in Mexico. So I'm guessing Drake has used them to smuggle human remains into the States."

"Yes. And certain psychotropic drugs."

So Tony Fournier was right.

"Some cartel bosses like Rodriguez practice black magic. In brutal ways. So there was a lot of common ground between Drake and those people. Rodriguez is a Nicaraguan American, originally from Mobile, Alabama. The fact that he's done so well in Mexico suggests just how ruthless he is."

"So what do Tico Rodriguez and the Mexicans get out of their relationship with Drake?"

"Looted bones and skulls from Maya archaeological sites. The skulls of kings, artifacts that belonged to old sorcerers. Precious things, some of which they use in their black rites."

"The Agency approves?"

"Well, they did, but that was way before my time. But, yes, they wanted access to the cartel leaders who have performed favors for us. Including recent favors in the War on Terror."

"Terrorists on our borders?"

Twee didn't answer.

"So Drake is an active CIA asset, meaning you want me to do what? Back off?"

"If he's guilty of murder, then arrest him."

"He contacted you for help?"

"I've never had any contact with him. He's not run out of NOLA Station. But I got a call, yes. From a person in a powerful position at Langley."

"How much trouble can I expect from you or the CIA if I don't let it go?"

"None from me. I just can't protect you. I'm short on field operatives. The Skulls might have a contract from Drake for your death. I'm trying to confirm that."

"A contract? For what, doing my job? Does he think if he eliminates me, his problems will go away?"

"Maybe. The Skulls are forming cells in cities all over the country. And they won't become schoolgirls just because they crossed the border. The eight men here were doing groundwork for a substantial cartel presence in New Orleans. Wish I had followed my instinct."

"Which was?"

"Establish contact. Do them a favor. Get a favor in return. I can think of a dozen scenarios where I could use their services. Don't forget, the founding members of the Skulls were originally disgruntled ex-Mexican special forces operatives. They are the most technologically advanced cartel, period."

One thing I'll say for Twee, she never papered over who and what she was.

"I understand that the CIA has to turn a blind eye to who they do business with, as long as the intelligence obtained is good and the results positive. But getting into bed with the Skulls?" I shook my head.

"You don't approve. But if I had done that, I could get them off your back. Now that four of them are dead, others will be sent, looking for payback."

I didn't say anything, just took another sip of pinot.

"The CIA has been making deals with the devil since forever, to realize larger goals. All intelligence agencies the world over do the same. Stansfield Turner tried to purify the CIA when he was DCI and fired nearly a thousand operational employees—covert-action people. I guess it appeased the politically correct crowd, but it was a disaster for American intelligence. It took decades for the Agency to recover from that misguided blunder. Even Turner now regrets what he did. When my late husband saw Turner here in New Orleans walking on the street, he had three words for him: 'Fuck you, Stan.' So, sure, I'll use drug cartels or anyone else to get the job done."

Who was I to take the moral high ground? Intelligence is a dirty business. If you don't want to get dirty, don't play. I'd played a dirty game as a cop and investigator for years. Even on this case, I'd already crossed lines most detectives wouldn't.

The cute waitress finally arrived with a wineglass and poured one for Twee. I'd always meant to ask the waitress out but never got around to it. So I was happy she was seeing me sitting with a woman as attractive as Twee Siu. The waitress finished and moved off.

"You like her," said Twee, as if reading my thoughts.

"Just eye candy. *I* need to find a sitter so I can get out more and have a social life again," I joked.

Twee glanced at the wine. "I'm not much for pinots. I like bold tannins. You have a nice bottle of Chalk Hill Cabernet-Carmenère at your place."

How did she know that? Maybe Twee had hacked my security video. As I ran possibilities through my mind, Twee put her hand over mine. "Like I said, I have until eleven."

What the hell . . . I signaled for the check.

CHAPTER EIGHTEEN

I was at my desk by 7:30 A.M., mostly out of guilt. Even though Honey and I weren't lovers, I always felt bad after sleeping with another woman. Kate Townsend had been right, and it was an issue I felt a strong need to resolve. But how had Townsend guessed that? None of my friends, *no one,* knew how I felt about Honey or the issues between us that I'd been wrestling with.

After Twee left my place promptly at eleven last night, I'd driven out to Tony Fournier's house in LaPlace. He was either a sound sleeper or had gone out, because he didn't answer his cell and ringing his doorbell from the locked front gate produced no results. I'd gone back home and done more research until two this morning.

I took a healthy gulp of hot coffee and then checked in with the lab and got a shock. Of the more than thirteen sets of unique fingerprints lifted from Becky Valencia's acupuncture office yesterday, five sets matched people with criminal records, although none were violent criminals. And one set belonged to someone we knew: Gina Sanchez.

Clearly her husband, Felix, knew Valencia, so it wasn't beyond the pale that Gina Sanchez may have gone for an acupuncture appointment. But it was a fact I'd need to check up on.

Honey must have been running late, because she hadn't yet come in when Chief Pointer strode into the Homicide Section at 8:42. The chief's visit was not a usual occurrence, but even more unusual was that Heckle and Jeckle were nowhere to be seen.

"Saint James," he growled, "let's take a ride."

The chief told me to drive the Bronco. I carefully logged my starting mileage as we left headquarters. Neither of us liked small talk, and while I wasn't nervous, since I didn't consider the chief to have power over me (I'd been shot in the line of duty, so I couldn't be fired), it was highly unusual to have him sitting next to me in my truck.

"If you need the Internet, I have a computer there, Chief," I said, indicating the unit I had built into my dashboard.

"No thanks. I have my BlackBerry if I need the Internet in the next hour or so."

Okay, so this would take an hour. I remained silent as he gave me the occasional driving direction to a liquor store on Loyola Avenue. Seemed a little early in the morning to be hitting a liquor store, but this was New Orleans.

"Ever hear of Evan Williams Single Barrel bourbon?"

"I've heard of Evan Williams, but never tried it."

"The single barrel is its classier cousin. Let's go."

I followed Pointer into the shop, where he purchased three bottles of the bourbon from the owner, his brother Morris Pointer. The chief made a quick introduction, I shook hands, and then he ordered me to put the bourbon in the Bronco.

"Take us back toward headquarters."

I learned patience through all of the stakeouts I've pulled and through years of martial arts training, where learning the weakness of an opponent took time. We got back into the Bronco, I pulled into traffic, and we rode in silence for a few blocks.

"We're riding alone in your truck, but I don't hear you asking for any favors or bitching about something or someone," said Pointer.

"You never will. I figure in the NOPD, we make do with what we got. End of story."

"That's about right. I'm in a similar situation right now, and I've decided to do something about it. I'm going to stop ignoring a problem but instead address it by making do with resources we already have."

Now he had my interest. *How did I fit into this?*

"I may not be well liked, but I take my job seriously. I've had many discussions with my pastor regarding my responsibility to the community." His BlackBerry chimed, he checked the call, then ignored it.

"Behavioral scientists tell us the underlying motivation for murder is shame and humiliation. They say the perpetrator is trying to get back some self-respect. Think that reasoning applies to the killer of your three victims?"

"For my first theory on who the killer might be: no. For the second theory: yes. Seems to me law enforcement understands very little about ritual crime," I said as we cruised along Tulane Avenue.

He nodded vigorously. "I can't tell you how many conferences I've attended where police chiefs can't agree on the extent of it, can't agree on what ritual crime consists of, and can't even agree on the motives of the perps."

"Forget shame and humiliation. Some of the ritualistic killers are deliberately trying to gain power through their violence. It's these beliefs about magical power that they have."

Pointer pursed his lips. "We have a major problem here in New Orleans. Too many drugged-out freaks who watched too many vampire or zombie movies. I've been covering a lot of things up the last couple years, but that's finished. I want to go proactive. I don't want to discriminate against anyone's ethnicity or religion— there are plenty of decent people who practice hoodoo and the like, but I'm not going to let a small minority of those folks terrorize the city, either."

I started to get a bad feeling about where this was going.

"The department needs an interdisciplinary, cross-cultural approach to this wave of ritual crime. We need someone who can interpret the violence through a familiarity with world religions and theories of sacred violence and rituals."

Uh-oh.

"Meaning you are the department's *official* occult specialist, as of now. That doesn't mean you only work the 'woo-woo' cases. You will continue to partner with Detective Baybee on every Five Alarm case that comes down the pike. But every occult issue that pops up will be yours."

The chief looked out of the window and gestured. "Park in the side lot there at the criminal courthouse."

I turned right from Broad into the lot the chief indicated. We were a block from police headquarters, and I was starting to get the picture.

The chief reached for his door handle. "So, Saint James, to establish your credentials with the rank and file, I need you to stop farting around and nail Drake or whoever you need to nail, okay? Now grab the bourbon and follow me."

We exited the Bronco, and I tagged along behind Pointer through a side door. We wound through the entrails of the seat of NOLA justice and into the private chambers of the Honorable Benjamin X. Soniat, whom I had always affectionately referred to as "The Old Drunk Judge."

The chief gestured to a mahogany table where I was to place the bottles of Evan Williams Single Barrel. Soniat reclined on a forest-green corduroy sofa wearing jeans, a blue denim work shirt, and looking like a poor man's Willie Nelson. Like Hans Vermack, he had long hair in a ponytail tied behind him, but Soniat's hair was decidedly more silver. He looked over his bifocals, first at the bourbon, then at me, then at the chief, but he didn't speak.

"Ben, this is Detective Saint James. He needs some help going after a murdering shithead. Next time, he'll be coming alone with the whiskey."

Pointer pulled an envelope from inside his suit-jacket pocket and tossed it on the coffee table next to Soniat. "Here's the particulars for some search warrants."

"All right. Tell him to wait in the commissary."

"Tell him yourself, he's right there."

"Wait in the commissary, detective. It won't take long."

And that was that.

The good news was I now had multiple warrants for Drake's properties and possessions. The bad news was, no warrants for Kate Townsend or Hans Vermack.

As we drove up St. Charles in Honey's unit, I filled her in on Twee's appearance at Tommy's and what she'd said about Drake.

"That's it? She didn't ask you to back off?"

"She didn't. Said she's never met Drake. She did warn me that the Skulls cartel wants to see me six feet under. I tell you that only because you are my partner and it could impact you. I'm carrying an extra piece, extra mags, extra knives. I know you don't carry a backup gun, but maybe you should start."

"Okay. Then what happened?"

"What do you mean?"

"At Tommy's," said Honey, her eyes glued to the road.

"She picked up the tab."

"And after that?"

"What are you suggesting?"

"Did she go to your place?" Honey asked the question as casually as asking me if I slept well.

"What do you think?"

"I think she did," she said, without hesitation, as she stopped at a red light.

"You have a dirty mind."

"You're obfuscating."

"Hey, now, don't use those ten-dollar words on me."

"You know what I mean," she snapped.

And I snapped, too, but in a different way. I'd had enough; I needed to erect some boundaries. "I have asked you to marry me, how many times? And how many times, when I was expressing how much I loved you, how much you meant to me, did you step on my neck? Thus establishing the following facts: (A) It's none of your business who I do or don't invite to my home. (B) You have no right to even ask the question. Those have been our unspoken ground rules for almost two years, which you are now violating in the middle of a murder investigation."

She blanched. The traffic light turned green, but she just sat there. A horn honked behind us. I reached to the dash and switched on the red-and-blue emergency flashers mounted in the grille and the front and rear windshields.

"But I have never lied to you, and since I never will, I'll answer your question. Yes, she came to my place. For privacy. For what we were discussing."

"That being?"

"She asked me to join the CIA. And I'm seriously considering it. It's not the first time she's tried to recruit me, but this time she got more specific. And that is all I can reveal. Period."

"You'd quit the department?"

"Twee said it's not necessary. But if I ever leave for three months with some story about wanting to see the world or joining some exchange program, it means I've gone to spy school."

Honey and I stood waiting next to a wooden classroom door with a large frosted-glass window in the eerily quiet second-floor hallway of Tulane's Dinwiddie Hall. The occasional muted sound escaped from inside, where Drake was teaching his Magic, Witchcraft, and Religion class.

A large corkboard mounted to the pastel yellow wall was covered with flyers promoting worldwide anthropological conferences, seminars, lectures, and graduate programs at other schools. One of the flyers announced that Professor Robert Drake from Tulane University would be presenting a lecture on "Sexual Politics of Human Sacrifice" at Chichén Itzá, the famous Maya archaeological site near Cancún, Mexico. The date was about a week away. I ripped the flyer from the board and handed it to Honey. We had yet to speak since the heated exchange in her car at the traffic light.

Before she could respond, the classroom door opened and students began to filter out, not in an explosion of released energy and high decibels, but in soft spurts of humanity simply ambling on to a new location.

Drake finally emerged and froze with a scowl at the sight of us. He stood silently holding his briefcase until the last of his students had cleared the doorway. I handed him the search warrants.

"I can't believe you have the audacity to come here, to harass and embarrass me at my place of work, an institution of higher learning."

"I can't believe that two dead Las Calaveras members have your phone number in their cell phones," said Honey. "Care to explain?"

Drake didn't answer.

"Shitface here has no answer for us, Honey. He doesn't even get that we're here as a courtesy. Would you rather we bust down your front door and drill your safe open, or would you prefer to open them for us?"

"Finals start tomorrow. I can't—"

"Have an alibi for yesterday morning, Drake?"

"You can direct that question to my attorney."

"Screw you, then," I said. "Hand over the briefcase and your laptop."

"What?"

"You're holding the warrants, smart-ass."

I ripped the items free of his grasp. A few students turned around to watch.

"Wait!" He quickly scanned the document, frowned, then lowered his voice. "What do you need me to do?"

"Go fuck yourself."

He looked shocked. Honey and I spun away from him and marched toward the elevator. I felt a mean satisfaction deep inside. Like a lot of people who have achieved some station in life, however inconsiderable, Drake clearly regarded himself to be superior, and he didn't hide his pedantry well.

He reluctantly followed us to the fourth-floor faculty office area, where Mackie and other detectives stood bathed in soft light filtering down from renovated skylights. But the light didn't soften the seriousness of their features, as they patiently waited with empty plastic tubs and a hand truck. Onlookers gawked but remained silent.

Drake provided the password to his office computer, and Mackie and his team went to work.

"What's the password to the laptop?" I asked Drake.

"You'll have to ask my attorney about that."

I'd anticipated that response and handed the laptop to a female patrol officer who already had orders from me to take it to Kerry Broussard at the Jefferson Parish Sheriff's Office Crime Lab.

"If you're okay here, Mackie, we're moving to location number two."

"Yeah, we're good."

"What is location number two?" asked Drake. He managed to say it without sounding like a smart-ass.

"Ride with us and find out," said Honey.

It surprised me, but Drake accepted the invitation. Maybe he was getting accustomed to riding in the back of police cars.

We left the building without further delay, and within a few minutes Honey had pulled her car out onto St. Charles Avenue. The first stop would be a curious curio shop in Riverbend where Tony Fournier's obsession began fifteen years ago.

CHAPTER NINETEEN

Kruger and a large team would be meeting us in Riverbend with an empty police cargo van, since we didn't know how much stuff we'd be hauling out from the curio shop. As Honey turned onto Leake Avenue, my cell rang. I checked the caller ID; it was Kruger.

"We'll be there in a couple of minutes," I said into the phone.

"Then you might already be close enough to smell the smoke," said Kruger.

I heard sirens in the background on his end of the line as Honey made another turn.

"Tell me you're joking."

"The whole building is an inferno. The closest water main is busted. The nearest hydrants have been sabotaged. FD is doing their best, but it's a write-off. The way it's burning, they're already calling it arson. They say accelerants had to have been used."

I was sitting in the back with Drake and stared at him. He didn't make eye contact, but a slight look of smugness took hold of his face. *The prick knows. He arranged it.*

I hung up without breaking my gaze. "Your fire insurance is up to date, I take it?"

He wouldn't look at me, but his smugness spread like a bad fungus.

We kept Drake locked down in the back of Honey's unit while we checked in with Kruger. He lit a cigarette and I joined him with a cigarillo.

"May as well add a little smoke to the smoke," he said, as the fire raged behind us.

Since this was a residential street, there would be no security video to check. Lots of neighbors milled around rubbernecking, and I was reminded of how fires used to be the bread and butter of newspaper reporting. I guess car chases were the modern-day equivalent for TV news, but the NOPD was so backward, we didn't even have an air unit to track fleeing felons.

"Let me guess. None of the neighbors saw a thing," said Honey.

"Today they didn't," said Kruger, exhaling. "But yesterday, Mr. Jimmy Washburn, the black gentleman in the white T-shirt standing on the porch across the street, noticed four guys in an unmarked box truck. Heavily tattooed Mexicans."

"Could be the remnants of the local Skulls gang," I said.

"Sounds like it. They cleaned out the shop. Upstairs and down. Mr. Jimmy got curious because he could use some furniture. When he went over to ask if they were selling anything, he noticed two guys hauling a freezer out of the downstairs."

"Gee, wonder what was in it?" asked Honey, sarcastically.

"I got descriptions here," said Kruger, holding up a pocket

notebook. "One of the perps has a front gold tooth with three stones in it: diamond, ruby, and emerald."

"Classy," said Honey.

"White, red, and green. The colors of the Mexican flag," I noted.

"Mr. Jimmy said the Mexicans had keys to the place. I'm thinking they placed incendiaries when they moved the goods out, and today, somebody used a remote device to ignite them."

"Did Drake use his cell?" Honey asked me.

"Not that I noticed."

"Grab his cell and see who he's called. It's within the scope of the warrant," said Kruger.

I nodded. "Better if we don't talk to Mr. Jimmy while Drake is watching, but did he ever see any activity here?"

"Only at night, including the other night. Never in the day, is what he said."

I scanned the crowd. Kruger was one damn good cop. He'd covered all the bases for us here. "Wait a second. . . . Is that Tony Fournier?" I asked, looking up the street. The lone figure of a man in a down jacket, baseball cap, and sunglasses leaned against a parked car about half a block away.

"That's Tony, all right," said Kruger. "What's he doing here?"

I took a step forward, but Fournier abruptly turned, got into a white sedan, and sped off.

"I don't like that. At all," said Honey.

"We need to talk to Tony," I said. "But first, what say we hit Drake's house? Before it has a chance to burn down, too."

"I'm sorry," said Honey softly, looking me in the eyes. "I . . ."

We stood in Drake's home office. The entire house was empty.

Nothing remained except dust bunnies and crud. The freestanding safe that had been here was gone. As we had wandered through the vacant house moments ago with Kruger's team, no one had said a word.

I could tell Honey felt horrible about the situation.

"I've handled this case badly. Should have given you freer rein to go after Drake."

"No apologies. You didn't do anything wrong. It's just the breaks," I said, pulling out a hard pack of Partagas mini cigarillos made in Havana and a gold-plated Bugatti lighter that had once belonged to a drug kingpin I shot.

"I didn't think it was murder," she said. "I didn't push like I should have."

From the start, Honey had agreed with the chief on the overdose scenario, and now the whole case was unraveling before our very eyes. Guilt was clearly dogging her.

"Forget it. I'm going out for a smoke."

I walked past Drake silently standing in the living room with his hands in his pockets.

"What a pity. I just had everything moved from here to my curio shop the night before last. And now I've lost it all."

"My ass bleeds for you. But don't even think about leaving town."

"I wouldn't dream of it. I have unfinished business with a few people."

I stared at him. The prick was threatening me.

"It's not what you're thinking," said Drake. "I told you that a demon might have been summoned, and if so, we'd all be in danger. And I was extremely sad to learn today that Mr. Jackson, the UPS driver had a fatal accident. It might be a coincidence, but what if it wasn't? I'd be very careful if I were you."

"You're not the only one with unfinished business," I said, giving him a look like I wanted to kill him. A part of me wanted exactly that.

I walked out to be met by a chill, sharp wind. A quick call confirmed that indeed the UPS driver Jackson had been killed in a traffic accident. *Damn.*

A black storm cell rolled in fast as I started to walk a circle around the house. The dozens of cat graves reminded me that we might make a cruelty-to-animals charge stick, but I wasn't sure we could nail Drake with much more than that. And I'd be calling the arson investigators to make sure they crawled up his ass.

Before I'd gotten back to the front door, icy rain lashed me with a sobering cold. I ignored the rain, scanned the property, and drifted again toward the backyard. The shed stood empty, and all the yard tools, everything, was gone.

I exhaled deeply, letting go of my anger toward the professor, letting it wash down into the earth with the rivulets of rainwater. I reconstructed the murder scene in my mind all over again, working out possible scenarios for how a third person could have gotten away undetected. The Fish and Game warden we'd brought in had found no evidence of anyone exiting Drake's property on the back side, and she was so good at reading sign that I took it for gospel.

After ten minutes, Honey found me near the back door and pulled up the hood on her Gore-Tex jacket. Before she could speak, I flashed my chronograph at her and then dramatically pushed a button. I bolted, running all out, toward a tree line about fifty or so yards away, then pressed the button again. I jogged back to Honey and showed her the stopwatch feature.

"The killer panicked as soon as the doorbell rang. He or she then popped off three rounds; could be the gun was firing blanks. Maybe it was only a prop in the little passion play here. Anyway, the shooter hustles to the back door. Which you found unlocked when you and I arrived that day. The killer then ran balls-out for the tree line like I just did. It took me six point three seconds. The UPS guy was still hauling ass in his truck up the long driveway to the road, where he then had to turn around his big, brown step van with no rear windows. Then he parked facing the house, watching. I believed him when he said he didn't see anyone leave the house from that moment on. But by then, the killer was already well out of sight, following the tree line over there all the way to the front of Drake's property, right up to the road, around the bend.

"Hell, if we had stayed put the other morning when we heard the shots-fired call, we would probably have seen the murderer."

I lit a cigarillo quickly, sheltering the slim, brown stick from raindrops, then continued. "Our perp then runs across River Road and over the levee, unseen. It would be a piece of cake to track along the river, back toward town. If Drake is the killer, he simply calls Townsend, tells her where he is on the levee. She picks him up, then brings him back and dumps him into the middle of our investigation."

"What if Townsend is the killer? Or Vermack? You saying one of them arrived here early in the morning with Sanchez and Ruiz?"

"No, I'm not saying that. If we exclude Drake, then the killer arrived here on foot. The getaway car could have been parked somewhere along the levee. Our murderer never intended to park at what would become a crime scene."

Honey nodded slightly, considering. "How was the poison administered?"

"Orally. They shared some 'sacred' wine or something together.

Except the killer didn't drink the doped stuff. I figure the killer was acting as a 'guide,' like Becky explained to us, and didn't partake in the sex. Maybe Felix and Roscindo didn't touch each other, maybe they just masturbated and did that thing where they sent their energy to the guide."

"If you want two guys dead, why go to the trouble to kill them that way?"

"Exactly. That is the million-dollar question. That's why the overdose scenario seemed logical to you." I flicked ash from my cigarillo. "And this takes us back to my latest thinking about what kind of ritualistic killings we have on our hands. I have two theories. If the killer did it for religious reasons, then maybe it's all about 'death energy.'"

"What?"

"People who practice chaos magic use something called a 'death posture' to achieve what they call 'gnosis.' That is part and parcel of how they charge a sigil. They put themselves in a state of exhaustion or depletion or elation to get this gnosis. No gnosis, no magic—that's how important it is. And the Crimson Throne members claim they can move energy from others, or *take* it. What if the killer's plan was to bring a victim to the edge of some horrific death, and then take this intense gnosis energy generated from that?"

Honey looked skeptical, but she motioned for me to continue.

"And if they thought orgasmic energy was strong, good for their magic, then imagine how much more powerful fear or pain energy from a person dying in agony would be."

Honey raised her eyebrows and nodded. "Okay, whether it's real or not, it seems like a plausible motive. Given who the suspects are."

"It's not only plausible, it's happening. A standard tenet in magic is that strong emotion creates energy, so the nonviolent outfits like Wiccans, neo-paganists, chaos magicians, and so on use sex magic or whatever to do their thing."

"Which is what the Crimson Throne did."

"Right. But some who practice Santeria, some Satanists and some in the vampire cults use sexually sadistic acts to gain power by stealing energy from their victims. These folks believe the strongest emotions are fear, sexual stupor, and religious ecstasy. So has our killer developed a ritual that combines all three emotions? Because with our Mexican friends inside, there was sex, there was the religious element of being on the altar, and there was fear and/or pain. The looks on their corpses were something out of a horror film. Hell, the one guy's hair turned white."

"The question is," said Honey, "what the perp wants to achieve with the energy."

The rain suddenly let up, and I glanced at the sky, then back to Honey. "That's right."

"And it could also apply to Becky Valencia's death?"

"Yes. The coroner said she had an orgasm before she died. She was surrounded by thirteen black candles, giving us the religious element. And collapsed lungs would have been a hellish, excruciating experience."

"Sex, religion, and fear. All three elements." Honey absent-mindedly rubbed her temple. "You said you had a second theory."

"It involves secular ritual killing—no religion involved. I'm still working out the kinks. You check Drake's cell?"

"He didn't make any calls or texts after we picked him up," said Honey.

"Someone was watching him. Or us. Maybe one of the Skulls."

"Could Fournier have set the fire?"

"Why would he? As a vendetta?" I asked. "He couldn't put Drake away after trying for fifteen years, so he burns down his curio shop instead? I don't buy that."

"Could Drake and Fournier be working together?"

I smiled at Honey and pointed my finger. "Congratulations! That is the single most cynical, jaded, paranoid speculation I've ever heard you make. I like that. And it might explain why Fournier's niece is hooked up with Townsend."

I looked up at the sky, working my brain as I considered the possibility. "Based on the facts we have now, I'd have to say no. But we should keep the notion open as a remote possibility."

"Okay. But I want Fournier brought in. He's got some explaining to do."

I nodded.

"Do you believe Drake moved all of his possessions into his shop and then burned them up?" Honey asked.

"Absolutely not. Might be worth getting some people on the phones, checking the storage facilities, furniture movers, freight forwarders to see if we can find where Drake is stashing his goods."

"Agreed."

"One more thing. We have another death to add to this case. Jackson, the UPS driver, was killed in a traffic accident today. Drake practically told me I was next."

Honey looked shocked.

"Kruger can take Drake downtown. Let's you and me go find the patrol officers who responded to Jackson's accident scene."

Honey motored her unit along General De Gaulle Drive on the West Bank. As we approached the light at Holiday, we hit a pot-hole and the talisman Fournier had given me fell from the rear-view mirror.

"Crap," I said. "That's not a good omen."

Honey slowed the vehicle a moment as I retrieved the charm and hung it from the mirror.

"You have got to stop with the omens and charms and ghosts—"

A sickening crash exploded in our ears, and the world went into slow motion as the car was violently torn asunder. Our append-ages flopped as our bodies were wrenched where we sat, but our seat belts held us in place, our air bags deployed. Then I couldn't see anything.

CHAPTER TWENTY

I never lost consciousness, although I can't say I could recall everything exactly as it transpired over the last few seconds.

The air bags quickly deflated, as they were designed to do. We'd stopped moving sideways, and a loud hissing sound filled the interior of the twelve-year-old car.

The windscreen, or at least the place where the windscreen should have been, was filled with the sight of a beer truck, and not a brand I cared for. I could have reached right through and grabbed a cold one, since our engine compartment didn't appear to be there anymore.

Honey appeared dazed, and I gently touched her arm.

"We're okay. We got creamed. Nearly T-boned. Can you feel your feet? Your hands? Everything still connected?"

After a moment she nodded. "We'll feel like crap tomorrow."

"Who cares, we're alive today."

"Jesus H. Buddha and a smiling fat Muhammad, are you guys hurt?" A crusty guy who looked to be in his seventies and wore a

173rd Airborne Brigade Vietnam Veteran baseball cap, stood outside my door, trying to open it.

"I've felt better, sir," I said.

"If you can move, you might want to try and crawl out this window."

"Maybe we should wait for the fire department," I said.

"You got gas leaking all over the pavement."

"Then I like your idea better." I looked to Honey. "Can you do it?"

"Let's try," she said.

Other brave bystanders surrounded the car and tried to open our doors, but no go: The car's frame was tweaked and the doors frozen in place. Considering the state of our luck, there would be no time to wait for the Jaws of Life. As quickly as we could, and with lots of help, especially from the Vietnam vet, who took charge of the scene, Honey and I extracted ourselves from the wreckage of her unit, but not before I grabbed the talisman from around the mirror.

It felt sobering to see the extent of the carnage once we got out of the car. The huge beer truck had literally demolished the engine compartment, crushing it under its large wheels.

Within seconds after we cleared Honey's unit, a flame ignited, spread like hot butter, and the car burned like an offering to Kali, goddess of destruction. As we backed farther away, the uniformed beer truck driver came over.

"I'm so sorry, I . . . I don't know how to explain this. Guess I had a brain fart. I saw the red light but went anyway. I don't know what possessed me to run that light."

Honey and I looked at each other. Interesting choice of words he used.

Then it hit me that maybe our luck wasn't so bad after all. "If you hadn't slowed for that brief second when the talisman fell down," I whispered to her, "we would have really been T-boned. We'd be dead."

She just shook her head.

A few onlookers started to help themselves to the cases of beer stacked on the truck, lest it go to waste, as flames licked at the long undercarriage.

"Hey!" I yelled, holding up my gold shield. "Police officer! Bring a couple of those beers over here."

By the time Honey and I got back to the Homicide Section, Drake already sat parked with his lawyer in an interrogation room being interviewed by arson investigators. Kruger monitored the exchange, waiting for Homicide's turn to get in our questions for the professor, through his lawyer, of course.

Chief Pointer was not happy to learn he spent cash on bourbon and political capital getting search warrants, which turned out to be a waste of time, but at least he joined us in concluding that Drake was a no-good dirtbag with something to hide. Pointer didn't seem to mind that Honey's unit had been totaled, mostly since the beer company had deep pockets—pockets the chief would soon be picking for exaggerated compensation. He also bluntly told us that filing any Workers' Compensation claims would be a huge mistake on our part. Nice to know the guy at the top had our best interests in mind.

Pointer kept *seven* unmarked units in reserve as his own personal carpool. He graciously issued Honey one of those units until a permanent replacement could be found, which put Honey up to her elbows in paperwork that needed to be filed before she could get the keys. Pointer's graciousness would engender a lot of resentment from detectives who had no unit assigned to them, but then those officers had not generated banner headlines and positive TV coverage of crimes solved, as Honey had, so screw them.

I crossed toward my desk and felt my body stiffening up thanks to the car wreck. A wave of fatigue lapped at my consciousness, so I found a vending machine down the hall, chugged a couple of Red Bulls, and wolfed down a Snickers bar.

Breakfast and lunch finished, I got a cell call from Vice with the location of Townsend's house of ill repute.

"Right smack on Saint Charles Avenue," I said to the detective, then rang off. Staking out Townsend's bordello was now on my agenda for this evening, along with finding Tony Fournier. It had been another slam-bang day, and as I tried to remember all of the things I'd forgotten to do, I saw Gina Sanchez walking toward the entrance to the Homicide Section, escorted by a uniformed officer.

"Miss Sanchez!"

"That's the man," she said to the uniform, who I waved off.

"We've been worried about you. You should have let us know you were moving."

"Did you arrest the witch yet? Did you find my money?"

"No arrest yet. And sorry, the money hasn't turned up. Where are you living now?"

"Can I go home to Mexico? Do I have your permission? It not safe for me here."

"I'd rather you didn't go back to Mexico just yet. And I promise you're safe now."

"How you can promise that?"

"The Las Calaveras, the Skulls are . . . you heard that four of them were killed?"

"Yes, I see on TV, but only four."

"So the chances are they're not going to cause any trouble right now."

"Four cartel killers dead and you say they no cause trouble? And the witch, she still around, yes?"

"Yes."

"I hear about Becky Valencia. I scared."

"Did you know her?"

"I go for acupuncture few time. Felix do some small work at her house, so she pay with money and with five appointments for us. Needles scare me but make me feel good."

Gina Sanchez just explained to me why her prints were in Valencia's office. So much for that lead.

"I can still give you protective custody."

She waved off that notion. "Why you no arrest the witch? If you no do your job, then I must to run and hide."

"I heard you haven't made any arrangements for your husband's body." It was a cold thing to say so bluntly, but I needed to see her reaction.

"I no have money!" She burst into tears and reached for a tissue in her purse. "You arrest Kate Townsend and I can get my money back, give Felix a good burial. And I will piss on her grave."

Sanchez started sobbing again and shuffled off. I raced into the Homicide offices and made a couple of quick calls. Sanchez would be detained in the lobby until undercover detectives could take up surveillance. I didn't think she was guilty of murder, but I'd been wrong before.

"What was that all about? We all heard the crying from in here," said Honey as she came up to my desk.

"We've got a tail on Gina Sanchez now. I told her not to go back to Mexico."

"That made her cry?"

I ignored the question and watched as Honey popped a couple of pain pills.

"Vice came up with the address of Townsend's pleasure palace." I said. "What time is good for you?"

"I can't think clearly. I haven't eaten all day. Again. I've been full throttle since six this morning when I got to the crime lab to push along some of the evidence evaluation. I need rest. I'm going home."

What could I say? Honey looked like she'd been rode hard and put away wet. Maybe she got knocked around in the car more seriously than I did. I also knew she was still raw from our discussion about personal boundaries. It was a talk we needed to have. The decision had simply snuck up on me that I wasn't going to wait around forever for my work partner to come around on the personal front. And I didn't want to be in a position to have to lie or hide my liaisons with females for fear of hurting Honey.

"Good idea. Get some rest. I feel okay, so I'll check it out, check with the coppers who responded to Jackson's accident, and drop in on Fournier too."

She left without saying another word.

CHAPTER TWENTY-ONE

The details of Jackson's fatal accident were eerily similar to the nearly fatal wreck Honey and I just had; a semitruck ran a red light instantly killing the former Marine in his step van. No foul play was suspected, but how could one explain it?

As I sat parked outside Townsend's apartment building on St. Charles, I draped Fournier's talisman around my neck, an illogical thing to do. I didn't believe that an object or good-luck charm could protect me, but I believed that it acted as a reminder that I was responsible for protecting myself. And that was good enough.

I then turned my attention to the task at hand. Within an hour, by around ten o'clock, I had figured out the process. Johns would park on the street and make a cell-phone call, probably to tell Kate Townsend they had arrived. They'd wait in their vehicles until they got a call back, usually within fifteen minutes. Then they'd walk to the front door and get buzzed in.

One of the johns was an NOPD captain I recognized. Maybe that's how Townsend got my home address, if it was Townsend in the Anonymous mask; she asked for a little favor from a highly placed police client.

I clocked a fortyish businessman get out of a new Mercedes and go in, and I decided he would be the one. The guy would have a wife, kids, social standing—a lot to lose in a vice arrest. When he emerged smiling forty-five minutes later, I stood waiting at his Benz and flashed my gold shield.

"NOPD. Put your hands on the hood."

"What?"

"You just had sex with a hooker. Now put your hands on the damn car!" I gave him a little shove, and he quickly complied.

"Spread your legs farther apart." I stood behind him and kicked his right foot to give him the idea. "Don't move."

I fished out his car keys, wallet, and a little something extra from his pockets.

"What do we have here?" I set the vial of cocaine on the car hood in front of him.

He hung his head sadly. "Shit."

"Well I hope it was good shit, because you are in a lot of trouble, mister." I checked his ID. "Mister Jon Harol." I glanced at family photos in his wallet then tossed them next to the coke. "Taking a little walk on the wild side tonight?"

He didn't answer. I could tell he was the kind of guy who'd never been in trouble with the law. He kept trying to swallow, but I guess his mouth had gone dry.

I spun him around to face me. "Here's the deal. Looks like you got a nice family. And I bet you'd like to keep things good with them, wouldn't you?"

He looked up at me. "Yes, I would. I'd be willing to give you—"

I grabbed him by his lapels and got right in his face. "Don't you try to bribe me, asshole!"

"I'm sorry, I . . ."

I released him with a little shove. "Who is this woman?" I showed him Townsend's mug shots.

"I only know her as Susan."

"She's the madam, right?"

He nodded.

"What about this girl? Is she in there right now?" I showed him an eight-by-ten still I had generated of Anastasia, taken from my hidden video the night I saw her in LaPlace.

"Yes, that's April."

"You bang her?"

"Yes . . . no. Not tonight. But I have, yes." Harol was shaking, he was so scared.

"Okay. I'll throw the cocaine in the street and let you walk. In return, you call Susan, tell her you have a good friend who wants April to come to his place. Tonight. Doesn't matter what it costs."

"Would you rather I just call April? I have before."

"Thank you, Mr. Harol," I said with a slight smile. "That would be even better." He gave me April's number; I gave him a piece of paper with a phony name and one of my throwaway-cell numbers on it. "Give April this name and number and tell her to call me. If she doesn't pick up when you call, leave a message."

Harol performed flawlessly. I handed him his photos back. "I'd change your cell number if I were you, and never contact these ladies again. They'll figure out you helped me. Understand?"

"Yes," he said quickly. I could tell he wanted to get into his car and run home to the safety of his home and family.

I turned the cocaine vial upside down and tapped the contents into the street as he watched. "You think this blow and that piece of ass you rented in there are worth going to jail for?"

"No, I don't."

"Then keep that in mind for future reference."

He nodded, relieved, and I melted into the darkness.

A dark sedan pulled to a stop directly across the street from my building just as my throwaway cell rang. I knew this was Anastasia/April calling to tell me she had arrived outside my place. Her first call to book the liaison had been about thirty minutes ago.

"Hi, this is Steven," I said.

I zoomed in using night vision. Most escort services used drivers, and the guy sitting behind the wheel looked like a scuzzy punk. I made out Anastasia sitting next to him in the front seat.

"It's April, I'm here," said Anastasia over the cell phone.

"Slight change in address. You see the black awning across the street?"

"Yes."

"Push the button and I'll buzz you in. Come up to the second floor."

I'd long ago removed the sigil from next to my front door, but if Anastasia had placed it there or had a connection to those who did, then she would know my building and know this was a setup. I watched from a darkened window in my loft as she crossed the street toward my front door without hesitation. That told me she didn't know who I was. I buzzed her in.

The first floor of my building was a work in progress. My Ford F-350 diesel dually extended-cab pickup truck with a five-inch lift and wraparound custom grille guard and bumpers sat parked, surrounded by a world of junk, uh, I mean, collectibles. Upon entering from the street, you could either attempt to penetrate the vast wasteland of the ground floor or walk up the cypress stairway with a brass railing. At the top of the stairs, another security door awaited, and I'd cracked it open for Anastasia to come right in.

"I'm in the kitchen, mixing a drink," I yelled as she peeked through the doorway. I'd been disguising my voice slightly, on the slim chance she might recognize it from the brief encounter we had in LaPlace. "I put your fee on the coffee table."

The fee was five hundred dollars in cold cash. A more-prudent professional would have balked at the last-minute change of address and at the fact I wasn't at the door greeting her, but Anastasia entered and went right for the money. She quickly counted and pocketed the dough, then made a quick cell call, presumably to the driver downstairs.

"I'm in and everything's okay."

As she tossed her cell phone in her purse, I entered holding two martinis.

"Good to see you again, Anastasia, or whatever your real name is."

You can't fake the kind of utter shock that swept across her face. She quickly looked to her purse.

"Don't even think about it," I said, closing in quickly. "I want this to be a friendly visit."

Since the department still held my Glock and the Colt .45 for testing, I had my Browning .380 tucked into my rear waistband on a permanent basis now, thanks to the Skulls. I added the Ruger to my arsenal whenever I left the loft, but the only weapon I figured I'd need tonight with Anastasia was my brain.

I could almost see her mind racing as she searched for an explanation to give me. Not the truth, necessarily, but an explanation that would fly.

"Let's start with your real name," I said, setting the drinks on the coffee table and sinking into my brown leather sofa. She still stood there, looking confounded, worried, and a little scared.

"Am I under arrest?"

"I'd rather not do that, but I have you on video taking the money to perform sexual services. I recorded our calls and, if you remember, I was pretty explicit in telling you what I wanted. So why don't you just sit down? You're involved in something a lot more serious than a prostitution beef. Cooperate, be truthful, and things will work out better for you."

She sat on the other end of the couch.

"I make excellent martinis, that is, if you like them dirty," I said, taking a sip. After a moment, so did she. Good. I now had her fingerprints on the glass. I don't allow smoking in my home, but tonight I'd make an exception. I'd already set out an ashtray and lighter. If she was a smoker, I could get DNA from her cigarette butts.

"I'd like to call my uncle."

"Not yet. And maybe not at all."

"Uncle Tony means everything to me. After my parents died, I . . . I was a mess. He saved my life, actually."

I didn't say anything. I'd still be checking with personnel to confirm Fournier's family history.

"When was this?"

"About three years ago. We argue sometimes. But . . . what family doesn't? So I owe him a lot, and that made it easy to say yes."

"Yes to what?"

"To go undercover and gather information so he could arrest Robert Drake."

The notion had occurred to me, but I'd rejected it because I couldn't believe Tony Fournier would be willing to use her as bait. But to prostitute his brother's daughter in an attempt to make an arrest that had eluded him for years was beyond low.

I glanced at her purse. Had Tony planted tracking devices in Anastasia's things, since he had her working clandestinely? Was he tracking her cell phone? Even though Fournier didn't know where I lived, I wouldn't want him clocking my address electronically.

"So exactly how did you set out on your task?"

I casually stood and crossed to a cabinet where I kept a portable cell-phone-jamming device. Out of her line of sight, I switched it on and picked up a cigar lighter, so she would assume I'd gone to the cabinet to get the lighter.

"I started stripping at a club on Bourbon. Let it be known I was broke, living in my car. That my ex had abused me. I wasn't hooking then, just dancing. Kate Townsend showed up there within a week. Said she'd heard about me and my problems and asked if I needed a place to stay."

"And you said yes," I said, sitting back down. I lit a Dominican panatela in an effort to encourage her to light up.

"Sure, that was the plan."

Recalling what Vermack had said about Drake and Townsend having split long ago, I asked, "Why did Tony think you could get to Drake through Townsend?"

"She was his high priestess. They saw each other all the time, even though I learned they weren't as close as they used to be."

"You know Drake well?"

"Not well, but I know him."

"You've had sex with him?"

"Yes."

"How did your uncle feel about that?"

She looked away from me, started to reach for her purse but stopped. "Mind if I get my cigarettes?"

Excellent. I nodded for her to go ahead. She retrieved a Cartier lighter and a pack of super-slim smokes and lit up. "I don't think he felt too good about that."

"Did they try to recruit you into the Crimson Throne?"

"They asked me to come as a guest. I don't know anything about magic, just what Uncle Tony has explained to me, so I didn't fit in to their group."

"How many times did you attend one of their meetings?"

"Eight or nine."

"Since you don't know anything about magic, why did they keep inviting you back?"

"Because they like doing me. They use me to get themselves all worked up, I guess."

"You had sex with all of the members? Townsend, Valencia, Sanchez, Ruiz, Vermack?"

"Yes," she said, without embarrassment.

"Are you sharing Kate Townsend's bed?"

She looked downward and flicked some ash into the ashtray.

"In a way. I didn't want to work as a clerk in her shop, so she taught me the ropes of being a call girl. I work very late every night and usually go out and party. Or I'll drive back to LaPlace and sleep at the house. Make a report to Uncle Tony in the morning. Sometimes I sleep at Kate's during the day and she . . . joins me."

It all added up. Pathetic that Fournier had done this to his niece, but it added up.

"What have you told Tony that could help nail Drake?"

"I report everything to him. Everything I see or hear. All kinds of details. I don't know what might be important, that's up to him."

"What have you learned about the deaths of Felix Sanchez, Roscindo Ruiz, and Becky Valencia?"

"Kate says Felix and Roscindo OD'd. And Becky accidentally put a needle in the wrong place. Isn't that true?"

"What does Tony say about the deaths?"

"He hasn't said anything, really."

So Anastasia didn't know there was a ritualistic killer on the loose and that the killer was probably an acquaintance of hers.

"What do you make of Hans Vermack?"

"He's cheap, that's for sure. And I wish he wasn't so cruel. He's into a lot of fetishes. He likes to make a sex partner feel pain."

Throw in the religious connection and you have the MO of the murderer. I certainly wouldn't remove him from the suspect list.

"So there's no master plan to lure Drake or any of the others into some kind of trap? You know, get them to commit a crime so your uncle could make a citizen's arrest?"

"Nothing that I know about." She took another drink, draining her glass faster than a fat Russian.

At the very least, Fournier had taken a calculated gamble. Even if she wasn't found out, if Drake was really a killer of transients, Anastasia was a prime target.

Still, I had to consider if Anastasia could be the murderer. But her name hadn't come up with any of the suspects. And I couldn't fathom a motive. She didn't appear to be involved in the cultish aspect of the case, and I doubted she acted as some kind of avenging angel for Tony Fournier. Besides, Tony had no revenge motives against the group's members; he only wanted to see Drake behind bars.

"Can I use the ladies' room?"

"Through the kitchen, to your right."

She reached for her purse.

"Leave the purse," I said with a tone suggesting there was no room for negotiation on that point.

She walked into the kitchen area. And yes, I admired her figure as she went, but there was no way in hell I would touch her. I held fast to the theory that the victims had all been poisoned or drugged—in Valencia's case, in addition to having a fatal acupuncture needle inserted. So I'd looked carefully to note Anastasia had no pockets in her outfit and wore no jewelry that could function as a secret vial full of some exotic toxin.

I looked to her purse and calculated an excuse to search it. I'd tell her she might be being monitored by Drake or Townsend and I needed to check. So I rifled the bag. Cell phone, keys, makeup, small wallet, condoms. No weapon, nothing out of the ordinary.

It would take time to look for a tracking device, and the issue became moot as Anastasia suddenly reappeared, wearing only high heels, red bra, and red panties.

"Whoa, whoa. Put some clothes on. The five hundred bucks is yours, but not for sex, okay? That's not my game."

She walked right up to me and leaned over, so I had an eyeful of substantial cleavage.

"But I want to play with you. Not because of anything else, except . . . I wanted you since I first saw you with the blond detective going into Crafty Voodoo."

"You told Tony I'd seen you in the window at Townsend's?"

"No, because I wasn't sure what you saw. But when you came to LaPlace, you undressed me with your eyes. I know you want it, and so do I."

"No, Anastasia, I don't 'want it,' and that's not going to happen. So please go put your clothes on. We're almost finished here."

As she moved her hand behind my neck, the door to the stairs opened.

"I tried to call you, Saint James, but . . ."

Honey stepped into the room. She had her own keys to my place. She took in the sight of me with a half-dressed Anastasia leaning over me, her breasts in my face and arm around my neck.

Damn, she tried to call, but I had a cell-phone jammer blocking Anastasia's cell signal . . . and my own.

Honey seemed to implode into herself and backed away quickly, slamming the door behind her.

I sprang up from the couch. "Where do you keep your car parked?"

"I didn't bring my car."

"I know, but the Lexus, where do you keep it parked?"

"Private lot off Chartres at Toulouse."

"Okay, get dressed. You have to go. We'll talk again soon."

"Should I tell Uncle Tony about this?"

"No. Let me handle that. I need to have a serious conversation with him."

CHAPTER TWENTY-TWO

When I arrived at Honey's house her car was nowhere to be seen, but a voodoo doll was nailed to her front door. *Damn this fucking case!* I ripped the cloth figurine free, set fire to it with my lighter, and dropped it into the gutter where it burned quickly, releasing a thick, inky smoke.

I moved into the shadow at the edge of Honey's house, a house that I had purchased for her myself after coming into a financial largesse. I had keys, I could have waited inside, but tonight was all about establishing new boundaries, so I stood waiting for over an hour, listening to drunken laughter and ribald conversation coming from inside Vaughn's Lounge, which sat right next door.

Finally, Honey's borrowed police unit rounded the corner and parked right in front of her doorstep. The voodoo doll had burned to ash and I don't think she even noticed it.

She must have stopped to pound a couple somewhere because she staggered slightly as she got out of the car, and then stumbled on the sidewalk. Good. I sprang from the darkness and stood between her and her front door. I hit "play" on my digital audio recorder with the sound turned up all the way.

"Whoa, whoa. Put some clothes on. The five hundred bucks is yours, but not for sex, okay? That's not my game."

"But I want to play with you. Not because of anything else, except . . . I wanted you since I first saw you with the blond detective going into Crafty Voodoo."

"You told Tony I'd seen you in the window at Townsend's?"

"No, because I wasn't sure what you saw. But when you came to LaPlace, you undressed me with your eyes. I know you want it, and so do I."

"No, Anastasia, I don't 'want it,' and that's not going to happen. So please go put your clothes on. We're almost finished here."

"I tried to call you, Saint James, but . . ."

I clicked off the recorder. To ease out of confrontational mode, I simply sat on her front steps and watched her closely without staring. Honey tottered slightly as her rage melted into something else. Embarrassment? Her eyes were red; she'd obviously been crying. She took a tentative step forward. After a moment, with some determination, she sat down next to me.

We sat in silence, enveloped by the scent of whiskey and cigarettes seeping out from Vaughn's rotting clapboard facade. The first licks of "Green River" by Credence Clearwater Revival twanged on the bar's sound system.

I looked to Honey and knew that she wasn't going to say anything, that I couldn't pry a word out of her with a crowbar. We could sit here and listen to the entire repertoire of Credence and she'd just remain mute. So to make things easier for us both, I launched into a machine-gun fast explanation of how I'd staked out Townsend's bordello and set up the sting with Anastasia. "Now would you please listen to the whole recording, beginning to end? Because we have a serious problem."

She nodded and didn't say a word as we sat on her steps listening to the recording. When it finished, I pocketed the recorder and looked at her.

"We need to come down hard on Fournier before he gets his niece killed. And maybe screws up our official investigation. So please think about that tonight and be ready to discuss our options tomorrow."

She nodded.

I could see her demeanor had softened a bit. Maybe she wanted to say something, maybe apologize, but I wasn't going to let her. I'd been waiting long enough, in more ways than one.

"On a personal note, it's obvious that we haven't been getting along since the morning this case fell into our laps. Okay, every relationship has bumps, but what I realize now is that the nature of our relationship has to change. For me, starting now, it has changed. I love you, you mean the world to me, but I'm not waiting for you anymore. I mean, how long has it been without you explaining *anything* to me? You won't even discuss having a real relationship. So no more sleeping together without sex, no more kissing without sex, no more sexual stuff without the payoff. And I'm not asking you to give me the payoff. I'm not asking for a damn thing. We're best friends, period. Nothing more. I'm through with the guilt. I'm declaring my freedom, do you understand?"

I was starting to get worked up, but I didn't care. I wanted to get this off of my chest.

"For you to even imagine that I might have sex with Anastasia, a suspect in our murder investigation, means that you don't think too highly of me as a professional. So I'm not even sure we should keep working together. Because if you don't trust my judgment . . . maybe I'll be taking that three-month vacation a lot sooner than I planned."

I stood. "Green River" had segued to "Proud Mary" then to "Born on the Bayou," and as John Fogerty sang about an old hound dog chasing down a hoodoo, I turned away from Honey and walked up Lesseps toward Burgundy, where I'd parked the Bronco. I heard her front door slam shut behind me as the laughter and music from Vaughn's faded in my wake. So be it. I hadn't meant to mention the CIA stuff, but screw it. In a way, I'd be protecting Honey in the future by not becoming romantically linked, since my inclination was to accept Twee's offer. It would be better if I entered the clandestine service as a single guy, not a family man.

My destination now was B.J.'s Lounge, a place where you could show up in your underwear and be overdressed. B.J.'s sat on the corner of Lesseps and Burgundy, and I felt like I could use a couple of pops.

But I never made it to B.J.'s.

As I traversed a dark stretch of Lesseps, walking in the middle of the street as I always do on poorly lit, deserted roads to make it harder to get jumped, I felt the sting of Taser darts puncture my back, and my body snapped rigid as thousands of volts and who-knows-how-many milliamperes zapped me. Wracked with excruciating pain, I fell like a stone to the pavement, flat on my back, unable to control muscle function. Some guys scream when they get tased, but I couldn't. In spite of the pain, a million thoughts raced through my mind: Were they using a police or civilian model? Was I going to get a five-second cycle or thirty? Were they dialing up the juice to really hurt me? How could I regain advantage when the tasing stopped?

Damn, they were giving me thirty. My arms started to flop. I was drooling. It felt like a thousand banshees fought inside my nervous system, screaming to escape.

And then it stopped.

Recovery is generally quick, especially for guys in good shape who've been tased before, meaning me. But I wasn't quick enough.

A foot slammed into my groin. Two Mexican guys grabbed my wrists and gift-wrapped them with gray duct tape, aka gaffer's tape, aka thousand-mile-an-hour tape, effectively handcuffing me. They pulled me to my feet.

Las Calaveras. The Skulls.

A third gangster stuffed into my mouth a dirty rag that stank of gasoline and caused me to gag. Four strong men carried me toward a dark van. No matter how much I struggled and tried to kick and break free, they held on.

They threw me face-first into the back of the van. I cushioned the landing as best I could since my taped hands had some freedom of movement. As I tried to spring to my feet, a devastating blow rocked my right kidney.

They were beating me with a steel pipe.

Massive pain shot all the way into my upper abdomen, and I collapsed, retching, the vomit rising in my throat.

But there was a rag stuffed in my mouth and the vomit had nowhere to go.

Shit, I was about to drown in my own vomit in the back of a dirty van at the hands of the Skulls. *Jesus God, help me. Please help me.*

Searing pain as another blow landed. The worst pain I'd ever felt in my life caused tears to spurt from my eyes as I heard them speaking in Spanish. I was about to pass out, maybe forever, when the rag got pulled from my mouth and I puked.

My head spun. My eyes were closed, but bright shafts of light stabbed at my consciousness. The van was moving, somebody driving. I opened my eyes but couldn't see, it was so dark. Hands searched my many pockets, relieving me of wallet, keys, two knives, cell phones, digital recorders, and all the many gadgets that I always carried. My Ruger semiauto was pulled from the paddle holster under my shirttails and the Browning drawn out of the inside-the-pants holster at the small of my back.

Miraculously, somehow—and this gave me a glimmer of hope—in the dark of the van as it jostled on a bumpy road, they missed the karambit tucked into my waistline above my groin. It had to be due to the placement of my taped hands—a big mistake to tape them in front of me. Since they found the other two knives, I doubted they expected to find a third. And how many guys carry a knife tucked over their penis? I had a weapon. They missed it.

I'd almost gotten to use the karambit on a Russian assassin once. Now I had to figure a way, and fast, for that karambit to draw its first blood. If I could get one finger into the hole in the handle of the karambit, I'd be in business.

I strained to reach it but realized it would be impossible in my current position. So I reviewed my situation: They'd taped my feet together with duct tape, and they weren't stingy with the tape. The van reeked of gasoline and some other chemicals. Why? *Oh, shit, I hope they aren't going to set me on fire.*

They could have already killed me, so I was being kept alive for now. To be taken to Drake? To hang me on a hook in his taxidermy room and take a chainsaw to me? Or maybe just a simple beheading with a dull knife. Drake was into heads, after all.

Whatever it would be, it would be excruciating. Extremely painful. Much more agonizing than everything so far, and I promise you that the last ten minutes had already earned top ranking on my World of Hurt list. Physical pain was something that I could often tune out, although tonight didn't seem to be one of those times. I wasn't at all sure that I could ignore a rusty hacksaw to my neck.

The van lurched to an abrupt stop, way too soon for my liking. Only the faintest sliver of light trickled in from the windshield.

Then the side doors opened, and a bit more light was quickly blocked by the hulking figures that pulled me outside.

I heard traffic sounds. We were close to a thoroughfare. Possibly a major one, but at this hour of night, traffic would be light. I stole a fast glance at where I now stood shoulder-to-shoulder with two killers. A dirty concrete slab, old tires, piles of junk, a Dumpster, freeway overpasses in the near distance. The drive had been short, and I suddenly knew with certainty we were standing behind a gas station, maybe on Franklin or Elysian Fields or Almonaster, near the I-10/I-610 interchange.

Didn't seem like a place to whack me, but maybe a transfer to another vehicle made sense. I needed to act, but my muscles told me I was operating on only 50 percent power. I'd already been stiff from the car wreck but was in much worse shape now. Still, I surreptitiously strained to get at the knife. Then my escorts kicked my feet out from under me, and I dropped to the cement. I managed to land so my left arm absorbed most of the fall.

I watched as my four captors got busy. Two of them hauled out five-gallon cans of gasoline and a rubber mallet from the van. Another one muscled out what looked to be a thirty-pound pail. The fourth gangbanger rolled a fifty-five-gallon drum that had already been sitting on the concrete in my direction.

My stomach lurched. This was no vehicle transfer.

They were going to kill me, here and now.

And it wasn't going to be pleasant.

CHAPTER TWENTY-THREE

Careful to show no sign of strain, I fought with every grain of strength I had against the duct tape to get my left index finger into the hole on the karambit's small haft. My wrists were tightly taped together, but they weren't taped to my body, giving me enough freedom of movement to generate the hope that I could do this. Only minutes remained to my life unless I succeeded, because I knew what was coming.

A "stewing." The homeboys here were going to make *guiso* out of me.

The cartels used many gruesome ways to kill their adversaries. Beheading enemies and innocent victims on video was clearly only one. Tonight they planned to stuff me into the fifty-five-gallon drum, add gasoline and lye, hammer the lid down shut, then maybe roll me right onto Franklin Avenue. The chemical reaction of gasoline and lye would create an acid that would dissolve my body down to teeth and bones.

No doubt Drake would want the bones.

My finger edged closer to the karambit's hole, but the killers' prep was almost complete.

In case I managed to free the knife, this was my chance to size them up, decide who looked strongest, who might be the best fighter, who carried what weapon and where.

I named them Wart Face, Fatty, Goldie, and Flaco. The first two names were for obvious reasons. Goldie, I saw in a shaft of light, had a front gold tooth, like the description we got of the movers at Drake's curio shop. The fourth Skulls member I called Flaco because he was on the skinny side.

They all had semiautomatic pistols tucked into their pants, except for Fatty, who had a big-ass chrome-plated .357 revolver.

"Hey, Mister Policeman, know what this is?" asked Goldie in heavily accented English. "You like cooking shows? Maybe you seen Mexicans make stew before."

"It's for *guiso*," I said.

They all laughed at that, getting a kick out of my so-so command of Spanish and the fact that I knew what was about to happen.

"Don't forget to add salt," I deadpanned.

Nobody laughed.

"*Pinches* gringo, you a smart-ass?" asked Flaco.

"You going to kill the other policemen too?" I asked.

"What you mean?" asked Goldie.

"The SWAT cops who killed your homeboys in the raid."

"We'll be killing a lot of people here. Starting with you."

His response told me they weren't here as revenge for my participation in the raid. "How much is Drake paying you for this?"

"Hey, gringo, shut the fuck up or we gag you again. The only reason I took the rag out is, I want to hear you scream when the magic starts," said Goldie.

"Put the lye in first," said Wart Face.

"No, pour the gas in first. Then Mister Policeman, then the lye," said Flaco.

"That's not how we do it in Tamaulipas."

"That's because you *pinches putos maricones* do everything the hard way."

"It doesn't matter which you put in first," said Fatty coldly, speaking for the first time. "Same thing will happen to the *pinches* asshole cop."

Flaco started pouring lye flakes from the plastic pail into the steel drum.

"Don't breathe that *mierda,* unless you want your lungs to bleed," said Wart Face.

I loved the fact that they were arguing over how to cook me, because I needed every extra second I could get.

I jerked my head violently and fearfully said, "Don't do it, please." I did this as a distraction to mask the violent wrenching of my left hand to loosen the duct tape.

"Don't be scared, *niño pequeño.* It only hurts like a mother-fucker for about five minutes," said Flaco.

I almost had my finger in the hole, when Fatty and Wart Face, the two biggest guys, lifted me to my feet.

It was just about now-or-never time.

I jerked my left hand; my index finger felt the edge of the knife hole. I had to get my finger fully through the hole to be able to pull out and deploy the knife.

I also couldn't struggle too violently or they might coldcock me unconscious. They dragged me toward the barrel as Flaco finished emptying in the lye.

"That's some nasty shit all by itself. Fuck," said Flaco, lapsing into a coughing fit.

"You pissed off the wrong person, you *hijo de puta*," said Wart Face to me.

Damn, he must have fifty warts on his face, and his breath reeked of a bad abscess.

Flaco grabbed my legs and they lifted me off the ground. *Crap, if they load me in headfirst, it's over. I'm dead.* I caught sight of Goldie unscrewing the top from a gas can, smiling, the diamond, ruby, and emerald in his gold tooth all glimmering with an evil glow.

"Did he wet himself yet?" asked Goldie.

"The *pinches policía* better not piss on me," said Fatty. "Or I'll cut it off him!"

That brought a round of laughter. "I can't see if he pissed or not. It's too dark."

"Who's got a light?"

"I do."

They almost dropped me as Flaco pulled out his lighter and lit it.

"Not a cigarette lighter around gasoline, *pendejo de mierda estúpido*! Stop fucking around and put his legs in."

I wasn't happy to be going into the drum, but at least it was feetfirst. A cloud of lye dust rose as they dropped me in.

"Sit down."

I didn't want to be hit, so I quickly squatted in the barrel. Almost instantly the lid went on and light was cut off, except for a tiny amount streaming in through the open bunghole in the lid.

This was the opening they would pour the gasoline through any second, sealing my fate.

My body started to cramp, the stiffness from the traffic accident locking my leg and back and neck muscles as if in a vise.

I heard the rubber mallet pounding the lid tight on the barrel as my body involuntarily convulsed in a coughing spasm from the lye.

A nozzle filled the sight of the open bunghole. A gas can nozzle. Then I heard laughter and the barrel flipped onto its side. I banged my head on the steel.

The barrel began to roll. No gasoline yet; they were toying with me, rolling the barrel on the concrete.

I banged around a couple of times before bracing my legs, taped hands, and shoulders up against the perimeter of the steel in order to stop bouncing around inside the big can.

Lye dust rose to my nostrils, and I held my breath and squeezed my eyes closed, struggling to fight off motion sickness as they rolled the barrel around and around, laughing.

Then suddenly I was upright again.

My shoulder pressed against the lid and felt the jab of what had to be a gasoline can nozzle. And I figured, with what little cognitive ability I had left, that this time they would pour the gas.

My current position inside the barrel had changed the angle of my hands in relation to the karambit. My finger instantly found the hole in the handle. I heard the men speaking in Spanish, happily, not a care in the world. I fought unconsciousness, squatted as low as I could, and then launched myself with one massive thrust, using my powerful legs like pneumatic pile drivers, and slammed my right shoulder into the underside of the barrel lid.

The lid shot into the air as I stood up, lye flakes flying up, right next to Wart Face and Fatty. The gas can got knocked out of Wart

Face's hands, and all four gangbangers looked on in total disbelief.

With a smooth motion my bound hands pulled the karambit free of my waist, instantly opening the supersharp steel blade, and I angled the weapon toward Wart Face, cleanly slicing through his throat and severing his jugular.

I didn't stop my momentum and quickly swung right, repeating the process with Fatty.

In a slow-motion world punctuated by gasping and gurgling and geysering sticky red liquid, I saw Flaco and Goldie reaching for their pistols. With my hands still taped together, I let loose my blade and snatched the .357 from Fatty's pants as he stood wobbling in his last moments of life. I went for his wheel gun and not Wart Face's semiauto, knowing it would not eject superheated spent shell casings that could ignite the gas.

I sighted the heavy sidearm on Flaco's heart and punched his ticket straight to hell.

Goldie was trying to draw a bead when I shot him three times, aiming low. He went down, his gun skittering away.

Nauseous beyond belief, I puked again, then retrieved my karambit and cut myself free of the duct tape binding my wrists. The gushing gasoline from the dropped can made me nervous, and I wanted out of that barrel of lye, fast. But there was no way to climb out without the barrel falling over. So I lurched the barrel over away from the gas, crawled out in another cloud of lye dust, and cut the duct tape around my feet.

I staggered to my feet, coughing, head spinning, and it took a minute to get my sea legs. I lurched more than walked, and found Goldie groaning and bleeding heavily from where I'd shot him in the thigh and groin.

I dropped to my knees, teetering, and put the barrel of the pistol against his face. "Who sent you?"

He looked at me with no fear, only hate.

"Who sent you?" I jammed the pistol into his groin wound. When he stopped screaming he just gasped for breath.

"Who sent you?!"

I jammed the pistol again, and the screaming didn't stop until he passed out.

So I searched him and pocketed his wallet and other goodies. When he came to, I was ready. He blinked, watching me cover his body with lye flakes. He lay still, very weak.

"It's a little different from stewing, but when I douse you with gasoline, the acid will form and eat you alive," I said casually. "I have to hurry and do this before you pass out from loss of blood."

His eyes glazed over. He knew he was dying, knew it would be painful, knew he had lost.

I set a gas can near his face and unscrewed the lid.

"Who sent you to kill me?"

His eyes searched my determined face, then shifted to the gas can as I screwed on the nozzle.

I stood up and hefted the can. Drops of gas accidentally sloshed onto the ground near his face. I was so weak, the gas can felt like it weighed a hundred pounds.

"Last chance to die without pain. Who sent you?"

I tipped the nozzle toward him.

"Tico Rodriguez," he said quickly. "Old *compadre* of El Professor Negro."

"Professor Robert Drake."

"*Sí.*"

"How much is Drake paying to have me killed?"

"Nothing. He just call Tico and say 'Kill this *pinches* cop, please.' Tico, he just laugh, say, 'No problema.'"

I put the can down, glad I didn't have to hold it any longer.

As a trained medical first responder, I knew that without immediate medical attention, he would bleed out and die. So I did the decent thing for humanity and sat with him as he bled out.

At last I stood, drenched in blood, but curiously, not my own. I heard deep base thudding from a passing boom box on the street, the muted roar of traffic from the interstate overpass exchange, the far-off laughter from girls probably hanging out on a street corner. A faint whiff of chicken frying in a deep fryer told me I was gloriously alive, and I decided I'd be eating fried chicken tonight.

I absentmindedly fingered Fournier's medallion around my neck. Check that; it was *my* medallion, given to me by Fournier.

Yes, for sure I'd eat fried chicken, and for sure I was not calling this crime scene in to the New Orleans Police Department. For many reasons. This needed to be handled on the down-low. So I returned to the van and gathered up my weapons, electronics, and other stuff and used my cell phone to call a number I knew well but seldom used.

"It's me. I need a cleanup. The head count is four," I said as my hand holding the cell phone shook.

"Are you hurt?" asked Twee Siu.

"I've been better. But mostly it's my feelings. I thought I was charming, but apparently Professor Robert Drake really does want me dead."

Twee dropped me at my Bronco parked under a street lamp at the corner of Lesseps and Burgundy, across from B.J.'s. As she drove off, a dog barked from the shadows, and I saw Honey standing there with Chance, her rottweiler/shepherd mix. I'm sure I looked pretty rough, and there was no hiding the blood all over my clothes and in my hair.

But my face was a mask of stoicism as I met Honey's stare. She took in the sight of me, and it must have registered that something bad had just happened, and I hadn't turned to *her* for help but to Twee Siu. My intention had not been for Honey to see this, but there was no hitting rewind. Knowing Honey as well as I did, I knew she would feel very guilty about what had just happened to me, since she was my partner and hadn't been there to back me up. No reason to add more guilt to what she already carried, so I wordlessly turned away, got into the Bronco, and drove off.

CHAPTER TWENTY-FOUR

I'd gotten two and a half hours of sleep before the buzzing woke me. I could barely focus. The computer monitor next to the bed showed views from my security cameras. After rubbing my eyes for the third time, I made out Honey standing outside my front door, ringing the bell. She had keys, but I guess she wouldn't be using them anymore, and maybe that was a good thing.

I buzzed her in and groaned as I forced myself from bed. The pain from pulling on a sweater and a pair of jeans was sufficient to wake me up, like a couple of cups of coffee and a slap in the face.

She stood in the front room when I shuffled in.

"I've been trying to call."

I spotted my phone on the coffee table next to my pistols, knives, an empty takeout box of fried chicken from the Wing Shack on North Claiborne, and a half-empty bottle of Crown Royal that had been full three hours ago.

"Sorry, I didn't hear it."

"How do you feel?" she asked, trying not to show concern. I knew I looked like death warmed over.

"Like I've been tased, beaten with a pipe, and stuffed in a steel barrel full of lye."

"It's Hans Vermack," she said solemnly.

My mind raced. "Give me five minutes."

"Nothing like the smell of grilled meat."

"They say burnt meat is carcinogenic, but it tastes so damn good."

"Ever watch any of those comedy roasts on TV? This is a different kind of roast altogether."

"This will be an autopsy you take a fork to."

"Or mustard."

"A-One, anyone?"

"I like my meat well done, but this guy is burnt black."

"All right, knock it off," I snapped at the squirrelly crime-scene photographer and another CSI tech. "I had more questions for this guy and I'm not too happy that he won't be answering them."

Honey and I stood in Hans Vermack's apartment kitchen above the Voodoo Cave. Han's head, hands, and feet sat in a big turkey-roasting pan on top of the stove. Some of the flesh had been picked away.

The rest of Hans still filled the bathtub, where he'd been butchered. His girlfriend, Patrice Jones, who should have been institutionalized long ago, would be soon. The patrol officers who responded to the 911 call had found her sitting at the kitchen table, eating a plate of Hans amandine. Both coppers had tossed their cookies.

Mackie and Kruger had taken Patrice away moments ago to book her for murder. She had made the call to 911 and told us that Hans had fallen asleep in his chair, and that a ghost had come into the house through the back door and killed him. She claimed the ghost had told her that since Hans was so cheap, he would have wanted her to eat him and save on grocery money. And so she did.

"Is there any chance Patrice could have killed the other victims too?"

"No. None," said Honey. "I've already talked to the chief about that. He knows that dog won't hunt."

Honey was acting matter-of-fact, neither warm nor cold. Since she'd showed up at my place this morning, she had behaved like there were no issues between us. And maybe there weren't.

"I agree Patrice couldn't have whacked the other victims," I said. I paused, trying not to wince as my lungs and sinuses burned from my having breathed the lye dust last night. I'd already snorted about a pint of water trying to rinse out my insides. "Which begs the question: What are the odds this would happen? You and the chief are so big on percentages. What are the chances that Vermack, one of a handful of remaining Crimson Throne members, and one of our suspects, would be butchered and eaten by his crazy girlfriend the day after Becky Valencia got wiped?"

"The facts suggest the odds were beaten here today," said Honey. "Where's the MO of your ritualistic killer? Your triumvirate of religion, sex, and pain?"

"The facts aren't all in," I said. "The coroner will tell us if there was sex. There was definitely pain. Religion is tattooed all over his body. But I want to hear more about the ghost she was talking about."

"We're going from demons to ghosts?"

"She called it a ghost. What was it that she really saw?"

Honey shook her head in disagreement. "You know how Vermack treated her. Maybe she just had enough."

I pursed my lips, took a step, then pulled my cell phone from a cargo pocket. I took a photo of Hans's body parts in the turkey pan and then turned to the CSI techs who were watching. "Wasn't there a British pop group called Heads Hands and Feet? I'll send this photo to their fan page."

Honey looked slightly aghast, but the CSI techies smiled; I didn't want them to think I'd lost my sense of humor.

"C'mon," I said to Honey, "let's take a look at the bathroom again."

Mere walking hurt like hell, but I kept that to myself. As we entered the bathroom, the stink almost overpowered me. Since the coroner was running late, Vermack's remains remained.

"So you think, what? He comes in to use the can, she follows, then knifes him. Then her rage flows out and she dismembers him?"

"She had blood on her. Her shoeprints are in the blood on the floor."

"Why was he naked?"

"You never went into your bathroom naked?"

"Wait a second, wait a second, wait a second! Damn if my mind isn't scrambled eggs this morning. Vermack told me he didn't keep knives in the house. There had been an incident, so he removed every last knife from the building. So where did Patrice get the butcher knife?"

The back door had already been dusted for prints, but I wanted to look for pick marks on the lock. We opened the door, revealing a tiny gallery with exterior stairs leading to ground level. The French Quarter was a warren of buildings crammed together, often in odd and illogical configurations, and when one caught a glimpse of what stood behind the historic storefronts, it brought home just how densely packed the place really was.

I gingerly bent over to check the lock, then stood and gazed outward. "Look," I said, pointing. "There must be fifteen or twenty units with a direct line of sight to right here. We need to get officers canvassing all of them. A neighbor could have easily seen someone coming through this door."

"Patrice's ghost sighting?"

"Check out the lock. I don't think ghosts make those kinds of scratches. And they're recent, although I can't tell how recent. This lock has been picked."

Honey looked, then shook her head. Her easy arrest of Patrice was growing questionable.

"Why can't we catch a break?" she asked.

"Maybe we need to hire a witch to brew us up some good-luck spells."

I nosed around downstairs in the voodoo shop and immediately noticed significant items missing that had been there before, primarily items from the altars Vermack had maintained. I checked the photos in my phone, photos I had taken the first day Honey and I came into the Voodoo Cave. The entire skeleton from one large altar was gone, as were important pieces from other altars.

I called Honey's cell and asked her to come downstairs. When I showed her the discrepancies, she nodded, remembering.

"You're right, but could he have sold the stuff?"

"That altar had been there for years. I doubt he sold it. It's just like at Valencia's place, where the silver baskets her father made were missing."

"Was theft the motive? Fifty thousand that Felix had stashed is gone. Then the pieces from Valencia's and Vermack's murders."

I shrugged. "I suppose it's possible. Aside from the money, the missing articles hold a lot of value to a fellow sorcerer or a collector."

"That doesn't narrow it down. Does it?"

"Not at all." My mind had already narrowed down our suspect list to one person, the man who'd almost had me killed a few hours previous by some Mexican gangbangers, but I had to keep that information under wraps. And I reminded myself to remain open to the possibility that Drake had accomplices, even unlikely ones.

As I glanced out the shop's front window, I saw a familiar figure across the street talking to an older crime-scene tech.

"That's Tony Fournier," I said.

"Like a bad penny," said Honey, already on the move.

We hurried out of the shop, through the front door of the Voodoo Cave, and made a beeline toward Fournier. When he glanced over and saw us approaching, he made like he was going to run, then stopped, as if giving up, knowing he couldn't get away.

"You have a lot of explaining to do, Tony," I said.

"He knows I'm closing in."

"He who?" I asked.

"We're getting close."

"I'm getting close to thinking bad things about you." I looked to the CSI guy in his fifties. "If you've been giving him privileged information, you've got a problem."

The tech didn't say a word. I gritted my teeth from pain that shot through my body as I started to muscle Tony toward Honey's borrowed unit.

"Heard you had a bad car accident. Glad to see you're okay," said Fournier.

"I'm not sure whether to thank you or arrest you," I said. "Maybe both."

CHAPTER TWENTY-FIVE

Patrice Jones was arrested and booked for murder. Due to the gruesome nature of the crime, the media frenzy had gone viral, so Pointer, in one of his trademark press conferences, trumpeted the quick arrest and hard work of NOPD and reiterated, as he always did, how no tourist visitors were ever in danger.

Just about everyone in the city was in danger, as far as I was concerned, and not from Patrice Jones. But I kept that to myself.

I'd just arrived back to the Homicide offices after making a quick trip to the Jefferson Parish Sheriff's Office Crime Lab. I dropped off the martini glass and cigarette butt to my old friend Kerry Broussard to get Anastasia Fournier's prints and DNA. Kerry was faster and more accurate than the NOPD lab, and often did such favors for me. In return, I tutored his daughters in aikido and made frequent donations to his church on St. Claude. Kerry had apologized for not yet hacking into Drake's laptop but said he almost had the job done and would messenger it to me later today.

Honey had Tony Fournier chilling in an interrogation room.

Must have been uncomfortable for the retired detective to be sitting on the other side of the table. There certainly wouldn't be any attempt at gaming him; Fournier knew the tricks as well as we did.

So Honey and I entered the room and sat across from him. I opened my laptop so he couldn't see the screen.

"Tony, forget about any talk of demons or curses. You need to come clean with us, right now. You've been lying. You know it, and we know it."

Tony was chewing gum, and he worked it pretty good. But he didn't speak.

"Tell us about your brother again."

"Died when he was twelve. Drowned in a lake," said Tony, matter-of-fact.

"So who is Anastasia?" asked Honey.

"She's not my niece, she's my wife. Her maiden name was Tiffany Mouton."

"Your wife," Honey stated.

"For how long?" I asked.

"About three years now. She was a runaway, a transient. Had a fake ID. She was heading for a life of crime. Started hanging out at a place in the Quarter where I knew Kate Townsend trolled for fresh meat. I gave her a home instead."

"And?" I asked.

"You had to do this down here?" exploded Tony, coming out of his chair. "At headquarters? With the tape recorder running to make sure the whole department finds out! You assholes couldn't have just asked me?"

"We did ask, outside of headquarters, shitbag. And you lied to us. Because we weren't supposed to see you and Anastasia together, right? That was not in the plan as to how you were going to spin us, influence our investigation. You must have known we'd come across her as we nosed around, but you never figured we'd connect her to *you*. So you made up some bullshit about your brother dying in a boat accident."

He sat back down. In what must have been a nervous tick, he flexed his fingers for a good five seconds. "She told me about your sting. That you know she's hooking, working undercover for me to gather intel on Drake and the Crimson Throne. Told me you had it all recorded. She tells me everything."

"How long was she undercover?"

"She still is. Don't forget that," he said, looking me in the eye.

"Which is a mistake, Tony. Bring her in."

"I can't. She's . . . confused. She still debriefs me every day, still comes out to the house several times a week. We still have sex and talk about the future, but—"

"But she's been seduced by the dark side," I said.

"It's the thrills, the adrenaline. She's young and immature. She's making all this money, partying nonstop. It's why we were arguing when you guys showed up unexpected at my house. I wanted her to spend the night. She wanted to go party with Townsend."

Maybe Anastasia had fallen victim to an old scenario of identifying too closely with the undercover role she was playing. Maybe she'd grown addicted to the excitement of her new life.

"Gee, all of this was left out of the files on Drake you gave us," said Honey, sarcastically.

Fournier looked at her but said nothing.

"Why were you at the curio shop as it burned?" I asked.

"I have a police scanner in my car. I was in town, heard the calls, recognized the address. I had mixed feelings about seeing it burn."

"Why?"

"On the one hand, to hell with Drake. Anything that hurts him is obviously okay by me. I only wish he'd been inside the burning building. On the other hand, I heard you guys were getting search warrants. For the first time, PD was going to see what was in the place. I was curious to know what you found."

"And why were you outside Hans Vermack's place this morning? Scanner again?"

He shook his head. "I got a call. Twenty years in the department, I have friends at the coroner's, the lab, EMS, the fire department. You know how it is. You going to try and get my friends in trouble?"

"It's not a witch hunt, no pun intended. You caused this yourself. You came to us and lied through your teeth. Keep that in mind."

"Since you planted your wife on the inside of Drake's inner circle, who killed our victims?" asked Honey.

"Professor Robert Drake. He's got money problems. He owed Felix Sanchez and Roscindo Ruiz about ten grand for work they did on his house."

"Felix's wife Gina said Drake didn't owe any money."

"Felix probably kept it from her. I can tell you with certainty that they wanted to get paid and were ready to pull out of the Crimson Throne because they weren't happy with how some things were being done. They felt Drake and others lacked integrity. Drake knew Felix kept tens of thousands hidden in his truck. First he took the cash from the truck while the Mexicans were in the house, then they had a sex-magic session, and Drake killed them.

"He killed Becky Valencia because she broke her vows. I figure he broke into her house the night before and drugged her juice or drinking water or something. He comes back the next morning while she's incapacitated, but still conscious, still alert. He sets up his sex-magic session, and puts in the needle that kills her.

"Hans Vermack, I'm not sure yet, because I haven't heard the details of the case. His girlfriend is a nutjob, but she's never been violent."

"Why would Drake kill Vermack?"

"I'm not the only one with friends in the department. I always suspected the professor had inside sources, the way he always out-maneuvered me over the years. So Drake heard, just like I did, that Vermack was giving it all up like a virgin on prom night. Drake doesn't tolerate people who rat him out. In that way, he's just like his buddies, the Skulls."

"Drake introduced Felix Sanchez and Roscindo Ruiz to the Las Calaveras cartel?"

"Of course."

"So the heads in the ice chest weren't going to Drake."

"Drake could buy direct from the Skulls. He didn't need Felix or Roscindo for that. I assume the heads were for Kate Townsend."

"If Drake needed money, why didn't he sell to her himself and keep the profit?"

"Because he wouldn't have gotten paid. She would have just kept the heads. She's been squeezing him for years. She never forgave him for what he did."

"You talking about the abortion?"

Fournier nodded. "He drove her all the way down to Reynosa to have a cartel doctor do it."

"Why?" asked Honey.

"So he could gift one of the Skulls kingpins, Tico Rodriguez, an old friend of his, with the fetus. Tico either ate it or used it in some black-magic ritual."

I looked to Honey. There was a reason police officers were the way we were. Partly it was from having to deal on a daily basis with the scum of the earth and the things they did. Even so, Robert Drake had just been enshrined in the pantheon of slime.

After we cut Tony Fournier loose, the chief called Honey and me into his office and read us the riot act. He was using the "If I Yell Louder, They'll Work Harder" management philosophy today.

"Two naked dead guys, an acupuncturist with a million needles in her, heads in an ice chest, a botched raid shootout with four dead Mexican gangbangers, a Dutchman filleted and eaten by his Creole girlfriend! Not exactly the kind of publicity the tourism board or the mayor's office or the city council likes to hear!"

"And you're not going to want to hear this, but there might be some NOPD involvement."

Pointer fell silent.

"Tony Fournier, a retired homicide detective."

"I remember Tony," said Pointer.

Honey and I filled him in with all the pertinent details, including the doings of Anastasia Fournier/Tiffany Mouton/April the hooker.

He shook his head. "Okay, what do you need?"

"How about paying for a rush job on the toxicology reports and sending them to a better lab?"

"I'll see what I can do," said Pointer, suddenly preoccupied with shuffling some papers on his desk. The meeting had ended, and I knew the chief wasn't going to do a damn thing to help us.

Kate Townsend and Anastasia Fournier were currently at Townsend's apartment above Crafty Voodoo, but our surveillance team had lost them until little over an hour ago, when a taxi deposited them at the shop's front door. They obviously knew they were being watched and had somehow snuck out of the bordello late last night through a rear entrance. Or perhaps they had left in disguise; it wasn't clear.

Drake was still missing in action. The professor hadn't been seen since he left the Homicide Section and drove to his lawyer's office. All places of lodging within fifty miles of the city had been notified, and Dinwiddie Hall at Tulane was under surveillance, but since it was finals week, he wasn't due in class until tomorrow. Honey put out a BOLO on Drake, that if sighted, he was to be detained. His lawyer was refusing to cooperate in any fashion.

And then there was the troubling issue of Gina Sanchez. I wanted to let her know, unofficially, that the last of the New Orleans-based Skulls gangsters were no longer a problem for her. But Gina had deliberately ditched her NOPD tail yesterday. She'd taken a taxi from police headquarters to the French Market, joined a large group of tourists, and then melted into the crowds in Jackson Square. Fred Gaudet was diligently trying to locate her new place of residence.

After easing into my desk chair, I washed down a handful of anti-inflammatories with my fifth cup of coffee. I felt like shit-on-a-stick as I shook my head, trying to disengage creeping memories of what the Skulls had almost done to me, and to instead remain focused on the case.

A growling stomach reminded me I hadn't eaten today. I reached into a drawer and fished out a bag of kale chips I'd bought for some obscene amount of money at Whole Foods on Magazine Street. You needed to take out a bank loan to shop there, their profit markup was about 10 million percent, but they sold good stuff.

I started munching and looked down at Drake's laptop sitting on my desk. A messenger had just delivered it. Kerry Broussard had hacked the password, but the computer had been sanitized and held few files, none of interest. Drake's briefcase and Tulane office computer had also yielded a fat zero.

I waved Honey over to my desk and gestured to the laptop. "No *grimoire,* no journal of magical workings, no business records listing sales of body parts to nefarious buyers."

"Drake is smart. He's had plenty of time to dump incriminating evidence."

"Hey, partner. Peace?" I offered Honey some kale chips. She took one, scrunched her nose for the sniff test, and then put it back in the bag.

"Peace. But you need to buy some nacho chips. Or some other good junk."

"Remember I said I had a second theory for the murders?"

"Right," said Honey.

"What if the ritual aspects of the crimes—the candles, the sex, the pain inflicted—was just a dog and pony show?"

"You mean the killer actually had a motive. And wasn't killing for magical power."

"Right. But he or she incorporated the ritual trappings to deflect suspicion or lead investigators in the wrong direction. Fournier did a good job of outlining possible motives Drake might have for the killings." I made loud crunching sounds as I gobbled down another kale chip.

"Except Vermack said quitting the Crimson Throne wasn't a killing offense."

"Maybe Drake felt otherwise. Anyway, setting aside the ritualistic nature of the crimes, let's look at the possible motives of Kate Townsend. Question one: Why kill the two Mexican members of the Crimson Throne?"

Honey thought for a moment. "She's greedy, but I don't buy theft."

"Me either. Could this just be about getting even with Drake? To pay him back for what he did to her unborn child?"

"The Crimson Throne was important to Drake," said Honey. "A big ego thing for him. And he wanted his students' energies for his black magic."

"So getting rid of the group's members removes his power base." I reached for another chip. "When I think of other possible suspects on our radar screen—Tony Fournier, Anastasia, Gina Sanchez—I don't see any motives."

Honey nodded. "Fournier might want Drake dead. But what beef would he have with the others?"

"And Sanchez might kill her husband for fifty thousand bucks, but Vermack and Valencia?"

"Percentages say it's Drake," said Honey. "He burned his shop down, emptied his house so we couldn't find incriminating evidence. If he's been whacking people for as long as Fournier believes? Maybe the professor has snapped. Gone round the bend."

I logged on to the Internet. "I want to check his Web site again. Maybe there's a clue as to where he might be hiding."

Honey sat next to me as we slowly scrolled down the long home page containing hundreds of links to Drake's accomplishments: articles, books, papers, abstracts, reviews, lectures, seminars, presentations, interviews, awards, grants, memberships, case reports, and more. We hadn't had time to check all of these closely.

"Damn, if this guy makes a shopping list, he'll put up a link to it," cracked Honey.

"A lot of these papers he wrote are in Spanish. And I recognize some of the words in the titles: *sacrificio humano* and *desmembramiento.* 'Human sacrifice' and 'dismemberment.'"

"Looks like he published something in *El Bruja Bulletin,* in the Yucatan. Sounds like a magazine for sorcerers."

"No, wait. *El Bruja* means 'the witch.' But it's an archaeological site. Looks like Drake did extensive field research there."

Honey clicked the link, and we came to a page with photos of Drake in the field, and more links; each year for the last thirty years had a link.

"Pick a year," I said.

Honey clicked a link about twenty years back, which took us to a page with dozens of photos of a smiling, much younger Drake excavating what looked like human remains.

"Well, he likes his work. You have to give him that," said Honey, about to click to another page.

"Wait! Look at the girl in this photo," I said, pointing. "That's a young Gina Sanchez."

It was a group shot, with Drake standing with his arms around what looked like local hires who aided in the excavation. Most of the photos had captions listing names, but this one and some others did not.

"And look here," said Honey, referring to another picture. "I'd bet that's Felix Sanchez." Again, this photo had no caption.

We kept looking and found more photos of Gina and Felix Sanchez and Roscindo Ruiz; they had all obviously worked with Drake in some capacity during his field expeditions.

"Where is this El Bruja, again?" I asked.

Honey clicked back to another page. "Not far from the famous Maya ruins of Chichén Itzá. On the Yucatan Peninsula, near Cancún. Where Drake is scheduled to present a lecture in less than a week, according to that flyer posted at Dinwiddie Hall."

"So he lied about how long he's known Felix and Roscindo. And about how well he knew them. In a way, so did Gina Sanchez. Why didn't she mention this to me? Instead, she very quickly tried to steer me in the direction of Kate Townsend as the prime suspect."

Honey and I looked at each other.

"So which witch is which?" asked Honey.

CHAPTER TWENTY-SIX

Fred Gaudet told us by phone he was closing in on Gina San-chez's location, so Honey assigned a couple of other Spanish-speaking detectives to back him up. Honey and I had returned to Casa de la Carne out on Airline Drive to talk to Alberto, the owner and former landlord of Sanchez.

We were in a no-nonsense mood and escorted Alberto into his office for privacy.

"I have already told you everything I know."

"No you haven't, not even close."

"You want to cause problems for me with Las Calaveras? The Skulls?"

"Those men are all dead."

Honey blanched at my remark. Now she could put two and two together and deduce what had happened, why I had been covered in blood last night as Twee dropped me off at the Bronco.

"You want to know who your problem is, Alberto?" I poked my index finger hard into his chest. "Your problem is me, unless

— 224 —

you answer my questions with the truth. *Está claro?*" I gave him a look that told him I meant it.

After a beat, he said, "*Sí.*"

"What's the real story on Gina Sanchez?"

He looked concerned. "You won't tell anyone I spoke?"

"You have my word."

"She is a very powerful *bruja*. A witch. Stronger than Felix and Roscindo, and they were strong. *Todo el mundo*—everyone—is afraid of her. And when you're afraid of something, you don't speak of it."

"Because she does black magic."

"*Sí.*"

"You know this man?" Honey asked as she flashed Drake's photo.

Alberto nodded. "He came to eat sometimes. Sometimes with Felix and Roscindo and Gina. Sometimes just with Gina. People call him El Professor Negro, 'The Black Professor.'"

"Why do they call him that?"

"Because he is one of them. A sorcerer, a *brujo*."

"Could Gina and the professor have been . . . ?"

"*Adulteros?*"

I motioned impatiently. "Yeah, you know, getting it on, on the side."

"Maybe. Two times I saw the professor go up the back stairs to the apartment. Why else would a man go into the home of a married woman when the husband is not there?"

A couple of days ago, Fred Gaudet had located the money transfer service used by Gina Sanchez to send cash back to Mexico. It was just down the street from Casa de la Carne.

I left Honey in the parking lot of Número Uno Check Cashing with clear instructions, and then went in alone. Half a dozen Hispanics were waiting in the single line to do their business with the cashier sitting behind thick Plexiglas. I cut to the front of the line, flashing my badge. My adrenaline was pumping, so I felt a little better, except for the burning in my lungs from the lye dust.

"I need to speak to the manager."

"I'm the manager," said the chubby gal in her thirties with way too much makeup on.

"You have a regular customer named Gina Sanchez. I need to know exactly where she sends her money to in Mexico."

"I can't give out that information."

I turned, saw Honey through the window, and gave her a wave. She lit up the red-and-blue flashers and wailed on the siren.

"*La Migra!*" I announced to everyone in the room. "Show me your ID, or get out!"

The entire room emptied in less than ten seconds.

I looked at the manager. "I can arrange to have a police car parked outside with lights flashing all day long. Might cut into your business, though. Seeing as how there are so many other money transfer places around town."

She gave me a dirty look and then went to work on the computer.

"She sends her money to Banamex, Calle 41-206 Centro, 97780 Valladolid, Yucatán."

I entered the address into the map software of my smartphone. The bank was about twenty kilometers from Chichén Itzá and even less from Drake's site, El Bruja.

The front desk area looked to be on the grungy side, which probably didn't bode well for the condition of the rooms. Honey and I had just arrived after Fred Gaudet's call that he'd located where Gina Sanchez was staying. The shabby motel that proudly advertised it featured cable TV sat next to a pawnshop on a stretch of Jefferson Highway in Metairie. The manager, Chadna, wore traditional head covering and had the red-dot-in-the-middle-of-her-forehead thing going on. Fred stood with the two Spanish-speaking detectives and made quick introductions.

"Was this the man who was with the Mexican lady?" I asked, showing Drake's photo.

"Yes, that's Manuel. They were a very nice couple. I'm so worried now, is there a problem?" said Chadna, with a heavy Indian accent.

Fred handed me a photocopy. "Here's the ID they used."

"Manuel Hernandez and Maria Gonzalez," I said, reading. "Chadna, why did you ask for the ID of the woman?"

"Because this is a proper establishment."

The remark almost made me laugh, since we were standing in a no-star dump.

"Every adult who stays here must show identification."

"They paid in cash?" asked Honey.

"Yes, Manuel paid in advance for one week," said Chadna.

"They cleared out," said Fred. "There's nothing in the room."

"What time did they check out?" I asked.

"Very early this morning," said Chadna. "Before five o'clock."

"They were driving a rental," said Fred. "I ran the plate and was on the phone to the car agency just as you rolled up. The car was returned to the airport lot at five ten this morning."

"Crap, they're in the air as Manuel Hernandez and Maria Gonzalez!"

"Maybe, maybe not," said Honey. "I'll call the JP sheriff's office at the airport."

"Take your guys and get over there," I told Fred.

The detectives left quickly as I called Kruger at Broad Street to fill him in. He and other detectives would work the phones to track Robert Drake/Manuel Hernandez's and Gina Sanchez/Maria Gonzalez's destinations.

"Five will get you ten they're in Mexico by now," I said to Honey.

"We have an international airport in name only. They'd have to stop in Houston or Atlanta or Miami first. We may still have a chance."

Honey and I sat down at Kruger's desk in the Homicide offices to confer with the veteran detective. Turned out our luck held.

Our bad luck.

Drake had flown as Manuel Hernandez with a Mexican passport to Charlotte, North Carolina, where he changed planes for the flight to Cancún. He'd already touched down in Mexico. There was no record of Gina Sanchez/Maria Gonzalez flying anywhere. Only Drake appeared on the security video at Louis Armstrong. Was Gina Sanchez still in town?

"They're being careful," said Honey. "Not traveling together."

"This is a well-thought-out plan of two guilty people," said Kruger, waving a piece of paper.

"More bad news?" I asked.

He nodded. "None of us believed Drake burned up his life's collection of gris-gris and bones and furniture in that arson fire, but the storage facilities or freight forwarders didn't have any record of Drake, Townsend, or any other suspects, right? So where did Drake stash his goodies? Well, one Mr. Manuel Hernandez used Trans-National Shipping and sent a couple of shipping containers to Veracruz, Mexico. I figure he shipped to Veracruz since Cancún is not a container port. The ship left yesterday."

"Along with all the evidence," I said. "And Mexico won't cooperate on a capital murder case." Since Mexico had no death penalty, they routinely refused to extradite murder suspects to the United States.

I slammed my fist down hard on Kruger's desk, then stood and started to pace. "Drake is following a plan. Vermack hinted Drake would start a new group with a new high priestess he could trust. That would be Gina."

"Is it possible they've been carrying out the killings together?" Honey speculated.

"We can't rule it out. Gina's prints were at Becky Valencia's crime scene," I said. "Are Drake and Sanchez permanently relocating to Mexico?"

"That would be my guess," said Kruger.

I punched up a number on my cell and put it on speaker. "This is Homicide Detective Saint James. Is this Donna, at the anthropology department at Tulane?"

"Oh, hi, detective. I've been waiting to hear from you to tell you the news."

"Donna, I've got you on speaker with other detectives here. What news would that be?"

"It's the talk of the department. Professor Drake resigned yesterday, effective immediately. He did it by e-mail! My boss is pissed.

Some of his grad students will be administering his finals this week, but the professor left clear instructions, so it's not total chaos."

"Thanks Donna, I—"

"The jerk left us in the lurch, but he has funding for the next three years at his site in the Yucatan."

"At El Bruja?"

"Yeah, but, where does anybody get funding for three years in this economy? He must have rich connections."

"Thanks, I'll be in touch." I rang off and looked at the others.

"Rich connections like the Skulls cartel?" asked Honey.

"Could be. This may be part of a plan, but I doubt Drake would bug out of Tulane at the last minute if he didn't have to. Makes him look bad in academic circles."

"Yeah, he moved up his timetable because things were getting hot," said Kruger.

"This means his girlfriend, Gina, has a plan, too. Apparently, getting rid of her husband was part of it. She was lying about being afraid of the Skulls and the Crimson Throne. She made like she wanted to surrender to me, but that was bullshit, too." I stopped pacing. "You know, she came right out and told me she should just surrender to Immigration and let them send her back to Mexico."

We all looked at each other.

"I have an old drinking buddy works for CBP over on Canal Street," said Kruger, reaching for a phone.

In only a few moments, Kruger had his Customs and Border Protection pal, Roger Ensenbach, on the line, told him who we were looking for, then put the call on speaker.

"Maria Gonzalez? She was waiting outside the damn door when we got to work at seven thirty," said Ensenbach.

"Her real name is Gina Sanchez," said Kruger. "So she's detained?"

"Not here. We processed her."

"Where would she be now?" I asked.

"Let's see what time it is. . . . Well, she's somewhere in the Gulf of Mexico."

"What?"

"We have some leeway on how we return illegals. For example, when I worked in Nogales and we apprehended a bad guy who we couldn't arrest, we might send him all the way to Brownsville, Texas, and repatriate him there. Make it harder for him to get back to Sonora and resume his dope smuggling."

"Why couldn't you arrest him for being illegal?"

"What have you been smoking, pal? When I worked Nogales Station in Arizona, I personally apprehended the same guy *twenty-three* times for illegal entry! He was a drug mule who would dump his load at a drop point and then surrender to the first BP agent he saw for the free ride back to the border. The dirty little secret is that these people don't get prosecuted, they get *processed,* a sack lunch and an air-conditioned bus ride back to the closest point of entry. Like I said, once in a while we'd screw with a guy we knew was dirty, and bus him to the other end of the country."

"Not much of a punishment."

"You got that right. Anyway, I tell you all this because Gonzales—you say her real name is Sanchez—surrendered to us, was cooperative and apologetic. More than a few Mexicans who came here to work after the Storm have done exactly the same— turned themselves in so they could get the free ride home. These are good, hardworking folks who helped the city out when we were down. Anyway, we accommodated her request. She got put on a regular charter service boat we use. To Cancún."

"Free cruise to Cancún. Can I get one of those?" asked Kruger.

"When did the boat sail?" asked Honey.

"Hold on. . . . About ninety minutes ago."

"That puts them in international waters," I said, shaking my head.

"Thanks, Roger," said Kruger. As soon as he hung up, the phone rang. "Homicide, Kruger." He looked over at Honey and me. "Yeah, they're right here." Kruger jotted something down, hung up, and then handed me the note.

"Mackie said get your ass over to the Quarter. There's a gay chick that's gonna shove a two-by-four up the chief's ass."

Honey and I looked at each other.

"Finally, a lead I'd like to follow."

CHAPTER TWENTY-SEVEN

Buzzed Salon operated around the corner from the Voodoo Cave. Chris Huff, the lady who owned the place, wore black army boots, and her hair was shorter than a marine in boot camp. Mackie made the intros as Huff snipped at the green hair of a heavily pierced client.

"Ms. Huff here lives upstairs. She saw somebody going into the rear second floor door of Hans Vermack's apartment at about four A.M. this morning."

My mouth almost dropped open. Were we actually catching a break?

"Could you tell if it was a man or a woman?" I asked.

"It was a person," she snapped. "I don't like profiling of any kind, okay? I can't say man or woman or transgender, okay? I know a little something about gender issues."

I believed that. Chris Huff had a short fuse and clearly ran with the politically correct crowd. No problem; I needed her information.

"Hey, no offense intended, it's just that descriptive modifiers like white, Asian, female, tall, husky—those kinds of words—are facts that help us apprehend bad people. We're not profiling. What you tell us might match up with suspects we have, and that could help us save lives."

"I'm sure you saw it in the news. What happened to Mr. Vermack was pretty horrible," said Honey.

"I've met Hans. He was an asshole."

"I agree he was an asshole. And maybe he deserved to have his head cut off and cooked in a pan. But his girlfriend has been booked for the crime. I'd hate to see her go to prison for something she didn't do," I said. "Regardless of what you might think of the police, my partners and I are not interested in arresting innocent people."

I could see Huff softening, just a little.

"It looked to me like this person was trying to be quiet," she said. "I figured it was either Hans or his girlfriend sneaking home late from a costume party, okay?"

"The individual you saw was wearing a costume?"

"Yeah, a white suit, you know, like an astronaut, or . . . like the kind of suits the cleaners wore after the Storm, when they went into the Convention Center with power washers and hosed out all of the crap and piss and garbage."

"A biohazard suit."

"Yeah. With a hood and a mask."

"What kind of mask?"

"You know that character they call 'Anonymous?'"

I nodded. "I know it. By any chance, did the person in the white suit spend extra time at the back door before going inside?"

"Now that you mention it, yeah. I thought it was a case of being too drunk to get the key in the lock. It took a couple of minutes for whoever it was to open the door."

I looked to Honey. She knew I'd been right; the killer had been picking the lock.

"Ms. Huff, you just saved an innocent girl a lot of grief. Thanks for talking to us."

I extended my hand. She looked at me suspiciously and then gave me the most masculine handshake she could muster. I felt so grateful I almost didn't want to let go.

Mackie, Honey, and I walked out onto the sidewalk. I lit a cigarillo, then immediately put it out. I was in no condition to smoke.

"We caught a break. I hope there's more to follow."

"A hooded white suit. It's the ghost Patrice Jones told us came in the back door," said Honey.

"You were right, Mackie. That lady in there just ruined the chief's day. Pointer will look like a fool after everything he said about Jones at the press conference this morning."

"Our two main suspects are safe in Mexico. The chief is not the only one who looks like a fool," said Mackie.

"True," I said. "May I suggest that we move Jones into a private room in the jail ward at Touro Hospital? We make sure she gets exceptional care, but sit on Huff's information for now. Jones has no family, nowhere to go, and can't provide for herself. VIP treatment in the jail ward is not the worst experience she could have. We quietly tell the DA to put the brakes on moving forward while we clarify a few details."

"We have to tell the chief," said Honey.

"Thank you for volunteering," I said. "I'm sure the chief will go along for the short term and give us some new unrealistic ultimatum to find the killer."

My cell rang; it was Kerry Broussard, my JP Crime Lab buddy. I'd dropped the martini glass and cigarette butt from Anastasia off with him only a few hours ago.

"That was quick," I said into the phone.

"Drago's. Grilled oysters on the half shell and beer, on you. Twenty minutes. We have an anomaly."

Seventy-two oysters, eight beers, and two shots of medicinal whiskey for me later, Honey, Kerry, Mackie, and I got down to the reason for his call, at a corner table in Drago's at the Hilton on Poydras. We sat in solid wooden chairs in the large, open plan restaurant that usually had a mix of tourists and locals. During the last hour we'd regurgitated the facts of the case to Kerry, accompanied by the background soundtrack of oyster shuckers in fast tempo behind a stainless steel counter.

The long and the short of it came down to Robert Drake and Gina Sanchez on the run, traveling under false identities. Once again, I had to keep secret from fellow investigators the fact that Drake had ordered a contract on me.

"The DNA I couldn't rush, but I got three hits on the prints from that martini glass," said Kerry, squeezing some lemon over an oyster as big as a hamburger patty. Like many locals, I usually skipped the entrées at Drago's and just stuffed myself silly on grilled oysters.

"Three sets of prints?" I asked, confused.

"No, three hits on the lady's prints. Tiffany Mouton from Gulfport, Mississippi, has a long juvenile record starting at the age of

twelve. Shoplifting, auto theft, assault, illegal possession of a fire-
arm. She was arrested four years ago for a series of burglaries in
the Marigny Triangle here in New Orleans."

The three of us stopped eating and listened intently to Kerry.

"Then two years ago she got a DUI. Her Louisiana driver's license was under the name Anastasia Fournier."

"The DMV didn't get a match on her prints as Tiffany Mouton?" I asked.

"Her juvenile record had been sealed, so no, they didn't. But I
have ways to pry open seals," said Kerry, smiling. He then diverted
his attention to the last and biggest oyster on his plate.

"Okay . . ." I said, silently willing him to hurry up and not put
the big-ass oyster in his mouth, but of course he did, so we all sat
there watching him chew. I hadn't been able to eat much, so Kerry
was finishing off my platter.

"A little over a year ago, there was an investigation by the Tulane University police force into rape charges against Professor
Robert Drake. The prints on that martini glass belong to the accuser, one Georgia Paris, a freshman."

My poker face failed me. I sat there silently, but my brain was
spinning, putting together a scenario. I felt dumbstruck, then just
dumb. "They played us, and everyone else, like chumps and suck-
ers from the get-go."

"Tiffany Mouton, Anastasia Fournier, and Georgia Paris are one
in the same?" asked Mackie.

"Absolutely no question," said Kerry, still chewing.

"But how could Anastasia be undercover? How could she infil-
trate the same group she'd accused of rape when she'd been a
Tulane student?" asked Honey.

"I'll tell you how, but let me paint the whole picture. The best liars salt a lot of truth into their lies, and I'm sure Tony did that to us. He probably did meet Anastasia—she was Tiffany Mouton then—when she was a transient. And he got her off the streets and married her.

"But his obsession with Drake was such that he enrolled her at Tulane under a false name—Georgia Paris—and signed her up for anthropology classes."

"Knowing she'd draw the attention of Drake," said Honey.

"No doubt. We wondered why Tony never ran a sting against Drake. Well, he's *still* running one. Anyway, back at Tulane, he planted her undercover, and it was a smart move."

"And before long, Drake invited her to one of the Crimson Throne meetings at his house," said Mackie.

I nodded. "At the meeting, Drake drugged her. She told Tulane police she hadn't agreed to have group sex and that she signed the waiver under duress. Everybody had sex with her that night, and some of the sex was pretty rough."

"Vermack," said Honey.

"And Townsend too. According to the Tulane report, she's a BDSM dom. She probably put all of those restraints in Drake's temple room to good use."

"I doubt Tony wanted Anastasia to press charges. She probably did that on her own," said Mackie. "Maybe it caused problems in their relationship, because Tony would have kept her undercover, I guarantee it."

"Probably. But it still suited Tony if he could bring Drake down with the rape charges."

"But the facts weren't strong enough. Tulane didn't pursue it aggressively," said Honey.

"So what could Tony do? He had to bide his time for seven or eight months, then get his girl back on the inside," I said.

Kerry took a sip of beer, then raised his hands. "How could he do that?! She'd already accused them of rape."

"Simple: He used what he knew about Townsend, the fact that she's always trolling for young women to recruit as call girls. Anastasia told me herself how she did it. She took a job stripping on Bourbon and let it be known she was in a money jam with no place to live. The Crimson Throne folks didn't know she was married to Tony. They didn't know anything about him. Anastasia—the woman they thought and still think is named Georgia Paris—was doing drugs and drinking heavily. It was probably very gratifying for Townsend to see a former accuser's fall from grace, now groveling for assistance. And let's face it: Anastasia is a great-looking young chick, sexy as hell, so Townsend probably saw lots of earning potential."

"Okay, I can buy Townsend. But rape is a serious charge. Why would the rest of the group let her return?" asked Honey. "I mean, she wasn't disguising herself. She returned as Georgia Paris."

"Kate Townsend is the Crimson Throne's high priestess. She took in her former accuser as her live-in lover. I think that spoke volumes to the rest of the group. Besides, they needed her."

"Needed her?"

"On the set of porn movies is a woman whose job is to make sure the male stars are 'ready for action' so to speak. Well, the Crimson Throne used Anastasia as a sexual object. She must have been pretty good, or they wouldn't have kept inviting her back. They didn't invite her for her magic skills—she doesn't have any."

"I can see how she could worm her way back in," said Mackie.

"I mean, they had to know that she could never accuse them of rape again. No cop, no prosecutor would believe a hooker who willingly returned to the same group she had previously accused of violating her."

I nodded. "It wasn't like they were befriending her. They just used her as a sexual stimulant. And don't forget, Anastasia is a good actress. I have no doubt that she sold them a very convincing bill of goods."

"I hate to say this," said Kerry, "but how do you know *she's* not the killer? She knew all of the victims. She would have known how to fake the ritual aspect of the murders. And she had a strong motive. Revenge. In her mind, these people had raped her. She was upset enough about it to disobey Tony and go public with those charges. I'm guessing she's dealing with huge rage issues."

"She suggested that Vermack brutalized her sexually," said Honey. "And the killer gave Hans very special treatment, right?"

"But does Anastasia know how to pick locks?" asked Mackie.

"The burglary arrests of hers—did the report say how she broke in?" I asked Kerry.

"The report said she'd been found with burglary tools."

"Read that 'lock picks,'" I said. "Where is Anastasia now?"

"At Kate Townsend's apartment," said Honey. "The question is, is Townsend the killer? Or the next victim?"

"And for that matter, are Drake and Sanchez on the run from the police or from a killer named Anastasia?" asked Mackie.

CHAPTER TWENTY-EIGHT

Honey dispatched detectives to locate Tony Fournier and bring him back to the station house. I paid the check at Drago's and brought Kerry along for the short ride to Crafty Voodoo. We checked in with the surveillance team to make sure Anastasia and Townsend were both still inside, then Honey, Mackie, Kerry, and I entered the shop.

The cashier refused to open the wooden door leading to the stairs, so I just elbowed her aside, jimmied the tang of the lock with a credit card, and we all rushed up the stairs.

The apartment stood empty. No Anastasia, no anyone. Alive, that is.

From a distance, Kate Townsend made for a pretty sexy corpse, sprawled naked on her red satin sheets. Upon closer inspection, her death mask was one of pain. It hadn't been a pleasant passing.

Kerry and Honey moved in carefully to examine the stiff.

"I'll call in the signal thirty," said Mackie, reaching for his BlackBerry.

"Tell Kruger he needs to play travel agent again, pronto. Find out if Tiffany Mouton/Georgia Paris/Anastasia Fournier is flying out of any of the local airports." I slipped on a pair of latex gloves.

"No obvious signs of death," said Kerry.

"Poisoned, I bet, just like the others," I said.

"This is a very fresh body. One hour, maybe," said Honey, and Kerry nodded in agreement.

"If you think she's been poisoned, I'd like to take a sample to the JP Crime Lab," said Kerry.

"What sample?"

"From this carafe here next to the bed. Looks like water inside, but who knows?"

"Please be our guest."

I checked Townsend's purse: Keys, cash, cards, cell phone were all present.

"She's naked, so maybe there was sex. And her face looks like she suffered. That's two out of three," said Honey. "Where's the third element of the MO, the religious-ritual connection?"

"Crap, look around the room. There's small statuary, esoteric paintings . . . even the magical symbols on the jewelry she's wearing."

"So how did your surveillance team let Anastasia walk out the door?" asked Kerry.

"If I were her I'd disguise myself. Hook up with a group of tourists in the shop downstairs and leave with them."

"So she's making a run?" asked Honey.

"Maybe she's after Drake," said Mackie. "The last person on her 'to do' list."

———

The United flight to Houston with passenger Georgia Paris was taxiing for takeoff at Louis Armstrong, when Honey and I pulled up to the terminal and bolted inside, yelling into our cell phones.

Jefferson Parish sheriff's deputies met us at the entrance, and we all ran full-bore toward the TSA security setup at Concourse C as I frantically explained over the phone to an air traffic controller that the plane needed to return to the gate.

And I'll be damned if we didn't catch another break. The United jet returned to Gate 35. Honey and I were waiting along with four uniformed JP deputies as the passengers deplaned. Since a dangerous murder suspect was on board, procedure was for the pilot to announce a mechanical problem and tell passengers a replacement plane was standing by to take them to Houston.

The wig was blond, the sunglasses large, but you just can't hide gorgeous. At least not from me.

"Don't make a scene," I whispered, grabbing Anastasia's wrists and cuffing her so quickly that few people noticed what had happened.

"We can't let them get away with it," she protested.

"I don't intend to let anyone get away with anything," I said, and led her toward the exit, as Honey and the deputies closed in around us.

"Kate drank something and died," said Anastasia. She sounded shaken, but I knew how great she was at role-playing.

"Don't say another word for a second," I said, and then Honey quickly read Anastasia her rights.

"You understand your rights?" asked Honey.

"Yes, I understand, but I didn't kill her. I didn't kill anyone. Yet."

"I'm recording all this, Anastasia, but why don't you save it until we get downtown?"

"We made love. She has a special water bottle. It has aloe, lavender, and lemon, and I don't like the taste. Only she drinks that. The bottle was on my side of the bed, and she asked for it so I handed it to her. Within a few seconds after she drank some . . ."

Anastasia teared up and bit her lip.

"So, your girlfriend is suffering horribly in front of you and you don't call for an ambulance. You don't call police. Instead, you commit a federal crime by buying an international air ticket to Mexico using a false identity and fake ID. What do *you* call *yourself*? Anastasia Fournier? Tiffany Mouton? Georgia Paris? I didn't catch April the hooker's last name."

"Please call Uncle Tony."

"Your husband isn't answering his cell. The police are looking for him right now. Where was it that you got married?"

The phony game was up, and her face showed she knew it. "Reno," she said, matter-of-fact.

"Okay, I'll tell you what. Since you're innocent, we won't go downtown, we'll go to your house in LaPlace. You can let us look around since you don't have anything to hide."

"You asked why I didn't call the police. If I had called them, I wouldn't be able to fly to Mexico to kill Robert Drake."

"You've finally said something I can believe."

"Because if I don't kill him, he'll for sure kill me."

CHAPTER TWENTY-NINE

Anastasia opted not to let us into her house, so we convened at Broad Street headquarters in an interrogation room. Other detectives and crime-scene techs were scouring Kate Townsend's apartment and her shop, Crafty Voodoo, for anything of interest relating to Anastasia Fournier or Kate Townsend.

Kerry Broussard had gone in after hours to the JP Crime Lab and had already confirmed Anastasia's prints were on the water bottle. He was testing a sample of the water for myriad exotic poisons and additives that were beyond the scope of the NOPD lab's budget.

"You know, I have to congratulate you—you're a convincing liar. I mean, when you came to my loft to have sex with 'Steven' and found out you'd been set up, you didn't miss a beat. 'Uncle Tony this' and 'Uncle Tony that' just rolled off your tongue like sweet syrup," I said.

"Your house in LaPlace is surrounded. We're getting a search warrant," said Honey.

"Good for you," said Anastasia.

"Where's the white biohazard suit you used when you killed Vermack?" I asked.

She just smiled. "Is it true that Patrice ate him?"

"You told her to, right?" asked Honey.

"I always felt so sorry for her," said Anastasia.

"Hope you're not disappointed, but she didn't really eat him, just nibbled a bit," I said. "We'll do forensics on your laptop. Did you use it to study the placement of acupuncture needles?"

"What are you talking about?"

The fact that Becky Valencia was found with dozens of needles in her hadn't been released to the public yet.

"What I'm talking about is this." I spun my laptop so she could see the security-camera footage from the auto-parts store on Carrollton of the killer slowly walking on the sidewalk, approaching Valencia's house.

Anastasia's eyes flashed, and a look of shock washed across her creamy skin.

"You didn't know we had you on tape?"

"This conversation is over. I want a lawyer. Now!"

The Old Drunk Judge told me to my face that I could easily have gotten the search warrant for Tony Fournier's home in LaPlace based on the facts.

"All you need to do is call a Saint John's Parish sheriff's detective with this information. He can get the warrant from a judge in his parish."

"I know that, sir. And I know their deputies have to accompany us when we serve the warrant."

"So why did you come to me with a few bottles of expensive bourbon when it wasn't necessary to do so?"

He was a smart bastard, so there was no point in being anything but truthful.

"I was hoping to invest in our future relationship, Your Honor. I know you can make a call to the courthouse in Saint John's to help pave the way. Anyway, if I only came to you with problematic requests, it would be insulting to you, sir."

"You want me in your pocket, is what you're saying, detective. Well, you're off to a good start."

And that was that.

Our first stop was the parking lot off Chartres, where Anastasia had told me she parked her Lexus. The vehicle looked clean, but we impounded it so CSI techs could go over it with a fine-tooth comb.

Next on the agenda was LaPlace. Tony Fournier remained at large while we raided his house, accompanied by St. John's sheriff's detectives. Not that Tony was a wanted man, although we had plenty to ask him.

"I've got the shoes," called Kruger from a room, as detectives and CSI folks swarmed the house.

"RUN DMC edition Adidas?" asked Honey.

"Just like on the video," said Kruger. "We'll get this to the lab for prints right now."

The killer's sneakers were something distinctive that we'd spotted when we enlarged the security video taken outside Becky Valencia's house. The killer wore a special-edition Adidas pair with

RUN DMC on the back panel. Only three hundred were made, though there were probably knockoffs floating around.

The veteran detective already had put the sneakers into plastic evidence bags, and Honey and I hurried into a spare bedroom. A quick look inside the closet revealed it to be full of women's clothes.

"You'll want to see this," said Mackie from the doorway. He held a receipt in his hand. "Anastasia Fournier rented a storage space here in LaPlace three months ago."

I took the receipt. "Well, well. What would she need storage for?"

The storage facility was a large fenced-in lot operated by an adjoining junkyard. RVs, boats, trailers, and cargo containers stood lined up in rows behind chain-link fencing topped with concertina wire. A guard dog sat chained, but there was no security camera setup or watchman. Renters were given a key to the padlock at the front gate, but there was no on-site manager. We had to get Mal Galusha, the junkyard owner, to open the gate and show us the twenty-foot container Anastasia had rented.

"I remember Miss Fournier, all right. We don't get too many customers who look like fashion models," said Galusha.

"You remember what she put into the container?" I asked.

"Didn't put anything in the day she rented it. Not that I recall."

"What about the other times she came in?" asked Honey.

"How would I know about that? When a renter comes in, I don't usually see it. Renters have their own key to the gate. I stay pretty busy in the junkyard."

"Can you open her container?"

"Nope. Customers provide their own locks."

On that note, Mackie used bolt cutters and snipped off the Master Lock padlock.

There wasn't much to see in the container. Except damning evidence.

I immediately spotted the skeleton and other items stolen from Hans Vermack's shop. A cardboard box contained the silver baskets made by Becky Valencia's father, which had been stolen from the acupuncture office waiting room.

"I got cash here," said Honey. She was squatting next to a paper grocery sack and held up a wad of cash for me to see. "Look at the small black sigils. On every bill. These look the same to you?"

I examined some bills. "Yeah, this looks like the mark on the five-dollar bill Gina Sanchez gave to me the day Felix was killed. I logged it into evidence control."

If we find Anastasia's prints on any of this, and I'm guessing we will," said Kruger, "she's going down. We got a wrap."

"I'm calling the chief," said Honey. "Give him the good news."

"What a waste," said Kruger. "She had a messed-up childhood and was already a hardened juvenile offender by the time she was fifteen. Then that sonofabitch Tony Fournier married her to use as a tool against Drake. The gang rape screwed her up even more and screwed up Tony's agenda. He lost control of his operative, to say the least."

"Some kind of liquid in unmarked jars over here," said Mackie. "Could be our poison."

I crossed over to him and nodded, eying the small, dark brown jars. My eyes darted around the container and I scowled.

"What's with you, Saint James?" asked Mackie. "You look like a monkey took a piss in your coffee."

"I'm wondering why these items are here, but not everything

else. Where's the black cape, the white biohazard suit, the Anonymous mask? Those are items we could get DNA from."

"The biohazard suit might have had Vermack's blood on it, so she tossed it or burned it. Ditto the mask," said Kruger.

"And do we really need DNA?" asked Honey, joining the debate after ringing off with Chief Pointer.

"So where's the stencil for the sigils? The spray paint?"

"Think about it," said Mackie. "She took precious things from the people who raped her. Maybe as trophies, maybe like counting coup. That's what we have here, along with the poison, which she would have to keep in a secure place."

"It all feels a little too convenient," I said.

"Convenient? Holy shit, we've worked our nuts off to get this far," said Mackie.

"We caught the big break. Why rain on it?" asked Kruger.

"Could Drake have planted all this?" I asked.

Silence, as Honey, Mackie, and Kruger all looked at me as if I'd lost my marbles. But then they hadn't been nearly dissolved in acid courtesy of killers sent by Professor Robert Drake.

"Drake is the guy with the master plan," I stated. "And he's not a forgiving fellow, much like his buddies the Skulls. Anastasia Fournier, aka Georgia Paris, publicly accused him of rape, almost costing him his professorship. So as I think about it, I can see Townsend and the others letting her back into the Crimson Throne because she was a hot, sexy young chick begging for forgiveness and asking for just one more chance to provide them free sexual services. But would Drake go for it? Really? Or would he incorporate her into *his* plan, with the end result being Anastasia gets death row?"

"You're suggesting that Drake knew she was working for Tony."

"All he needed to do was have her followed for a few days. The Skulls could have easily done that. And Tony Fournier was Drake's old nemesis. If Drake found out they were married, maybe he thinks Tony loved her and wasn't just using her. So by setting up Anastasia he gets even with *both* of them."

"Are you saying Anastasia is innocent? We pull her off a plane, in disguise, using a phony name, after fleeing a murder scene. We find items connecting her to all four murders—in a storage container she rented. Which brings me to the question: Why did she rent the container? In your theory, I guess Drake asked her to do it," said Honey, exasperated and maybe a little angry.

"I haven't named any murderer during this investigation. I float theories based on the facts at hand. The facts right now suggest Anastasia is our killer. Maybe she is. But something is telling me to keep digging. Remember how abruptly she changed her tune when I showed her the video from outside Valencia's house?"

"So? She knew we had her."

"How did that give her to us? I've watched that video. I couldn't see anything that told me it was Anastasia Fournier. We didn't show her the blown-up version that identified the special sneakers. And in case you forgot, Robert Drake and Gina Sanchez *did* flee the country using phony names. Why do that if you're innocent?"

"Drake's lawyer probably told him he could get ten years for mutilating all of those cats we found buried in his backyard," said Honey.

Mackie and Kruger both nodded. "He was facing a felony arson investigation. We could connect him to local members of a murderous drug cartel through the cell-phone calls. We threatened to resurrect the rape charges. E-mail forensics might reveal he trafficked illegally in body parts, because while it's legal for him to possess them if he purchased them properly, it's not legal for him to sell them or obtain them from Mexican drug dealers. He had plenty to run from," said Mackie.

I was losing this discussion but kept at it. "One thing we haven't had time or resources to properly examine is the disappearance of all those transients over the years. Tony Fournier didn't become obsessed with a guy who he suspected *might* be guilty. He became obsessed because he was convinced Drake was a killer who was getting away scot-free," I said.

"Drake's a probable felon. I'll give you that. But there is no hard evidence that Drake killed transients," said Honey. "I'm charging Anastasia with four counts of murder."

I could tell that Mackie and Kruger agreed with that pronouncement.

"I understand."

"I'll let the chief know you disagree."

"Okay. And as to why Anastasia rented the storage container, let's go ask her."

Being intimately familiar with the criminal justice system, Anastasia would not speak to us and referred all questions to her public defender, who also would not speak to us. So I could get no answer to my curiosity about the storage container. I'd seen enough perps behind the eight ball during my law-enforcement career to see through most of them, but I could not read her at all.

It didn't take long to confirm Anastasia's prints were found on the sneakers, the jars thought to contain poison, the paper sack that held Felix's cash, and on a cardboard box. A conviction looked fairly certain.

Tony Fournier walked into the Homicide Section right after the news of the print match came back to us. He stumbled in drunk, insisting that Robert Drake had set up his wife, Anastasia, and swearing that she was innocent. There was no evidence linking Tony as an accessory to the murders or to any other crimes, so he was let go. The conventional wisdom was he was a three-time loser, a broken man whose desperate machinations had backfired.

A ton of forensics testing and lab reports were still pending, but my part in the case was finished. Still, I reviewed the security footage again and again showing the killer approach Becky Valencia's house. My eyes watered, my sinuses dripped, my lower back ached. On about the fiftieth viewing, I saw something that—in my mind, anyway—confirmed to me that Anastasia was innocent. I kept this information to myself, since it wasn't strong enough to clear her.

I had four days off, but instead of checking in with a doctor, I checked in with the chief on a few issues and then flew to Mexico to catch the lecture "Sexual Politics of Human Sacrifice" from a guy protected by the most ruthless drug cartel on the planet.

The date of the event was December 21, the winter solstice, a pagan holy day and witches' Sabbath known as the Yule to occultists like Robert Drake.

I was traveling as a private citizen with no authority, just unfinished business.

CHAPTER THIRTY

The ancient Maya city of Chichén Itzá is a UNESCO World Heritage site that draws more than a million visitors a year. Like at the pyramids at Giza in Egypt, a sound and light show wows the tourists every night, meaning the tour buses arrive all day long like ants to spilled sugar. Vendors throughout the park sell everything under the sun; it's the Maya version of Disneyland.

In spite of the commercialization, a closed area of the site still functions as a working archaeological dig, and important conferences relating to Mesoamerican culture are held there on a regular basis. And to those in the know, like Professor Robert Drake, ancient ceremonies are still practiced in temples surrounded by jungle, as they were a thousand years ago.

At least he hinted that was the case during his presentation under the stars on the large stone platform that held the ancient, decaying observatory structure that had once been cylindrical—El Caracol, located in a more-isolated southern finger of the park. About one hundred people sat on folding chairs upon the smooth gray limestone listening raptly. A cool white ground-hugging fog had crept in unannounced, creating the illusion that we sat perched on mounts of the gods above the clouds.

Maybe only ninety-nine people were listening raptly, since I barely heard a word Drake said. I sat in a rear row and wore a fake blond beard, horn-rimmed glasses, and a boonie hat pulled low over my face.

I surreptitiously kept scanning the crowd and support staff looking for gangster-types, or anything that didn't seem right, but the attendees looked like an academic/student crowd of archaeologists and wannabes. Gina Sanchez sat beaming in the front row, not an obvious care in the world. If she was some heavyweight sorceress, why didn't she know I was there?

The sound and light show for the tourists had already finished before Drake's lecture had begun, sending the hordes scurrying to their plush tourist buses. So the grounds were largely empty and mostly dark. The most striking structure, the magnificent pyramid, El Castillo, Temple of Kukulkan, dominated the inky horizon like the dream of a lost city emerging from a netherworld, or in the case of the Maya, Xibalba.

Drake must have some real juice to get permission for such a late-night event, but that didn't surprise me. I'd gotten lucky earlier in the day and located his residence in Valladolid on my second day in the country by posing as a rich archaeology buff/dilettante bearing gifts. But Drake and Sanchez weren't staying at his house in Valladolid or at his work site El Bruja.

So tonight would be my first opportunity to act.

I'd acquired a couple of handguns my first night in the country by mugging two drunken thugs outside of a Cancún whorehouse. I'd handled them easily enough, but the physical exertion cost me, since I was still recovering from my run-in with the Skulls. I knew I needed rest, but that would have to wait. The pistols I'd taken from the thugs now both nestled snuggly in my waistband. However, if cartel bigwig Tico Rodriguez showed up with an entourage, two pistols would not be nearly enough.

The post-presentation chatter at El Caracol seemed to go on forever. Most attendees had already wandered along a two-hundred-yard stretch of jungle clearing directly behind the observatory toward the warm glow of hotel and café lights. I'd learned Drake was hosting cocktails on the veranda of the Mayaland Hotel, meaning he and Sanchez must have a room there, meaning they'd have uninvited company later, namely, me.

But I didn't want to let them out of my sight, so I worked the fringes, and since part of my cover was that I was filthy rich, I found myself welcomed.

A final cluster of about twenty of us descended the twenty-odd steps of the platform to soft earth and waist-high fog.

"Cocktails and *marquesitas* are waiting on the hotel veranda," called out Drake congenially to the group. "I've been informed by an oracle of wisdom—namely, the weather app on my smartphone—that a storm cell is moving in, so please make haste. Gina and I will join you all in a few minutes." He took her hand, and they hurried off toward the path leading north to the main body of the park.

I stooped down pretending to tie my shoe, and within moments the sound of the chattering group faded into the black night. I quickly moved off to follow Drake and Sanchez, scanning with a night-vision monocular as I walked.

I picked them up skirting Casa Colorada and quietly followed as an approaching thunderstorm rocked the jungle with a growling rumble suggestive of imminent trouble. They moved quickly and with purpose past the pyramid Ossario, the Temple of the High Priest, and up the path to central Chichén, as lightning flashes stabbed closer at the primeval city, like an errant laser attempting to lock on a target.

Without hesitation they made a beeline to the great pyramid, El Castillo, the Temple of Kukulkan, adorned with carvings of the feathered serpent god, an extremely important deity that spawned a cultlike following throughout Mesoamerica and was known to the Aztecs and Toltecs as Quetzalcoatl.

It was too risky to follow them up the ninety-one steps they were taking on the south side of the pyramid, so I darted to the west and started to mount the steep, narrow, crumbling stone stairs. Visitors had been prohibited from climbing the structure since a number of tourists had fallen to their deaths during the treacherous climb, but there was no one present to stop us now.

Kukulkan is not a complete pyramid but is flat on top, where a square high temple about twenty feet tall sits, so it looks like a pyramid that's had its top cut off and a box dropped on top of it. I'd studied the literature about the site and knew that the main entrance to this inner temple atop the pyramid faced north. Since Drake and Sanchez had climbed from the south, would they move toward the main entrance to the inner temple? If so, they would move around to the north side, but which way would they go to get there, east or west? If they went west, they would run right into me if I climbed onto the somewhat narrow walkway surrounding the high temple.

The climb caused my lungs to burn. Pain stabbed my lower back where the Skulls had beaten me with the steel pipe. I managed to ease into a low crouch, clinging to the stone stairs below the top in muted darkness. The lightning flashes to the east now pierced the night with the frequency of a strobe in a low-end Bangkok go-go bar.

I froze when slow footsteps sounded mere feet from me, just beyond the crest of the stairway. They were silently circling west, and my prey would have run right into me if I'd continued upward. I'd caught no glimmer of a flashlight beam, telling me Drake didn't want to risk being spotted by a caretaker or security guard.

I waited for a twenty count; the footsteps had faded. I slithered on my belly to the top of the pyramid, swept in both directions with my monocular, and then silently made my way toward the north entrance to the inner temple, whose smooth stone walls stood mere feet from me.

If Drake were here alone, my task would be simpler. Instead, I was running recon and making sure the couple didn't sneak off through the park entrance to a parked car with a destination unknown to me.

At the corner I chanced a look. Drake and Sanchez had stopped in the mouth of the portico to the high temple, between twin representations of Kukulkan carved on columns supporting the upper lintel. But instead of entering, Drake stooped to mark a circle on the stone floor, a circle he and Gina Sanchez stood in the center of. They held hands and gazed up at the approaching storm.

I couldn't move in any nearer from my direction without exposing my presence, and I wanted to get closer, to better observe what they were up to. So I quickly retraced my steps and used another entrance to the high inner temple. Once inside, the night vision enabled me to thread my way past richly carved support columns. I moved to within twenty feet of the couple, watching them from the dank confines of the ancient sanctuary where I could hear them intoning some invocation.

". . . and be obliged to seek me from afar, until you come to grant me my desire, and then you may return again to thy destiny."

Drake and Sanchez paused and then turned to look into the temple entrance, in my direction. "Detective, won't you join us? The show is about to begin."

Jesus H. Christ! They'd suckered me into a trap!

CHAPTER THIRTY-ONE

I pulled the Taurus .40 caliber I'd taken from one of the Cancún thugs and emerged from the shadows to the sound of thunder cracking as if it had ripped the fabric of the universe.

Drake and Sanchez turned toward me revealing they both had automatics pointed at my chest.

"Why the pistols? Can't you just put a spell on me or send a spirit to, you know, scare me to death and cause my hair to turn white?"

"That takes too long. I didn't spot you until after my lecture."

"So you brought me up here to do the deed on top of El Castillo. Nice view," I said, not really looking. I figured I could shoot Drake first, then Sanchez, if it came to that. "What gave me away?"

"Your aura. I know it well since I planted a marker in it."

"Is that right? Well, did you have a chance to plant markers with the eight federal agents who are down below, backing me up?"

"You're bluffing."

"I don't like poker and I don't bluff. I believe in attacking a target with overwhelming force."

Drake wanted to believe I was bluffing, but he looked like a guy who wasn't so sure. Gina Sanchez I couldn't read.

"I'm also an excellent shot. If either one of you fire, even if you hit me, I'll put a round into both of your foreheads before I go down. I promise you that."

"So it seems we have a Mexican standoff. For the moment."

"Why you come here?" demanded Sanchez. "You *estúpido*? You think Roberto kill Felix and other students?"

"I didn't say that, Gina. But killing comes easily for your boyfriend, 'Roberto,' doesn't it?"

"You idiot. You don't know anything."

"I know that you don't have much trouble shedding blood."

"You would know about the ease of killing, wouldn't you?" asked Drake. "I checked you out. How many have you killed now? Officially it's twelve, isn't it?"

"Unofficially, sixteen."

"I'm impressed that you murdered all of the Las Calaveras members in New Orleans."

"I've never *murdered* anyone. But let's talk about you, doc, because the human sacrifice thing with the missing transients? What's your number? Thirty? Forty?"

Drake smiled. "Human sacrifice is completely misunderstood, except by those performing the sacrifice."

"How touching. You're trying to make a case that you're not a psychopath."

"And you're trying to invalidate me, but I won't allow that. Human sacrifice, indeed most all ritualistic crimes are valid religious rites specific to different traditions. They have tremendous value, power, and the prevalence of these rites in society is actually more shocking than some of the individual acts themselves. It's humorous when law enforcement makes an attempt to figure out what's going on. Those attempts never last long, because, quite frankly, most police are pretty stupid. And if you're the best homicide detective the NOPD has, then that city is in a lot of trouble."

"I'll agree that the city is in a lot of trouble. But the word on me is that I'm like an old elevator: I'm slow, but accurate."

"Accurate? You don't even know who your killer is!"

"Sure I do. And I know who put a contract out on me with the Skulls. The guy with the gemstones in his gold tooth told me all about it during his slow death on a dirty slab of concrete. I have his confession recorded."

Drake darkened. "Germano was an old friend of mine."

"Then maybe you'd like to examine his remains, although there's not much left. Mostly just his teeth. That *guiso* business really is something. Speaking of which . . . I'm kind of disappointed Tico Rodriquez didn't come to your talk tonight."

He glowered at me for several moments, then seemed to set it aside, to compartmentalize his feelings.

"Perhaps my friends in New Orleans were too gentle with you. I can assure you that your treatment later tonight at the hands of my friend Tico won't be so pleasant."

"You didn't bring me here to kill me yourself?"

"I would have no hesitation to shoot you right now. But be patient. Perseverance pays off. It's been a long time coming, but this whole unfortunate episode is actually a blessing in disguise. Felix's death enabled Gina and me to come out in the open with our relationship. And that albatross Kate Townsend is off my back. It led me to move back to Mexico, which I should have done long ago. It's so much easier to 'operate' here."

"Hey, Mr. Sherlock Holmes, you want to know who killed my husband?" taunted Gina. "Well here's a clue. It's—"

"I curse you with the black heart of Satan!" screamed a man's voice from outside the temple entranceway in which I stood.

As Drake and Sanchez turned to look, a hurtling figure shot past me and slammed into Drake. El Professor Negro went hurtling to the edge of the pyramid, where he dropped his gun, struggled to balance himself, then screamed as he tumbled down the stone staircase of El Castillo.

Tony Fournier now stood in the magical circle, clutching Gina Sanchez with one hand as he held aloft a medallion with his other hand. "And you, old witch, will burn in the depths of hell!"

Gina Sanchez fired her handgun three times in rapid succession point blank into Fournier's midsection. He sank to his knees.

I sighted on her, ready to shoot from twenty feet away, when a bolt of lightning from the storm cell overhead struck her in the chest.

I looked on in stunned disbelief as a silent scream formed on her lips. Her body went rigid—as mine had done when I'd gotten tased—and she fell to the ground. I hadn't seen an arc jump to Tony Fournier, but after Gina collapsed, he toppled over from his knees onto the stone.

As I ran forward, the smell of burnt flesh invaded my nostrils. Her blackened face smoldered, her blouse had been blown from her torso, and the Christian cross she wore around her neck was melted, fused into her flesh. Her dead eyes stared vacantly skyward.

Fournier wasn't moving, and I chose to ignore him for now. I carefully descended the ninety-one steps to where Drake's body lay sprawled awkwardly, obscured in the white shroud of fog. The man who so loved bones would have been aghast, as his flesh was ripped in a half dozen places where jagged shards of broken pieces of ulna, fibula, and scapula had torn through the skin on his arms, legs, and shoulders.

I slipped on a pair of latex gloves and retrieved his cell phone. No calls or texts made or received in the last three hours. I found the number for Tico Rodriguez and sent him a text: *I'm canceling the hit on the New Orleans cop. Will explain later. About to climb El Castillo.*

I trudged back to the top of the pyramid and checked Sanchez, but she didn't have a cell, meaning there was an excellent chance they hadn't alerted the Skulls to my presence.

Fournier groaned and moved slightly. I hadn't been in a hurry to tend to him since he had killed all of the victims in New Orleans and had made my life so miserable since that morning out on the West Bank, which now seemed like eons ago.

His breathing was shallow, his eyes open slits. I took a cursory look at the gunshot wounds. At a trauma hospital in a major city he might survive. My audio and video digital recorders had been recording all night, but I checked them just to make sure.

"You got your last name on the list, Tony. Drake is lying at the bottom of the pyramid looking like he got put in a rock crusher."

A faint smile appeared on his lips. "Then I'm a satisfied man."

"You're a lying, murdering dirtbag is what you are."

"There's a letter in my back pocket addressed to you. Exonerating Anastasia. Explaining details only the killer would know, like how many needles I put in Becky Valencia, the placement of Hans's head and feet in the stove pan, things like that."

"As if that makes what you did okay."

"They drugged and raped my wife. And weren't held account-able. The system is broken. So I held them accountable."

"What about Felix, Roscindo, Becky—rape's not a capital of-fense."

"It was this time."

I shook my head. I certainly understood the emotion behind what he had done. Our eyes met.

"You let Sanchez shoot you."

"I cursed her with a lightning bolt from hell and killed her, is what I did. Give me some credit."

"She was standing outdoors, on top of an ungrounded structure in a lightning storm. Wearing a metallic object around her neck. I'll bet she's not the first person to get struck by lightning on top of El Castillo. People get struck by lightning all the time around here, is what I heard."

He shook his head slightly. "You saw with your own eyes what I did and you still don't believe in magic. You're a hard case. Like a lot of people, you think if you don't believe in it, if you ignore, it won't affect you."

A gentle rain began falling. I took off my boonie hat and held it over Fournier's face. "Why did you come after me?"

"Go after you? I protected your ass every step of the way."

"Come on! You painted the sigil on my doorway, stalked my home. . . ."

"Sure I painted the sigil, to try and spook you off the case. Why didn't you go along with the program?" he said, struggling to smile. "Maybe you don't believe in it, but Drake and Townsend were hitting you with heavy-duty magic. Ask Anastasia. I was the guy countermanding their efforts. Especially those first few days. I literally saw a demon enter your building on South Peters. A little before you ran out into the street."

The dream. A chill ran down my arms, but I didn't let on. "You saw that, huh?" I asked. "Well, the only things I've seen on this case are the usual pathetic, self-absorbed assholes hurting other people for selfish reasons."

"And the reason you came to Mexico was why?"

"You think I came here to kill Drake, to save my own ass because of the murder contract? I came here to catch *you*. Once I figured out Anastasia had been set up, I suspected Drake and made that case to the other detectives. But when I watched the security tape one more time I saw you."

"You saw me?"

"You flexed all ten fingers. Nervous habit. It was obscured from the best footage, which is the footage I paid the most attention to. I would have missed it, except Anastasia had a reaction when she saw the video. So I checked it again and remembered seeing you flex your fingers in the interrogation room.

"It must have been easy for you to get Anastasia's prints on all that evidence: a paper bag, a cardboard box, the sneakers. You put the jar of poison there yourself, since it was the toxin you'd been using. And she rented the storage container at your request, right? I mean, you saw the day coming months ago when you might have to set her up for the fall.

"Anyway, I knew you'd track Drake here, to his first public event. My plan was to bring you back to NOLA."

"Plan?"

"You mean your sources inside the department didn't tell you I was coming? That's because only Chief Pointer was in on it. He was open to the theory you were our guy. And as long as I traveled at my own expense, the chief went along. He gave me four days to wrap it up."

"Sounds like you can squeeze in two days of margaritas on the beach, then."

The guy was trying to make jokes as he died. It almost made me feel sorry for him.

"We don't have a definitive on Hans Vermack yet, but how did you get the victims to have orgasms before you killed them?"

"You wouldn't believe me if I told you, so why waste my breath—I don't have that many left." He punctuated that comment by making a short gasp for breath.

"Explain the gunshots at Drake's."

"I used a 9mm shooting blanks. I fired point-blank at Felix, and I think it scared him, yeah?" Fournier's eyes started to glaze over. "I'm getting cold, almost finished bleeding out."

"Yeah, I know," I said, hanging my head.

"You still got that pendant I gave you?"

I looked at him and nodded. "I'm wearing it."

Tony Fournier laughed out loud. Funny, but it had only been in the last few minutes, as he lay here dying, that I'd seen him display any sense of humor. Or perhaps I should say irony.

"You don't believe squat, but you wear that thing, huh?"

Then he closed his eyes and died smiling.

CHAPTER THIRTY-TWO

I abandoned the crime scene, slipped away in the darkness to my rental car, and drove to Cancún, where I caught an early morning flight to Houston and then on to New Orleans.

The chief wasn't thrilled I'd walked away from the three stiffs, but he understood it was healthier for me if the Skulls remained in the dark regarding my Mexican holiday. I sat in his office with Honey, Mackie, and Kruger as we all finished watching the lapel-camera video of events on top of the Temple of Kukulkan.

My three homicide compatriots had been in agreement on pressing for murder charges against Anastasia, but the chief had held off and only charged her with lesser crimes just to keep her behind bars. So now they sat across from me with a bit of egg on their faces.

"Damn it, Saint James, how do you keep pulling these things out of your ass?" asked Mackie, as the video ended.

"Fucking Tony Fournier," said Kruger, shaking his head.

"Exactly," said the chief. "Even though he's retired, Fournier was a serial killer. The department doesn't need that kind of publicity.

We're still getting bad press from officer-involved shootings that happened during the Storm. I'm fed up with the notion that we are a department of nothing but dirty cops."

I suppose it didn't occur to the chief that he was perhaps the dirtiest officer in the department.

"So you're suggesting what?" asked Honey, who clearly suspected the chief had a plan and that it was probably shady.

"What's the harm if Felix Sanchez and Roscindo Ruiz are ruled as accidental deaths due to a drug overdose? And that Becky Valencia's death be ruled accidental as the result of a misplaced acupuncture needle? Kate Townsend can be logged as having died of an allergic reaction to some herb she was taking. I don't think their families would rather be told their loved ones were murdered, do you?"

No one replied. The chief looked intently at each of us in turn. No, we weren't a department full of dirty cops, but he was asking those currently in the room to get a bit soiled right now.

"The heads in the ice chest never went public, but people talk," said the chief. "And the explanation is Drake's own. He was a skeletal biologist legally in possession of bones and body parts for scientific purposes."

"That leaves Patrice Jones on the hook for Hans Vermack," I said.

"Jones is an orphan, practically a vegetable. Evidence will emerge that she acted in self-defense. It's no secret that Vermack abused her. The DA will change the murder rap to justifiable homicide. I'll make sure she spends the rest of her life getting better care than she could get anywhere else."

The chief's suggestions would afford him no banner headlines, but he'd score big points with the mayor and the city council and the business community, so it was still a win-win scenario as long as he could keep the real facts buried.

"I'm in," I said, surprising Honey, Mackie, and Kruger. I completely understood Pointer's reasoning and didn't believe that the truth emerging would make for a better result. "On a couple of conditions: Honey, Mackie, and Kruger each get issued a new unit. Not a *different* unit, but a brand-spanking-new, fresh-from-Detroit unit. And I get relieved of any duties as the department's occult expert."

"Agreed," said the chief, looking a little disappointed by the last part of my request.

"Computers for the Homicide Section," said Kruger.

"Done," said the chief.

"I'm tired of going to Staples on my own dime," said Mackie. "Office supplies, business cards for all the homicide dicks, and one of those fancy Herman Miller office chairs, something that doesn't hurt my back so much. I've been sitting on the same damn broken chair for ten years."

"Fine," said the chief. "Saint James, you make any copies of that video from Mexico?"

"No," I lied. I had several copies stashed away.

"Delete it."

They all watched as I worked the controls. "It's gone."

"We drop all charges and release Anastasia. Agreed?"

Everyone nodded but Honey.

"Detective Baybee, I need to hear from you," said Pointer.

"I was just wondering. Why it wouldn't look good to the public? That we had hunted down one of our own," she said.

"If the murders weren't so sensational, and if Fournier didn't meet the definition of a serial killer, I might agree with that. Now are you on board or not?"

She bit her lip, thinking. "I'll go along with the guys," she said without enthusiasm.

"And what do you want?"

"Nothing."

"Take a week off with pay. If I see your face before then, I'll transfer you to traffic. Understood?"

She nodded, then looked at me like I'd let her down.

And I probably had.

As I stood waiting for Anastasia Fournier to get kicked out of lockup, I surfed the Internet on my smartphone. It only took a few minutes to confirm I'd been right about others being struck and killed by lightning while standing on top of El Castillo in the rain. It happened in 1978 to anthropologist and Maya expert Dennis E. Puleston. Lightning strikes were common at Chichén Itzá and it made it easier for me to dismiss Fournier's contention that he had been responsible for the bolt of justice. Nevertheless, I continued to wear the talisman he'd given me on a heavy silver chain around my neck. And that pretty much summed up my conflicted relationship, my cognitive dissonance, with things occult.

Anastasia had been informed almost immediately of Tony's death. She emerged from the turnstile looking like she'd been through the wringer emotionally. She glanced at me with uncertainty.

"I'm here for three reasons," I said. "First to apologize for the arrest. Second, to offer my sincere condolences. I'm truly sorry about your husband. He probably saved my life down in Mexico."

"You were with him when he died?"

I nodded.

"So he saved your life but he framed me for murder."

"No he didn't. Not at all. That's the third reason I'm here. If you want, I can show you some things, explain some things."

She looked like she wanted to believe me. But I could tell she didn't trust me. "I'd stopped loving him. I told him I wanted a divorce."

"Good thing you didn't divorce. You get to collect his pension for the rest of your life."

"Money is easy to get."

"Anyway," I said, "unless you want to call a taxi, I'd be happy to give you a ride, out to LaPlace or wherever you want."

"Vegas?" she joked, sadly.

"I like Las Vegas, but I'm not sure that's the place where Anastasia Fournier should start her life over."

I stood there thinking that Twee Siu should be recruiting Anastasia instead of recruiting me. The young woman had successfully penetrated a secretive group operating undercover with practically no support, was an experienced burglar, could think on her feet, and was a drop-dead-gorgeous widow, all at the ripe old age of twenty-one.

"What do you really want?" she asked.

"Tony wrote me a letter. I thought you might like to see it." I hadn't told the chief or anyone else about the letter from Fournier and had no intention of doing so.

"Did he really save your life?"

"He took three bullets that could have easily gone into me."

For a second she looked vulnerable. But then the practiced mask of a woman confidently in control took over, the facade I'd seen her wear before. "I liked that martini you made. Make me another."

She stepped up to me, took my arm, and we walked out together.

Saint James:

If you're reading this, then I'm dead, and deservedly so. I killed Felix Sanchez, Roscindo Ruiz, Becky Valencia, Hans Vermack, and Kate Townsend. With divine help, I'll kill Robert Drake too.

You probably think I'm a lowlife for setting up my wife Anastasia to take the fall, but I did it just to give me time to hit Drake, the hardest target. I've attached a few pages to this note explaining how I carried out the murders and have provided details only the killer could know. Anastasia was not an accomplice; she is truly an innocent. Everything she did, initially at least, was because she loved me.

And I truly love her beyond measure. What a fool I was to employ her in my quest to bring a serial killer to justice. God or Buddha or the Universe, or karma, or whatever it is one believes in—well, divine retribution is a fairly immutable process in most cases. I should have stayed out of it and let Drake keep killing, instead of appointing myself the agent of justice, because I have lost the only thing that meant a damn to me—my young, sweet wife.

Believe it or not, she was sexually inexperienced when we first got together. Later, when I enrolled her at Tulane under the phony name, she got invited to one of Drake's Crimson

Throne meetings. I knew it was all about sex, but Anastasia and I agreed she wouldn't participate. We figured they would let her stay and observe. Her being drugged and raped never entered my realm of possibility. And since the criminal justice system is rigged in this country and always has been, that left it to me to even the score.

The Bible has it wrong; the meek don't inherit diddly-squat.

What I did was wrong, but it was RIGHT. And that is something I can die with.

Please do what you can to look after Anastasia. My tarot cards tell me you two have a lot in common.

Anthony Xavier Fournier

Anastasia and I spent the next three days in bed together. Our relationship was the most natural one I'd ever experienced. Mature far beyond her years, she made me laugh with her sly sense of humor, made me sad with stories of her childhood, and made me think that our fourteen-year age difference might be surmountable. We shared secrets on lock-picking and breaking-and-entering, watched old bank-job movies, and she cooked me Eggs Sardou just the way I like it.

All of her exposure to the occult had left her open-minded but reticent to pursue that path. Exactly the way I felt.

I knew we had a future together. The future might only last a few days or a few months, but there was shared time waiting for us.

I spotted an ad on craigslist for a moving sale in which the lady pulling up stakes from New Orleans was selling "spiritual objects." I stopped by her place on Octavia and ended up with an armful: Buddhas in various postures, a bronze Quan Yin; A Tibetan dorje; a rose quartz Christian cross; a malachite pyramid; stone incense burners; a pewter Hanuman, the monkey king; Hindu prayer flags with the symbol for Ram; a soapstone statue of Isis; and about a dozen other items, including hawk feathers.

I'd decided to become a collector of sorts.

My reasoning had nothing to do with believing the objects were imbued with some power that could protect me or do my bidding or bring benefit. In a way, the things I bought were like sigils, in that they functioned as prompts to me, reminders of what I simply call the Divine.

Religion-specific items, like a Star of David or a brass statue of Ganesh, for me function only as symbols that connect me to some deeper reality, not as part of any particular dogma. And I'd decided that the only good-luck charm or talisman I need is the power of my will, the energetic intent that I hold in my personal space, a clarity that comes from within me.

I still pray, of course, and I still embrace divine intervention, but I'm the guy who has to do the grunt work; prayers are not always answered, so I believe it is a sucker's game to rely too heavily on things outside of oneself.

All of this reminds me of how quick so many people are to surrender their own power as human beings, as citizens. So many choose to believe that the government will save them. Or a new spouse or a pill or a cult or a fill-in-the-blank. Many people tend to put faith in anything but themselves, possibly because they don't want the responsibility.

I personally don't play the blame game, and I figure the only person responsible for the state of my life is me.

Anyway, it feels good that I'd faced my fear of the occult. It doesn't matter whether voodoo is real or if black magic "works." I've survived quite nicely.

I rolled up behind Honey in the Bronco as she walked her dog over by the levee at the end of Mazant Street. We hadn't spoken since that meeting in the chief's office, four days ago. The sunshine reflecting off the broken pavement made her look a bit peaked and pale. And troubled.

As the roar of a passing garbage truck faded, I heard a couple arguing on their front stoop, but a duo of cardinals played on an overhead power line and flitted among the tangle of wires. I chose to take the redbirds as a good omen for my talk with Honey. I held a couple of frozen granitas from PJ's and handed her one.

"I wanted to say I'm sorry I let you down," I said.

She registered surprise.

"You let *me* down? I think it's the other way around."

"C'mon, I know you wanted to go public with Fournier being the killer. You think I'm a sellout, corrupt like the chief."

"No. Well, maybe I did at first. But it was the right call. We both know there's no black and white. Truth is, I . . . I . . . you're my partner and . . . I got jealous. Emotional. So I wasn't there to back you up when the Mexicans came after you."

"Forget about that."

"I can't. I'm not sure I want to stay in Homicide. My instincts were all wrong on this one."

"Honey, this case was messed up from the get-go. I made my share of mistakes, that's for sure. But we worked it out, didn't we?"

"You worked it out."

"No. *We* worked it out. Me, you, Mackie, Kruger—the whole team. It's a group effort. I was just unlucky enough to be there at the end." I lit a cigarillo, in spite of the state of my lungs. "I have something to tell you: Anastasia's been staying at my place."

Honey didn't seem surprised to hear it. Our relationship had shifted radically in the last week. Maybe she saw something like this coming. I truly liked Anastasia and felt Honey needed to see me hooked up with a girlfriend, to make it concrete to her that things between us had changed. It was more insulation to protect Honey from ugliness that I knew would be coming in the future.

"I need to . . . I'm going to . . . work some things out," she said. "For myself. Long overdue personal things."

I nodded. "That's good. I'm glad to hear that." I stubbed out the smoke in my pocket ashtray and then bent down and patted her dog, Chance. "Hey, Chance, think your mom could give me a ride to the airport, like, right now?"

Honey stiffened as she drilled me with her eyes. "You're going away. For three months, right? Some kind of conference."

I smiled. "The chief signed off on the FBI putting me through a ninety-day counterterrorism program."

Honey gave me a look; she knew better.

"Anastasia will be house-sitting. My bags are in the Bronco."

"So you're coming back."

"Yeah. Unless you don't want me as your partner anymore."

She reached down to pet Chance. "You any good at construction? Mom and I took your suggestion."

I raised an eyebrow quizzically.

"I helped her put in an offer to buy Drake's property. If we get it, the temple room will have to go."

I now remembered having joked about buying the place when

Honey and I first responded to the shots-fired call. "Fitness room? Swimming pool? Racquetball court?"

"Mom was thinking of a couple extra bedrooms. Wait—" She smiled. "You don't think it's haunted do you?"

I just laughed as we walked toward the Bronco.